W9-CNU-100

By Tessa Bailey

Make Me

A Broke and Beautiful Novel

TESSA BAILEY

AVON

An Imprint of HarperCollinsPublishers

This is a work of fiction. Names, characters, places, and incidents are products of the author's imagination or are used fictitiously and are not to be construed as real. Any resemblance to actual events, locales, organizations, or persons, living or dead, is entirely coincidental.

MAKE ME. Copyright © 2015 by Tessa Bailey. Excerpt from WRECK THE HALLS © 2023 by Tessa Bailey. All rights reserved. Printed in the United States of America. No part of this book may be used or reproduced in any manner whatsoever without written permission except in the case of brief quotations embodied in critical articles and reviews. For information, address HarperCollins Publishers, 195 Broadway, New York, NY 10007.

HarperCollins books may be purchased for educational, business, or sales promotional use. For information, please email the Special Markets Department at SPsales@harpercollins.com.

FIRST AVON IMPULSE MASS MARKET PUBLISHED IN 2015.

Designed by Diahann Sturge

New York City illustration © wanspatsorn/Shutterstock
Title page illustrations © Kotkoa; Victoria Sergeeva/Shutterstock

Library of Congress Cataloging-in-Publication Data has been applied for.

ISBN 978-0-06-332941-6

23 24 25 26 27 LBC 5 4 3 2 1

Acknowledgments

I hate to see the Broke and Beautiful series end. HATE IT. Because I know all three couples are having adventures without us, and I want to write about them. But I hope readers know in their hearts that Louis, Roxy, Ben, Honey, Russell, and Abby will be together forever, causing trouble and continuing to build a friendship and relationships that will stand the test of time. Tessa xo

As always, I have to thank my husband first for being supportive and loving me despite all my faults. Thank you, Patrick. Your socks are in the upper right drawer.

Thank you to my super editor, Nicole Fischer, for cheering for this happy ending and being excited to read each installment of the Broke and Beautiful series. Thank you for trusting my ability to tell the stories and working your magic to enhance what I wrote.

Thank you to Jessie Edwards, publicist extraordinaire, for being so upbeat and positive about the series. And emailing me your ALL CAPS feelings during Russell's book—it was a huge boost of confidence.

Thank you to Laura Bradford for your awesome advice and input!

Thank you to Gail Dubov and Nadine Badalaty for designing this kick-ass cover for *Make Me*. It perfectly suits the characters and the story.

Thank you to Jillian Greenfield Stein for being a massively supportive presence and remembering the first line of all three B&B books by heart.

Thank you to the readers, especially my Bailey's Babes, who love these characters like their own. They are yours. They belong to all of us.

Chapter 1

Day one hundred and forty-two of being friend-zoned. Send rations.

Russell Hart stifled a groan when Abby twisted on his lap to call out a drink order to the passing waiter, adding a smile that would no doubt earn her a martini on the house. Every time their six-person "super group" hung out, which was starting to become a nightly affair, Russell advanced into a newer, more vicious circle of hell. Tonight, however, he was pretty sure he'd meet the devil himself.

They were at the Longshoreman, celebrating the Fourth of July, which presented more than one precious little clusterfuck. One, the holiday meant the bar was packed full of tipsy Manhattanites, creating a shortage of chairs, hence Abby parking herself right on top of his dick. Two, it put the usually conservative Abby in ass-hugging shorts and one of those tops that tied at the back of her neck. Six months ago, he would have called it a *shirt*, but his two best friends had fallen down the relationship rabbit hole, putting him in the vicinity of excessive chick talk. So, now it was a halter top. What he wouldn't *give* to erase that knowledge.

During their first round of drinks, he'd become a believer in breathing exercises. Until he'd noticed these tiny, blond curls at Abby's nape, curls he'd never seen before. And some-fucking-how, those sun-kissed curls were what had nudged him from semierect to full-scale Washington-Monument status. The hair on the rest of her head was like a . . . a warm milk-chocolate color, so where did those little curls come from? *Those* detrimental musings had led to Russell questioning what else he didn't know about Abby. What color was everything else? Did she have freckles? Where?

Russell would not be finding out—ever—and not just because he was sitting in the friend zone with his dick wedged against his stomach—*not* an easy maneuver—so she wouldn't feel it. No, there was more to it. His friends, Ben and Louis, were well aware of those reasons, which accounted for the half-sympathetic, half-needling looks they were sending him from across the table, respective girlfriends perched on their laps. The jerks.

Abby was off-limits. Not because she was taken—thank Christ—or because someone had verbally forbidden him from pursuing her. That wasn't it. Russell had taken a long time trying to find a suitable explanation for why he didn't just get the girl alone one night and make his move. Explain to her that men like him weren't suitable friends for wide-eyed debutantes and give her a demonstration of the alternative.

It went like this. Abby was like an expensive package that had been delivered to him by mistake. Someone at the post office had screwed the pooch and dropped off the shiniest, most beautiful creation on his Queens doorstep and driven away, laughing manically. Russell wasn't falling for the trick, though. Someone would claim the package, eventually. They would chuckle over the obvious mistake and take Abby away from him because, really, he had no business being the one whose lap she chose to sit on. No business whatsoever.

But while he was in possession of the package—as much as he'd *allow* himself to be in possession, anyway—he would guard her with his life. He would make sure that when someone realized the cosmic error that had occurred—the one that had made him Abby's friend and confidant—she would be sweet and undamaged, just as she'd been on arrival.

Unfortunately, the package didn't seem content to let him stand guard from a distance. She innocently beckoned him back every time he managed to put an inch of space between them. Russell had lost count of the times Abby had fallen asleep on him while the super group watched a movie, drank margaritas on the girls' building's rooftop, driven home in cabs. She was entirely too comfortable around him, considering he saluted against his fly every time they were in the same room.

"Why so quiet, Russell?" Louis asked, his grin turning to a wince as his actress girlfriend, Roxy, elbowed him in the ribs. Yeah. Everyone at the damn table knew he had a major thing for the beautiful, unassuming number whiz on his lap. Everyone but Abby. And that was how he planned to keep it.

"I know why," Ben said, causing Russell's stomach to catapult itself across the bar. Before he could change the subject, Ben pulled his student-turned-main-squeeze closer and continued. "He doesn't need to give us advice on girls anymore. His powers have been diminished."

"We've slain the beast."

Ben and Louis raised their plastic beer cups in a toast without a single glance at one other. Why was he friends with these two again? Oh right. The power of beer had brought them together. Praise be to Heineken. Smug as they were, though, Russell knew humor was their way of showing support. If it wasn't humor, it would be sympathy, aka dude kryptonite.

"What kind of advice did he give you about us?" Roxy wanted to know, shooting Louis and Ben stern glances.

"Uh-uh." Russell shook his head. "I'm calling bro confidentiality on you both. That includes pillow talk and supersedes any and all forms of sexual coercion."

Ben adjusted his glasses. "*That* reasoning, however, should lend some insight into what you ladies missed."

Honey leaned across the table and patted Russell's arm. "It all worked out in the end, big guy. Who knows? You might have had something to do with it after all."

Russell opened his mouth to respond, but whatever he planned to say withered in its inception because Abby spun in his lap again, sending the world around him into slow motion. A left jab of her scent—which after careful consideration he'd termed *white-grape sunlight*—caught him on the chin, and he barely restrained the urge to shout *oh, come on*, at the top of his lungs. Her big hazel eyes were indignant on his behalf, mouth pursed in a way that shouldn't have been sexy, but damn well was. She'd snapped her spine straight, hip bumping his erection in the process.

Please, Almighty God, just kill me now.

"Russell gives *great* advice," Abby protested, and Russell would have smiled if he hadn't been busy earning his master's degree in boner-soothing meditation. She really had no idea her outrage only made her sweeter because it looked so unnatural on her. "Remember the man on the first floor of our building? The one who used to clear his throat loudly every time we walked by?" She waited for Honey and Roxy to nod. "Russell told me the next time it happened, I should just shout *TROUBLE* at his door. I did. And it hasn't happened since."

When Louis and Ben started laughing into their beers, Russell flipped them off behind Abby's back. What his friends knew that Abby didn't? As soon as she'd told him the problem, he'd paid a visit to their downstairs neighbor and explained that *trouble* would find him if he so much as breathed in Abby's—or any of her roommates'—direction again. Hence, the single word's being so effective. Russell *was* trouble.

But as Abby turned a bright, encouraging smile on him, swelling his heart like an inflating balloon, he recognized that *his* brand of trouble had nothing on Abby's. She didn't even know how dangerous she was to his health. Because while Abby was the package that had been delivered by mistake, he'd gone and fallen for her, despite his attempts to simply be her friend.

And maybe it was his imagination, but the loss of her seemed to loom a little closer each day. Like any minute now, she would peer a little closer and realize he was an imposter. Loss was something with which Russell was familiar. Loss had cut him off at the knees at a young age, made him hyperaware of how fast it could happen. Whoosh. Chopped off at the knees. So he was already in damage-control mode, hoping to limit the fallout when she inevitably headed for a younger version of Gordon Gekko. For now, it was all about keeping a comfortable gap between him and Abby.

She scooted back on his lap to make room for the waitress, who had returned with a round of drinks, and Russell gritted his teeth.

Okay. *Comfortable* definitely wasn't the right word.

I HAVE FRIENDS. I have friends now, and it's glorious.

Six months ago, when Abby Sullivan had placed the ad on Craigslist, seeking two roommates to share her Chelsea apartment, her highest hope had been for noise. Maybe it sounded silly, but apart from the Ninth Avenue traffic trundling past and the occasional shouting match on the street, her life had been so quiet before Honey and Roxy showed up. She'd been hoping for hair dryers in the morning, dishes being tossed in the sink, singing in the shower. Anything but the void of sound she'd been living with, alone in the massive space.

Then, oh *then*, she'd gone and done something even more impulsive than placing an advertisement for massively discounted rent in cyberspace. She'd blurted upon meeting them for the first time that she didn't need help paying the rent; she merely wanted friends. Unbelievably, it hadn't felt like a mistake to reveal such a pitiful secret to a couple of strangers. There had been a feeling when all three of them first stood in the same room that it would work out, like a complicated math equation that would prove itself worth the work.

Now? She couldn't imagine a day passing without them. The guys had been an unexpected bonus she hadn't counted on. Especially Russell.

As they walked crosstown toward the Hudson River, where they planned to watch the Fourth of July fireworks, Abby smiled up at Russell where he towered over her. She received a suspicious look in response. *Suspicious!* Ha! It made her want to laugh like a lunatic. All the way back to her furthest memory, she'd been reliable, gullible, sugar-filled Abby to everyone and their mother. Even Honey and Roxy, to a degree, handled her carefully around subjects that might offend her or hurt her feelings. She was too grateful for their presence to call them on it, though. Sometimes she opened her mouth, the words *I'm not made of spun glass* hovering right on the tip of her tongue, but she always swallowed them. They meant well. She knew that with her whole heart. Maybe someday, when she was positive they wouldn't vanish at a rare show of temper—the way people *always* did when she bared a flaw—she'd tell them. Until she worked up the courage, however, she would stay quiet and appreciate her new best friends for the colorful positivity they'd brought into her life.

But Russell? She appreciated him even more for getting *mad* at her.

Such occurrences were her favorite part of the week. Russell's stomping into the apartment, grumbling about her not checking the peephole. Refusing to go out on a Saturday night until she changed into more comfortable shoes. Giving her that daunting frown when she revealed they'd had a leak in the bathroom for three weeks and hadn't yet called the super to repair it. He'd had it fixed within the hour, but he hadn't spoken to her the entire time.

It was *awesome*.

Because he kept coming back. Every time. No matter what—no matter what she said or did—he never washed his hands of her. Never got so fed up with her admittedly flighty behavior that he skipped a hang out. Or didn't respond to a text. He was the steadfast presence in her life that she'd never had.

No one spoke to Abby at her job. She'd been hired after graduating at the top of her Yale class and placed in a silent power position at a hedge fund. Her *father's* hedge fund. So she could understand her coworkers' reticence to invite her for happy hour. Or even give her a polite nod in the hallway. At first, she'd been prepared to try anyway. Force them to acknowledge her in some small way, even if it was just passing the stapler in the conference room. Then she remembered. When she forced her opinion on people, or had an outburst, they went away and didn't come back for a long time.

Her coworkers assumed she sat in her air-conditioned office all day playing Minecraft or buying dresses online. And why wouldn't they? She'd done nothing to change that notion. In reality, however, she worked hard. Showed up before the lights came on and stayed later than everyone else. Brought work home with her and often didn't get to sleep. She had no choice.

Stress tightened like a shoelace around Abby's stomach, but she breathed through it. Tonight was for fun with her friends. Tomorrow morning would be soon enough to face her responsibilities.

"It's the shoes, isn't it?" Russell demanded, encompassing Abby, Roxy, and Honey with a dark look. "This always happens in the eleventh hour. You girls started limping around, and we just have to watch it."

Ben sighed. "Here we go again."

"No, really. I think I've finally figured it out." Russell swiped impatient fingers over his shaved head. "You ever heard of sympathy pains? When my sister-in-law gave birth, my brother swore someone was firing a nail gun into his stomach. To this day, the guy has never been the same." He pointed at Abby's electric-blue pumps. "Women wear these evil creations around to confuse us. Sure, they make a girl's legs look good, but that's the black magic, my friends. They want us to feel their pain and not understand why."

Louis turned, walking backward on the sidewalk so he could face them. "I have to admit, I'm with Russell on this one." He smiled at Roxy's outrage. "You could go barefoot, and it wouldn't make a difference to me."

"I'll round it out with a third agreement," Ben chimed in. "I like Honey in her Chucks."

That statement earned Ben a kiss from Honey and a groan from Russell. "I'm thrilled you assholes have found a way to use my amazing logic to earn points."

Abby loved the familiar argument simply because it *was* familiar—a routine she had in common with others—but she had to admit her feet were throbbing. After a night of dancing, the crosstown walk was giving her blisters. She wore heels all day at the office, but they were sensible and low-heeled. Nothing like the stilettos she'd borrowed from Roxy. In fact, now that she'd acknowledged her tired feet, every part of her seemed to sag with exhaustion, as if she'd finally given her bones permission. "I can end this argument right here," Abby interrupted with a weary, but determined smile. The group stopped to watch as she slipped off her shoes and placed her bare feet back onto the cool sidewalk with a hearty sigh. For some reason, everyone's gazes swung to Russell who—God love him—was frowning at her like she'd just crashed his beloved truck.

"A new tactic, gentlemen. Take note." Their four friends laughed at Russell's ominous tone, but Abby stayed pinned under his scowl. Although now, his scowl had a hint of uncertainty behind it. "Put them back on, Abby. You're going to step on something. Broken glass, or—"

Abby breezed past Russell. Honestly, he worried constantly for no reason. They were only a few blocks away from the river, and the streets were well lit. What was the worst that could—

Her feet left the ground, her gasp cutting off as she was cradled against Russell's big chest. His expression was hidden, thanks to the streetlights shining blindingly above his head, but Abby knew from experience, he would be annoyed. She couldn't prevent the smile from spreading like wildfire across her face, feeling as if it reached as far as her chest. It seemed impossible, but somehow she'd earned a place among these people who cared about her. Friends. Good friends. The kind you can't live without.

Especially Russell. Her favorite.

"You were put on this earth to make me crazy, Abby. You know that?"

"I'm not sorry about it," she whispered. "Does that make me a bad person?"

"No. It makes you a woman."

She muffled her laugh with the use of Russell's shoulder. "Men make women crazy, too. It's not a one-sided affair."

He frowned down at her. "What would you know about it?"

That question coming from anyone else might have embarrassed Abby, but for all Russell's bluster, he never judged her. Not for her lack of a love life, anyway. Shoes were another matter altogether. "I know things."

"*Things*, huh? Maybe Louis and Ben should spend more time at their own apartments." His arms flexed as he hefted her higher, with minimal effort. "Do you actually like watching the fireworks, or is this just a patriotic custom we're upholding?"

"No, I *love* fireworks." She tilted her head back and looked at the sky. "Everyone forgets over the course of the year how incredible fireworks are. You know? They forget until they're standing beneath them again. You don't like them?"

He stared ahead as he answered. "I like that you like them."

Abby smiled, knowing Russell would have to be extra gruff for the remainder of the night to make up for that slip. And needing to torture him a little over it. "That's how I feel when you make me watch the Yankees." She laid a hand against his cheek. "It's worth it just to see your adorable man eyes light up."

His sigh was sharp, but she caught the corner of his mouth kicking up. "All this time, I thought you were enjoying it."

"The blooper reel is my favorite." Drowsiness settled more firmly over her, and she stifled a yawn against his shoulder. "Also, I love when kids in the audience catch foul balls."

"Crowd. It's called a crowd."

She hummed in her throat, eyelids beginning to weigh down. "I knew that. Just seeing if you were paying attention," she murmured.

Russell chewed his bottom lip a moment, worry marring his features. "You're so tired lately, Abby. Everything okay?"

"Totally fine," she lied. "Just going to rest my eyes a minute."

Positive he would wake her up when they reached the Hudson, she wound her arms around his neck and dozed off. It was the first time she'd slept in three days.

Chapter 2

*R*ussell took off his hard hat and set it down on the sun-heated truck bed. Knowing his brother would be joining him for their noon lunch break soon, he opened the cooler and snagged a second can of Coke, holding it to his forehead. It was Monday morning, two days since he'd carried Abby crosstown to the fireworks, and he was grateful for the work to distract him even if it was ninety degrees outside.

Hart Brothers Construction consisted of him, Alec, and a half dozen part-time guys. Based in Queens, the company had been started almost as a joke the summer Russell graduated from high school. Having learned quite a few remodeling and repairing methods from their father—who'd worked construction until he retired in his midfifties—they'd shown up to repair a buddy's deck when the guy's broken leg rendered him unable to complete the task himself. Hoping to soothe their friend's pride with a dose of humor, they'd had T-shirts made up. *Hart Brothers Construction. We'll get you nailed.* The very next week, they'd had a request to complete another job, this time from a neighbor. The requests had continued to roll in at such an increasing volume, they'd been forced to get their shit together by applying for a business license.

Nine years later, Russell was twenty- seven, and they'd just won the most lucrative bid of their professional lives. Until now, the majority of their work had come from the outer boroughs, but the current Manhattan job—renovating an empty, five-story office building in Tribeca—could effectively put them on the map. If he could convince his brother to expand. Alec wasn't exactly a fan of change. Or excessive labor.

A fire truck roared past with its siren blaring, heading downtown. Not an unusual occurrence in the city, but enough to derail his thoughts and send them crashing back into Abby. She'd fallen asleep with her head on his shoulder more than a dozen times in the last few months. He'd questioned her about it the first few times, but all he ever got was an excuse about being swamped at work. Not wanting the privilege of holding her to be rescinded, he'd dropped it. Saturday night had seen a new level, though. The feeling of her body curled against his chest, her breath puffing against his neck as fireworks went off above? That memory wouldn't leave him alone.

Several times, he'd replayed her waking up and sleepily asking him to take her home. Okay, a slightly higher number than several. Probably more in the neighborhood of infinity times infinity. His head wouldn't stop creating screwed-up scenarios, either. Instead of laying her on the couch and leaving the apartment as he'd done, Russell envisioned staying wrapped around her all night, gauging her reaction the following morning when she realized their bodies were in position to fuck.

Abby was not the kind of girl you "fucked," either. You didn't shove aside her underwear and enter hard, rocking with enough force to break the couch springs. You undressed her slowly and took your time. Kissing her in between thrusts . . . listening to her breathe. Okay, musing about how Abby should be taken wasn't helping his cause, either. In fact, the more he thought about it, the worse the images became. Holding Abby down. Sucking marks onto her skin. Her neck. Things he was ashamed of, impulses he'd never experienced before, but that always snuck up on him when Abby was involved.

He'd never wanted to impress on a girl that she was *his*. His *alone*. The only one who'd ever roused that instinct was Abby. These urges to dominate her seemed to stem from those possessive feelings. As if mere words wouldn't suffice. There needed to be actions. Firm, decisive *actions* to satisfy him. But he would continue to deny the need to take action because Abby wasn't his. Something he had an extremely hard time remembering.

His brother, Alec, hopped up on the truck bed beside him, rattling the tailgate and Russell's concentration all at once. "Don't think so hard, dickhead, you'll get a nosebleed."

Russell took the first icy-cold sip of Coke, nearly crying as it trickled through his overheated insides. "*Someone* around here has to think."

"Excuse me?" Alec paused in the act of unwrapping his sandwich. "It's a wonder my brain fits into this hard hat. And I can read you like a book, man. You're jealous."

"Jealous of what?" Russell asked, genuinely perplexed.

Alec slapped the side of the truck bed, letting out a loud *whoop*. "No one told you, little bro?"

"Jesus. Why do you still call me that? I'm a foot taller than you."

"You're four years younger," Alec half shouted.

"And when I was born, a name was bestowed on me by our parents. Use it."

"God, you are touchy today." His brother bit into his ham sandwich, grimaced, and tossed it into the truck bed. "My wife is hot, but she shouldn't be allowed to handle food. We should have built her another closet instead of a kitchen."

Russell waited. "So? What's this big news no one has told me?"

Alec adjusted his hard hat. "I'm not telling you now, you big fucking buzzkill."

Another two fire trucks blazed past, tearing right through the red light. An accident downtown? A fire? The bite of sandwich he'd taken suddenly felt like dust in his mouth. Honey was uptown, attending her afternoon classes at Columbia. Ben was on the East Side, teaching at NYU. Roxy had just wrapped filming her first television pilot, so she and Louis had played hooky that day, very likely putting them in Louis's bed on the Lower East Side. The only member of their group working in the Financial District today was Abby.

Worrying was ridiculous. There were thousands of buildings downtown. He had no reason to think those fire trucks were headed in her direction. None. At one time, he'd been just like Alec. Not a care in the world. Then he'd *found* something to care about, and he'd become the first to fear the worst. Those damn possessive instincts—so focused on Abby—wouldn't be muffled.

They were trying to remind him it was his *job* to worry about her. If he didn't, someone else might, and that was flat-out unacceptable. Who knows how much time he had left before she picked someone else to be the one who worried? Until then, shouldn't he make damn sure she never regretted letting him fill in for a little while?

"Tell me the news, Alec." *Distract me from my idiocy.* "You want me to beg?"

"It wouldn't hurt." Alec grinned as he removed his hard hat, plowing a hand through his bleached-blond hair. "Ah, screw it. I got the call man!"

"What call?"

"*American Ninja Warrior.*" He punched Russell in the shoulder. "They want me to compete next season. On television, man."

"You're kidding me." Despite his exasperation over Alec's two-year-long crusade to get on the program, pride and disbelief clobbered him over the head out of nowhere. They high-fived with their filthy, callused hands. Which turned into a backslapping hug. Which immediately turned into uncomfortable coughing and backing away. "When are you going?"

"Get this. The show isn't live, like we thought." Alec cracked his neck. "I'll admit I was a little disappointed to find that out, but I got over it when I remembered I can win one hundred grand. *One hundred grand.* I'll build Darcy another useless kitchen if I win that. Just for the hell of it."

"Sounds wise," Russell murmured.

"They film in a week," Alec continued. "I know it's short notice, and we've got this big job." His brother pounded a fist over his heart. "But I have to follow my lifelong dream, man."

Russell did some quick math. "That show has only been on five years."

"See?" Alec shook his head. "This is why I didn't want to tell you."

"Because I can subtract?" His brother hopped off the truck bed, and Russell followed suit, ignoring the buzzing in his skull when another pair of fire trucks flew past, sirens almost loud enough to break glass. "Look, I'm really happy for you. You know I am. It's just . . . we've got that meeting at the bank next week. It's kind of our last chance to get the loan we need to expand."

"If I win *American Ninja Warrior*, we won't even have to *work*."

Russell narrowed his gaze. "You do know that one hundred grand has five zeroes and not six. Right?" A beat of silence passed where all he got from his brother was a blank stare. "Right?"

Alec scratched the back of his neck and laughed. "If you know so much about money, you'll be fine handling the loan meeting on your own."

Russell started to point out that he'd handled the previous five unsuccessful bank meetings on his own but decided against it. Alec didn't feel the same urgency he did to expand, and Russell had already come to terms with that. The continual rejections were hard to shoulder alone. The same way renovating their childhood home in Queens without help was hard. But the hard work would be worth it if he succeeded. And lately, he'd become less and less satisfied with being stagnant. He needed to *move*.

No idea what to expect, Russell had gone into the first bank meeting blind, with little more than their accounting ledger and a rough financial plan. He'd thought the company's rapid growth would speak for itself, but he'd been dead wrong. Chalking up the first go-round to a learning experience, he'd scheduled another meeting and been far more prepared the second time, not expecting that first rejection to hurt him. But it had, following him from meeting to meeting, closing doors in his face. He suspected his rough edges weren't helping either, but he couldn't do anything about those. All options had been exhausted, save one, and he'd been doing research whenever he had free time, intending to make it count.

His brother started in again about an obstacle course, but when more sirens approached, Russell couldn't focus on the conversation any longer. As Alec looked on curiously, Russell dug his cell phone from his pocket and dialed Abby's number. He got no answer, so he dialed again. When Abby answered on the second ring, he deflated against the truck.

"Hi, Russell."

"*Abby.*" Why was he shouting? "Everything all right?"

"Kind of."

"*Kind of?*" He was shouting again.

Her hum reached him down the line, warming his ear. "There's a gas leak at the building across the street, and they're evacuating us. Maybe the whole block." A commotion in the background, the din of voices. Abby's high heels clicking. He knew *that* sound too well. "They're telling us to go home."

"Okay." A door slammed loudly in the background, and he swallowed hard. "Don't take the train. If something happens with the leak, you shouldn't be underground. Walk west and hail a cab."

"On it."

By unspoken agreement, they stayed on the line. Russell walked away from the job site, toward the street, looking downtown. From his vantage point, he could see the massive group of flashing red lights. Several people were stopped on the sidewalk beside him, watching the far-off scene as well. For some reason, that made him twice as nervous. "You still there?" he said into the phone.

"I'm—"

He saw and heard the explosion simultaneously. Like fireworks they'd watched less than forty-eight hours ago, white light shot out and tracked down in sweeping arches, moving in slow motion. No. No . . . *Abby*. Fear hit Russell with the force of a cannonball, propelling him backward several steps. His work boots crunched on gravel from the worksite, a ringing resonating in his ears. He yelled into the phone, but nothing. There was nothing on the other end. *I didn't do enough. I let her down. Can't take another loss. Not when it's her. Not her.*

Something banded around his arm, and he spun to find Alec right in his face, mouth moving, but no sound. Jesus, was she hurt? Worse? He tried to breathe, but the air had been sucked out of the atmosphere.

Having grown up with his brother, Russell should have seen the right hook coming, but his head was filled with visions he couldn't deal with, flashbacks of his early home life—that one day he wanted to erase, along with all the shitty ones leading up to it—merging with new, even worse images, crowding out logic. A second after Alec's fist connected with his face, the world snapped back into place. Sound and color rushed back in.

"There you are." Alec shook him. "What the fuck, man?"

"I need the truck," Russell managed.

WHEN ABBY WAS twelve, her father had remarried after a whirlwind courtship with his business partner. Abby's mother had given up custody in the divorce when Abby was too young to remember, moving back to California with her sizeable divorce settlement. Looking back, she recognized that her father and stepmother had distracted her from thoughts of her mother, sending Abby to music and language lessons. Dance class, painting courses, mini vacations. One summer, her parents—father and stepmother—sent her to "gifted" summer camp. One of her tutors had recognized her aptitude for numbers and suggested the trip, and since her stepmother had been in the middle of her let's-rediscover-my-Italian-roots phase, she'd been all too eager for a two-week sabbatical from parenting not only Abby but her own similarly aged son. She and Abby's father had gone to Florence, and Abby had been shipped off to Camp Einstein, while her stepbrother had stayed home with the housekeeper.

Camp had started off well enough. She'd made friends with her bunkmate, Patty, who didn't seem to mind Abby's quiet awkwardness or that she always got picked last for kickball. The food wasn't the calorie-conscious fare served at the Sullivan house. Plus, she got to wear T-shirts and khaki shorts every day instead of the pressed slacks and blouses of which her usual wardrobe consisted. Three days into camp, however, Patty had found the cool girls who used the F-word a minimum of three times per sentence and boys had been discovered on the other side of camp.

Abby could still remember sitting in the mess hall, harboring the distinct feeling that she had no idea what was going on around her. Secrets were being told in hushed tones, spots were being saved—was *she* in someone's saved spot?—and the girl who'd been her friend mere hours before no longer even glanced in her direction.

Camp Einstein had set the course for the next twelve years. Private school had been a concentrated version of summer camp, alliances being formed and disbanded so quickly she couldn't keep up. Any type of misstep or flaw could earn you a *get lost* card from your group of friends. She might have been able to overcome her fear of making friends and losing them, but her home life had only amplified the one fact she'd lived by her entire adolescence. Screw up and you'd find yourself eating alone. Often even living alone. Before meeting Roxy and Honey, that feeling she'd had sitting in the mess hall had never seemed to go away. That feeling was what had driven her toward the reliability of numbers and tempted her to hunker down and never come up for air. That, and the responsibility she had toward her family.

But right at that moment, with paramedics rushing past her on the sidewalk and chaos blooming around her, the insecurities she'd been trying so hard to suppress came circling back, leaving her unsure how to proceed. Should she try to communicate to someone that her ankle hurt or should she just go home? Was she required to give a statement? She couldn't see any of her coworkers amid the confusion. Thank God her father hadn't been in the office. Then again, her father hadn't been to the office in a month.

Oh, no. What if she had to answer questions about his absence? Finally encountering the sense of urgency she needed to take action, Abby tested her ankle and winced. Probably not sprained, though, or it would feel far worse. Using the stone building at her back for leverage, she rose slowly, but her foot slipped in the sooty sidewalk, sending her back down onto her bottom.

"Manache."

A string of further Italian curses—courtesy of her parents' insistence on a decade of lessons—were dying to burst free of her mouth. It always made her feel better, without the negative side effect of offending anyone who didn't speak the language. Outbursts had never been tolerated in their household. When Abby gave in and allowed her temper to show, her parents' displeasure usually resulted in their absence. Absences that could stretch for weeks, giving time for her defiance to fade and regret to appear. Even referring to her father's new wife as *stepmother* hadn't been allowed. She'd been required to accept her stepmother's new status as *mother* with no questions asked, disapproval being heaped on her when she failed to address her correctly.

Abby's litany of Italian curses was stayed when a commotion to her left captured her attention. Warmth flickered and glowed in her chest when she saw Russell arguing with a police officer, trying to get through the makeshift barrier. Oddly, a part of her had been expecting him even if she hadn't consciously acknowledged it. The officer seemed adamant about keeping him out, but Abby pressed her hands to her heart and gave the man a pleading look, finally succeeding in making him relent.

Russell was by her side a split second later, kneeling on the concrete and running his eyes over every inch of her. He was filthy, sweating, and breathing heavy. One of the most welcome sights she'd ever encountered in her twenty-four years. "Ankle?" he barked over the sound of shouting and sirens.

She nodded.

"How?"

Abby was so busy marveling over how good it felt to have someone there—just for her—that she forgot the question. "What?"

He appeared to implore the sky for patience. "How'd you hurt your ankle? Were you . . . were you close to the blast? Has a paramedic looked at it yet?"

"No to both questions. And I don't need a paramedic." She clapped a hand over his mouth when he started to argue. "It's really stupid. Are you sure you want to hear this?"

"No, but tell me anyway." His voice was muffled against her hand. "I need a moment."

She wanted to question him about that statement, but his deepening frown told her it wasn't a good time. "The blast happened across the street while I was going down the emergency stairwell. That's where I was when you called. I dropped my phone." It occurred to her then that Honey and Roxy were probably worried. "Can you—"

"We'll call them in a minute. Finish the story."

His irritable tone made her grin. Who needed continual approval? Not her. That she could continually piss off Russell and yet he kept showing up? Never staying away for long periods of time no matter what happened? It made her feel as though she was more than just a sum of her accomplishments. "When I bent down to pick up my phone—because I could hear you yelling at me—my high heel slid back and got caught in the gap between stairs. I fell forward, and my ankle stayed where it was."

Russell seemed to be counting to ten as his eyes closed.

"Are you going to do that thing where you pinch the bridge of your nose at me?" She tilted her head, studying his expression. "It seems like a good time for that one."

Instead of answering, his hands shot out and retrieved the high heels from her feet, taking special care not to jostle her hurt ankle. Then he snapped the heel off of each shoe, in turn, and threw them into the nearest sewer grate.

Abby's jaw dropped on a gasp and stayed that way as Russell scooped her up off the sidewalk. "You are unbelievable, Abby," he growled. "A gas leak leads to an explosion. The entire city block is being evacuated, and you think it's a good time to fall down some goddamn stairs. You could have broken your neck."

"Russell, those were Roxy's shoes."

"Fine by me." He turned them sideways, squeezing past the barricade. "So long as you can't borrow them anymore."

"She'll never let me borrow *anything* now."

"You see this?" His voice boomed down at her, but against the backdrop of police radios and emergency vehicles, it was a comfort. "Those shoes could have cost you your life, and yet you defend them. New theory. When it comes to shoes, women have Stockholm Syndrome."

"You're just trying to take my mind off being scared."

She thought she heard him respond with *I'm trying to take my mind off of it*, but he was temporarily drowned out by sirens. When they crossed the street into slightly quieter surroundings, he glanced down at her, then away. "You were scared?"

"Terrified." Abby forced herself to keep a straight face. "I forgot to back up my work on the computer. If the building had exploded, I would have lost a full day." That earned her a glare. She smiled and laid her head on his shoulder just as they reached his truck, which he'd essentially abandoned in the middle of a side street. "That was good thinking, parking outside the blast zone."

"Stop making jokes about it, Abby." He lifted her higher against his chest and opened the passenger-side door before setting her down easy on the ripped seat. The interior smelled like paint, sweat, and pine, such a pleasing combination that she took a deep inhale. She reached for the seat belt, but Russell beat her to the task, strapping the worn nylon across her body and securing it with a *click*. Without a job to occupy himself, he appeared at a loss for what to do with his hands, but eventually he crossed his arms high over his chest. Then he just looked at her. "I knew it as soon as I heard the sirens, Abby. Knew you'd somehow manage to be in the middle of all this. Do you know how I knew?"

"How?"

"There's a belief that men and women can't be friends. Have you heard that one?"

Abby shook her head. Russell shifted in his boots, a telltale sign he was getting ready to impart a crazy, new theory. She propped her fists under her chin in anticipation.

"This is the universe telling us we broke code." He nodded once, as if to emphasize his point. "I made friends with someone determined to step on broken glass or fall headfirst down a set of stairs, and now I have to run all over the place making sure it doesn't happen. I don't have to do this with Ben or Louis."

"Because they're men."

He narrowed his eyes. "You're thinking I'm sexist."

"I'm not thinking, I'm knowing."

"Ah, but I don't have to worry about Roxy or Honey, either." The corner of his mouth tugged. "See that? Maybe I'm not sexist. Maybe I'm just an Abbyist."

Hoping to disguise the hurt—even over an obvious joke—she pushed back her shoulders. "I'm glad you came, but I would have made it home on my own, Russell. I'm fully capable of taking care of myself even with these pesky ovaries." She laid a hand on his shoulder. "I hereby absolve you of any extra responsibility you believe my Abby-ness has burdened you with. You're off the hook."

His shoulder jerked beneath her touch. "I never said I wanted to be off the hook." Muttering beneath his breath, he leaned down to inspect her ankle. "Why were you sitting there alone? I thought your father worked in the same office."

Abby kept her features schooled, but her heart had leapt into her throat. "He had a meeting uptown. He and my stepmother are probably calling my phone nonstop."

"All right." Russell handed her his phone with a grim smile. "Call everyone and let them know you're alive. I'll worry about getting you home."

He started to shut the passenger door, but she stopped him. "Russell?"

"Yeah."

"I'm really glad we're friends." She clutched the phone against her chest. "Even if you are an awful chauvinist sometimes."

Chapter 3

The red light turned green, but Russell's foot felt glued to the brake. A car honked, effectively reminding him he was operating a motor vehicle and needed to stop zoning out. Although zoning out would have been a welcome change to picturing Abby cartwheeling down a staircase while chaos reigned around her. Picturing her huddled on the sidewalk, seeing her attempt to stand and failing over and over again. She'd been right across the street from a fucking *explosion*. Even now, emergency vehicles blew past him, heading toward the still-fresh scene while he and Abby drove toward Chelsea.

Russell focused on Abby's musical voice as she spoke into his phone, listing her symptoms to Honey—a premed student at Columbia. He was grateful she had phone calls to occupy her on the drive, mainly because it prevented him from relaying any more bonehead philosophies. *You're off the hook.* Goddamn, she had no clue how *on the hook* he actually was. He'd found her whole and healthy half an hour ago, and it still felt as though someone had taken a circular saw to his intestines. There was an inner voice chanting *you almost lost her, you almost lost her*, when in reality, he didn't *have* her. At all. *Couldn't* have her.

A newer, more intense awareness beat in his gut now, though. He might have put up a good front to Abby, but the truth was, he craved the privilege of being her hero. To not fail her, the way he'd failed on that long-ago day so firmly lodged in his memory. It was different with Abby, though. A different shape. Unique and . . . *mighty*. Looking out for her, taking her home to soothe her aches . . . it made his blood pump faster. Since they'd started driving, he'd had the same mental image several times, and it only got more explicit with each go-round. Carrying Abby up the stairs, laying her down on that pristine white bedspread and taking her mind off the pain. Getting rid of his own in the process. He wanted her legs spread, those wide, hazel eyes acknowledging that *Russell* took care of her, all while he drove his cock into her body. *Jesus*. As if he needed another reason for her to think of him as a raging sexist.

Even worse, Russell *knew* why the need for Abby was at a fever pitch today. He earned an honest living with his hands. A living he was proud as hell of. But he had nothing to offer Abby, whose family could buy his family home *and* Hart Brothers Construction a thousand times without breaking a sweat. His *protection* was his offering, and he'd been allowed to somewhat utilize that part of him today. His traitorous gut was attempting to trick him into feeling worthy of Abby. He had to resist that false notion at all costs.

Abby was meant for bigger and better things than him. Someone who could discuss *The Grapes of Wrath* or listened to that *All*

Things Considered podcast he'd seen on her phone. Hell, someone who shopped at Brooks Brothers instead of borrowing clothes from his *actual* brother. But he could keep her safe until those things came along, and he'd be grateful for it. Now he just had to ignore his every instinct and keep his hands off even if they begged for the chance to squeeze her curves, stroke the sweet, untouched parts beneath her clothes. Christ. Why couldn't he stay away from her? Russell knew the answer to that too well. Being around Abby was torture, but staying away was all-out murder.

They drew close to Abby's building and lucked out with a spot half a block away, on West 17th Street. He gave Abby a look that said *stay put*, before rounding the car and plucking her off the seat. She tried to stay stiff in his arms, probably in light of his recent condescension, but gave in after about ten feet.

"Did you get ahold of your father?"

He frowned when she stiffened again. "I left a voice mail. He probably didn't answer because of the unknown number." That struck Russell as odd. If his loved one were missing, he would answer every single call that came through, hoping for news. "Anyway, our building wasn't damaged, so my parents have to know I'm fine. I'm more worried about Honey's experimenting on me when she gets home."

Over his dead body. "When will that be?"

"Not until tonight. She's running a Little League practice at her baseball field in Queens," Abby explained, referring to the city-block-sized gift Ben had bestowed on her as part of the world's best apology. "And I told Roxy to stay put at Louis's. There's no point in their running home when nothing is wrong with me. And you're here."

I'm here. He almost laughed over how unthreatening she found him when he spent hours every day picturing her naked. Russell stopped at the front door to her building and waited as she searched through her purse for keys. Good God, the amount of shit these girls carried around in their purses. After he succeeded in getting them all to wear flats, downsized purses would be his next quest. His musings vanished as she turned those hazel eyes on him and moistened her pink lips.

"You probably need to get back to work, too, right?"

"Work," he rasped. "Right."

Why was she looking at his neck? The spot she stared at felt hot, and he barely quelled the urge to rub at it. "If you want, you can stay and watch a movie."

Worst idea in history. "Which movie?"

"*The Notebook.*" Abby laughed at whatever involuntary expression of distaste he'd made. "I'm kidding. *Magic Mike.*"

"*Abby.*"

"Kidding again." Her smile blinded him. "I could go all day."

She unlocked the front and second inner door, finding her apartment key on the ring as he carried her toward the third floor. Russell tried his best to ignore the dark, primal satisfaction of returning her home safe, but it thumped inside him, a fist on a drum. He should leave now. No, he *would* leave now.

That resolution was left in the dust when she wiggled free of his hold, giving him no choice but to set her down . . . and watch helplessly as she limped toward her bedroom. So much for primal.

Russell dragged a hand down his face, over the scratchy beard forming on his jaw. He would rather take a sledgehammer to his own ankle than leave her alone with an injury. The next few hours were going to hurt.

Russell went to the freezer and rummaged for a frozen bag of peas, tossing it once in his hand. Then, like a man marching to the gallows, he followed Abby toward her bedroom and hovered just outside her door. "You decent?"

"Fully clothed." Her yawn reached him. "Your virtue is safe."

Trying not to choke on the irony of that, Russell entered her room and came to a quick stop. Paperwork everywhere; on the floor, her dresser . . . every flat and semiflat surface. Stacks of it. Three laptops. Two whiteboards were propped against her closet, words and figures written on them that reminded him enough of high-school algebra to send a shiver down his spine. The last time he'd been in her bedroom was to kill a spider, but that had been months ago. He did everything in his power to keep their interactions as far away from a bed as humanly possible. But he remembered every detail of her room, and it definitely hadn't looked like a NASA command center the last time he'd been there.

He gestured to one of the whiteboards. "What is all this?"

Abby sat on her bed, surveying the mess with what appeared to be detachment, but there was tension around her eyes. Still, she shrugged. "Work stuff."

Something about her tone, less upbeat than usual, bothered him. "Working some overtime lately?"

"A little."

Why was she being so vague? A series of flashbacks from the

last few weeks hit him one by one. Abby falling asleep beneath the fireworks, Abby not able to make it through a two-hour movie without passing out on his shoulder. Abby showing up late to the Longshoreman, still in her work clothes. "How much overtime are you working, exactly?"

His slightly harsher tone seemed to break her out of a trance. "Russell, I love that you're always angry with me, but can it wait until tomorrow?"

Too much to process at once. "Always *mad* at you?" That was not true. Was it? Russell felt the sudden need to sit down. It seemed his life would be flashing before his eyes tonight because he flipped through every memory of Abby and couldn't recall a single time he hadn't been harsh with her. Of course, his attitude had only been a way to hide his sexual frustration. He'd never been *mad* at her, but she didn't know that. "Why would you love my being angry with you?"

She eased off her work blazer, letting it fall behind her on the bed. Just like that, he was a trapped animal, feeling the equal need to pounce and blow the joint at a full-out sprint. "Everyone is always happy with me." Her eyes squeezed shut for a moment. "That sounds vain, doesn't it? It's true, though. I do what is expected of me. What I'm told. I say the right thing and dress in an appropriate manner for all occasions, despite your opinion of my footwear. I'm predictable. People don't have any reason to get mad at predictable. But you . . . *do*. You get mad."

Russell was so focused on the words coming out of her mouth, he didn't realize she'd been unbuttoning her blouse until it came off . . . revealing a white tank top. Thank God. *Eyes up, asshole.*

She's telling you something important. Russell heard himself swallow. "Predictable people don't take a chance on two strangers as roommates, letting them move in the same day. Predictable people don't almost get blown up. Or did you forget about that part of your day?"

Her lips twitched. "I have a feeling you won't let me forget."

"I don't like that you think I'm always mad at you, Abby. That makes me feel like a dick."

She yawned again, tipping to the side. "Yes, but you're *my* dick."

Aw, shit. He knew—he *knew*—she'd meant that in the most innocent way possible, but it didn't stop his stomach muscles from knotting into a series of intricate patterns and pulling *hard.* Which made him a complete tool because the girl was clearly exhausted, eyes fluttering with the need to close. Worry beat back the majority of his desire as he surveyed the cluttered room once again. Was it normal for someone in her position to work so hard? Had she gotten a promotion?

"Russell, stop thinking so hard and put on a movie." She inched her way backward on her elbows and collapsed back onto a pillow, making her tits bounce. Come *on.* What had he done to be tested like this? Grabbing the closest distraction like a lifeline, Russell leaned down and placed the bag of frozen peas on her ankle, adjusting it so it would remain in place. She was wearing nylons, but no way in hell was he taking those off, so the ice would have to do its job through the sheer material. When he looked up at Abby, she was smiling that *my hero* smile at him. It put the fucking sun to shame. *"Wet Hot American Summer* is on demand," she said around a sudden yawn.

"We're watching it in *here*? What about the couch?" Code fucking red. Come up with an excuse to get her out of there. "Look at me." He gestured to his grimy construction clothes. "I can't lie on your white bedspread like this. I'll leave an outline."

"I don't care if you smell, but if you want to take a quick shower, there are extra towels in the hall closet. Don't use the purple one, though."

"Why not?"

"Louis's birthday gift from Roxy is rolled inside it. You don't want to know."

"I assure you, I want to know."

Her eyes twinkled, and he experienced some serious relief at seeing something besides fatigue on her. "Edible underwear. For him to wear, not Roxy."

Russell executed an overhead fist pump. "All the worry you put me through today just became marginally worth it, Abby."

Her drowsy laughter followed him from the room, knocking him square in the chest. As soon as he'd closed himself in the bathroom, he started with the now-familiar breathing exercises. A few hours. He could get through a few, measly hours.

Chapter 4

*R*eminding herself it was only three o'clock in the afternoon, Abby forced herself to sit up before she lapsed into a coma. Russell had blown off the rest of his workday to keep her company, and it would be rude to fall asleep on him. She could hear the shower spray drumming in the adjacent bathroom and pictured him scowling at her pink loofah and white-grape body gel.

Smiling to herself, Abby set aside the bag of peas and eased to her feet before limping to the kitchen. Her ankle had started to throb, and without any painkillers in the house, she would have to employ the ancient alcoholic remedy known as tequila. And *wow*, her roommates were really rubbing off on her. She'd never been much of a drinker and was still considered the resident lightweight among the super group, but she enjoyed the buzz a couple of shots gave her. Maybe it would take her mind off the avalanche of work she would have to complete when Russell left. Work that would probably take her until dawn.

Determined to ignore anything but a couple hours of laughing with her friend, Abby retrieved two shot glasses and the bottle of Patron left over from their last indoor summer barbecue. By the time she returned to her bedroom, the shower spray had quieted, so she poured two shots in anticipation of Russell's coming in and left them on her bedside table. Using the piece of furniture for support, she peeled off her nylons and flopped back onto the bed. Abby didn't realize she'd closed her eyes until Russell's heavy tread forced them open, and she saw him standing in her doorway.

Shirtless. Damp. Jeans sitting low on his hips.

A red-hot fist formed beneath her belly button. For *Russell*? She tried to shoot into a sitting position so fast, the back of her head bashed against the headboard, which really didn't help her confusion. Not a bit. She wasn't supposed to notice Russell in that way, right? But when a water droplet rolled down the center of his abdomen and vanished into the waistband of his jeans, she noticed. And she noticed *good*. Today marked the first time she'd ever seen him without a shirt. It also marked the first time they'd ever been alone, without their friends around. Both facts occurred to her simultaneously and out of *nowhere*, she wasn't just watching a movie with a friend anymore.

She was watching a movie on her bed. With an extremely well-built man. A man with chest hair. A man with his family name—Hart—tattooed across his chest.

Russell dropped the towel he'd been holding and came toward her. "What was that reaction about? Did you forget I was here?"

In a manner of speaking. "No. I just . . ." She sucked in a silent breath when he stopped beside the bed, reached out, and cradled the top of her bumped head, rubbing gently. A touch that would have comforted her two minutes ago but now felt very intimate. "I brought tequila."

He must have already noticed the filled shot glasses because he picked one up without looking and held it to her lips. "I would have gotten it for you."

Needing to buy herself some time before speaking, Abby tilted her head back and let him feed her the shot, another gesture that felt like . . . *foreplay*. Or what she'd always envisioned foreplay would feel like. She was grateful for the burn tracking down her esophagus because it distracted her, but as soon as the fire hit her belly, she wished she'd gone for iced tea instead. It only exacerbated the still-undefined problem. "Thanks," she whispered.

Russell watched her with suspicion as he rounded the bed and climbed in beside her, muscles flexing in the television's glow while he settled. Seriously, why hadn't she known about his chest hair? Why did she like it so much? It made him seem so earthy and masculine. Older than the rest of their group.

"I give up. Why are you looking at me like that?"

Shoot. She performed an imaginary search for the remote. "I didn't know you had a tattoo. Or chest hair. Who *are* you?"

Her joke eased the tension a little. Until he stacked his hands beneath his head and stretched out, like a big, contended animal, making her queen-size bed feel tiny. "I'm sure there are things I don't know about you, too."

She doubted there was anything underneath her clothes as exciting as tattoos and chest hair, but she declined to voice that opinion. Something else entirely popped out of her mouth instead. Something she wanted to lasso and drag back immediately into her big gob. "Why don't you ever bring girls around, Russell?"

He sat up without warning, jostling her on the bed. "Hand me that shot of tequila."

"What? Oh." She reached over and handed him the glass. "Forget I asked about girls. It's none of my business."

For some reason, that made him laugh, but it sounded strained. His throat muscles slid up and down as he took the shot. "Would you like me to bring girls around?"

No. The word was yodeled inside her head, echoing like it might around the Swiss Alps. "If you brought a girl around, could we still be friends the way we are now?"

"No, Abby." Had he moved closer? "Probably not."

"Then, no," she whispered.

Horrified she'd revealed a lack of desire to see Russell with someone else, confused she even *felt* that way, Abby busied herself pouring another round of shots. She felt Russell's gaze linger on her turned head a moment before he picked up the remote and started the movie. God, she didn't like feeling awkward around him. This was Russell. Maybe she *had* been affected by the explosion? They just needed a good subject change to get back on solid ground.

"How is the Tribeca job going?"

He looked kind of shocked that she'd remembered. "Really well. We should wrap up in a few weeks unless we get some unexpected rain."

"So I should stop my morning rain-dancing sessions on the roof?"

His lips tilted. "Yeah. Knock that off." Just when she thought they were back to normal, he started looking uncomfortable again. "Actually, we're looking to expand soon. Take on more jobs."

She handed him a shot. "Really? That's great."

"More jobs means more equipment, an actual office, a supply surplus. All that good stuff." Down went his tequila, almost as if he needed liquid courage to finish what he wanted to say. "I have a meeting at the bank next week to discuss a business loan."

Abby's shot sat forgotten in her hand. Just how many new things was she going to learn about Russell tonight? His pride and excitement had always been visible when talking about new contracts. She'd assumed he was satisfied with the current trajectory of Hart Brothers but not actively looking to expand or make the company more lucrative even if there was occasionally unspoken tension when money came up in conversation. She felt guilty now for underestimating him. "Do you need help?" When his head snapped up, and he pinned her with a dark look, Abby realized he'd misinterpreted her offer and felt herself flush bright red. "N-not with money. I meant help preparing for the meeting." She pressed a hand to her cheek, attempting to cool the heated skin. "Numbers are kind of my thing."

"Right." The tension eased from his big body. "I guess I could use the help, seeing how my brother would rather be filmed wearing spandex while completing an obstacle course."

"Huh?"

"Exactly." Russell stole the tequila from her hand and drained it. "Thanks for the offer. I bet you didn't think I'd say yes, huh?"

He leaned close and pressed their foreheads together. "That's me trying not to be a dick. Please take note."

"Note taken," Abby murmured, wondering when her lungs had stopped working. Oh, brother. She needed some time to acclimate to this new consciousness of Russell. He'd never loomed so large or . . . smelled so good. Even with the scent of her soap wafting from his bare skin, his usual maleness was making it seriously difficult to pull away. But she had to.

Nearly every time they hung out as a group, Russell spoke about women with such knowledge, he had to be experienced, whereas she'd only been kissed twice in her life—once by her intoxicated and immediately apologetic stepbrother—and both times severely disappointing. Common sense said that if Russell hadn't shown any romantic interest in her after six months, he didn't have any, and if she let her new awareness of him show now, she risked losing a friend. In addition to landing in a freshly fallen pile of rejection.

Abby moved away, throat tightening under the fear of that possibility. "Helping is the least I can do after forcing you to hang out with me." She lifted her chin. "And making you use my loofah."

"I didn't use it," he responded too quickly.

She poked him in the chest. "You *know* you did."

Russell snagged her wrist and drew her up against his side. When Abby's head landed on his shoulder, everything inside her relaxed, the same way it always did when she put her head there. His strong arm curled around her, and the paperwork stacked around the room vanished into nothingness. Having her face pressed directly to his skin was a new experience. One she'd likely think about later. A lot. But just then, while the movie played in the background, she felt safe enough to let the pressure she'd been carrying around drop off like heavy stones . . . and allow exhaustion to overtake her.

ABBY WOKE UP by degrees. Her head was filled with churning cement, but as the heaviness of sleep wore off, allowing her to open her eyes in the partial darkness, she became aware of *anticipation*. Deep in her belly, between her thighs . . . expectancy hummed like a motor. All over, her flesh was sensitized and warm, in a way that told her minimal effort would be required to ease the discomfort. She'd woken up like this before, usually after watching a racy movie or catching Honey or Roxy making out with their boyfriends, like the hormonally charged couples they were. How could she not be affected by the sight of them going at it, like they might expire if they didn't orgasm?

She could relate. It was how she felt at that very moment.

There was a fine layer of sweat on her forehead, a low pulse below her waist, taunting her hand to come closer. Her work skirt was tangled around her thighs, pressing her legs together, and she squeezed even tighter, a soft moan tripping past her lips. Abby shifted with the intention of yanking the skirt higher, reaching into her panties . . . and froze.

This didn't simply feel like another one of her fantasies. One of those sweaty, often confusing dreams where she imagined being held with such . . . possession. Sometimes more than just holding took place. Her limbs being pinned. Mouth being kissed hard. A deep voice ordering her to do . . . things. Intimate acts she knew all about but had never tried. Never had the opportunity.

Wait. Russell. *Oh God.* She'd fallen asleep beside Russell. Abby heard her thin, rapid breaths and forced herself to quiet down. *Calming* down was another story altogether. Instead of her need cooling upon discovering who had inflicted it? Oh, it was on a warpath now, blazing down her middle with a vengeance. Wetness rushed to the spot where his hand held tight, her body begging without words for his fingers, his palm, anything to provide friction.

This was wrong. Wrong, wrong, wrong. He wasn't even awake, probably would be horrified if he woke up and found his hand under her skirt. She should wake him up *right now*, laugh it off, wait until he left and finish herself off like a good, single lady. Her instinct should not be to move against him, tempt him and hope like hell he woke up needing sex enough to follow through, no matter that they were supposed to be friends. Only friends. *Best* friends.

Russell's hold at the juncture of her thighs increased, that hand tugging her back into his hard body, releasing a rumbling growl into her hair at the same time. Abby's pulse went haywire, making itself evident in every extremity, every private region of her body. And that was before his body even *moved*.

It started as a slow, unhurried roll of his hips, but it was so much more than that. The movement introduced her backside to his erection, full and long. Desire for her? Wow . . . yeah. Desire for *her*. She'd never had a man want her like this. Or if she had, none of them had ever done anything about it. *Russell has never done anything about it, either,* a stern voice whispered. *Stop this now.*

Abby slipped a hand down her belly, fully intending to remove his touch, much as it was going to kill her. Before she could reach her destination, however, Russell's hand dragged up the front of her underwear, over her throbbing clitoris—oh *God*—and slid inside the material. Rough skin against smooth. His middle finger pressed against her entrance, and Abby winced, hyperaware of the dampness he would encounter, but his guttural groan at the back of her head assured her it wasn't a bad thing. Not to Russell. He used the desire coating his finger to glide higher, higher, and find her clit, teasing it with lazy circles.

Abby turned her face and moaned into the pillow. Already she was starting to spasm, his touch so completely different than her own. Unexpected and perfect.

"How'd you get here, angel?" he muttered in a gruff tone, fueling her flaming body even more, when his asking why she was in her own room should have warned her he wasn't fully awake. Wasn't aware of his own actions.

Her body jolted forward as Russell's hips bucked behind her—*once, twice*—then started to move in tandem with his fingers' movements. A tight stroke of her sensitive nub, a sensual drag of his arousal up and down the curve of her ass. There was no ending this, no way. Reason had gotten tangled up in the lusty fog encompassing the bed. Her thighs were a restless mess on either side of his hand, her belly shuddering, her back bowing against his chest. She gasped and cried into the pillow as her body sprinted toward the finish line. Yes, *yes.*

When the orgasm crested over her, Abby's heels dug into the mattress to push herself back into the welcoming strength of his body, bearing down on his pleasure-giving hand at the same time. And God, even with the wicked climax turning her inside out, she wanted to feel his erection against her backside. Wanted to tempt him to do something about relieving the hunger she sensed in him. Already, his movements were growing uneven, staggered, his breathing ragged at the back of her neck.

"*Yes,*" he grated. "That's how I make you come. Hard as fuck when you're in my bed. That's the way I do it."

Still shaken, Abby found herself nodding, because holy crap, he was right. She'd never come that hard in her life. But this wasn't *his* bed, like he'd said. It was hers. Russell still wasn't fully awake, and she'd already let this situation go on too long.

"Russell," she breathed, biting her lip when he started to strum her clitoris with his thumb and her muscles tightened with antici-pation once again. "Russell, we can't—"

"I know, angel. *I know.*" He sounded miserable, giving her im-mediate pause. When had Russell ever sounded like that? "Can't get what I need in real life. Fuck, I won't even let myself take it when I'm dreaming."

"You're not dr—"

Russell rolled Abby onto her belly with one, whip-tight ac-tion. Then he . . . climbed on top of her, wedged an arm beneath her hips, and yanked them up into the cradle of his lap. *Ohhh.* Her insides were clamoring with the new, sudden position. It was bad. And incredible. She hadn't managed to get leverage with her arms, leaving her cheek pressed down into the pillow where her harsh breaths were absorbed. What was he going to do? She should stop him now, but if he did, she would always wonder what came next. Twenty-four years old and a virgin. This had been so long in coming, and she'd dreamed of it so many times. The flesh between her legs craved the feeling of fullness, didn't care if it hurt. God, at this point, she'd welcome the promised flash of pain just to feel *something*.

Russell took hold of her skirt's hem and lifted, leaving the material gathered around her waist. The arm beneath her hips flexed and tightened as his hips started to move, his denim-clad arousal using the damp friction to pump between her thighs, making love to Abby through the barrier of her panties. Light winked behind her eyes as a new, kinkier kind of desire burrowed itself under her skin, raising goose bumps as it went.

"*More, Russell,*" she cried out, shuddering as he drove against her faster. "Please."

"Can't have that pussy. Can't have it. Stop trying to give it to me." She felt his forehead press into the crook of her neck and turn, his mouth finding her ear. "This is my dream, isn't it, angel? Always a fucking dream." His hand worked between their bodies, his big fingers hooking into the top of her underwear and dragging it down, exposing her. "Maybe I'll work myself into your tight ass tonight."

Then he slapped her bottom. *Hard.*

"*Russell,*" Abby shouted, staggered by what she'd just heard. Felt. The unexpectedness of it, by the usually overprotective Russell making her flesh sting. Mostly her mind reeled over the fact that she *still* didn't want him to stop. One of the primary reasons she'd been attracted to Russell's personality was his irreverence. The way he treated her like she wouldn't break under a little disapproval . . . and his palm snapping against her backside took those feelings and turned them up full blast.

Abby's thoughts had distracted her from Russell's sudden stillness, but she noticed it now. Noticed his panting breaths echoing in the dim bedroom. His hardness was still nestled in the valley of her bottom, but he didn't move. With every ounce of her will, she silently begged him to continue but knew deep down, he wouldn't. She'd shouted his name for that very reason. Or maybe her conscience had forced it out of her. The situation had gotten beyond her. She'd already let it go too far, and any further would be catastrophic. Maybe it already was.

"What the hell, Abby?"

Chapter 5

*R*ussell had been having the best dream. When you're hard up for a virgin, dreams were really all you had, so he dreamed *a lot*. Fantasized more than was probably healthy. In bed, in the shower, while operating heavy machinery. It was *never* anyone but Abby. Christ, the pathetic truth was, he couldn't even get his cock up for anyone else. There had been opportunities in bars with flirtatious girls, chances for a possible hookup, and every time—*every single time*—he had walked away, gone home, and dreamed about making Abby come. With his hands and mouth, almost every time. Another sad detail of his fucked-up condition. His dreams were about making her come, all the while leaving her virginity intact. Fantasies that were more satisfying than some random one-nighter with a stranger.

Sometimes, though, he lost the ability to do right by Abby in his imagination. Once, after spending an entire day in her company, he hadn't even made it home before pulling over his truck and beating off to a picture of her on his phone. He'd taken it that day, trying to capture her smile as she flopped back on the grass in

Washington Square Park. But her dress had inched up at the last minute, and he'd gotten a flash of the pink-lace thong between her thighs, immortalizing the image on his phone. It had felt so wrong touching himself to the picture, but the wrong felt so *good*, and he'd kept going. And going. Until he'd been mentally on top of her in the grass, feeding inches into her, taking her roughly for everyone to see. So damn wrong. He'd made it three weeks before breaking down on fantasizing about going that far with her again.

This? This was no fantasy. He should have damn well known, too, because it blasted anything his imagination had ever conjured right out of the water. Lust had him by the throat, and maintaining his focus on *not fucking Abby* was all he could manage. At some point, he needed to remove his aching dick from between her perfect little ass cheeks and pull her goddamn skirt back down. How had this happened? How had it gotten this far?

Everything came back to him in a rush. Abby's falling asleep, her hand eventually coming to rest on his belly, giving him wood for days. His reaching for the bottle of tequila, hoping it would alleviate his condition and take away the residual fear left over from today's near disaster, but the liquor only succeeding in knocking him out. Then he'd woken up with Abby on her knees, him dry-humping her gorgeous, off-limits ass. No, there was more. More. *More, Russell. Please.* He hadn't imagined her moaning those words. Hadn't imagined her coming in his hand. Had he?

Fuck. The memory caused the oxygen to vacate his lungs—his cock to surge harder against his fly—and he fell forward onto her back. It had been real this time. He'd touched her pussy. Her clit. Might have gone further if he hadn't . . . if he hadn't . . .

Russell's eyes flew open, and he lunged off the bed, away from Abby. The sight of her kneeling with her ass up in the air was too much, so he spun around and faced the wall. But not before the image branded itself onto his brain for the rest of his lifetime. He'd never recover. *Never.* Especially not from the angry, red handprint on her unblemished skin.

"Jesus, Abby. I'm sorry. I'm so fucking sorry." He raked both hands down his face, picturing her traumatized expression. Unbelievable. He'd spanked a virgin and suggested an act she had zero familiarity with. Great job, asshole. If she never spoke to him again, he'd be lucky. Every time she looked at him now, there would be irrevocable knowledge. He'd never anticipated Abby's knowing he preferred sex to be hard. Aggressive. Why would she need to know? He'd never planned to touch her. "I thought I was dreaming. I can't believe . . . I laid hands on you like that. Are you hurt?"

"No. I'm fine." He heard what sounded like Abby fixing her clothing, shifting on the bed. "I'm the one who should be apologizing. I-I . . ."

Russell turned around to find Abby sitting cross-legged, hands in her lap. His masculine pride rejected her confession until he remembered the way she'd encouraged him. *More, Russell. Please.* He hadn't imagined her ass writhing around on his lap, either. That had been real. "Did you ask me to stop at any point, Abby? At *any* point. Tell me the truth." He held his breath, aware that if she said yes, he'd want to die, but needing to know nonetheless. When she shook her head, pink rushing over her neck and cheeks, he fell back against the wall.

"I knew you were dreaming, and I let it happen," she whispered.

He swallowed the growl trying to burst from his throat. She'd just confirmed her active participation, and his unsatisfied body demanded he approach the bed, flip her back over, and resume what they'd started. *Fight it, man. This is Abby.* Still, he couldn't let his curiosity go unchecked. "Why did you let it happen?"

A slight hesitation. "It felt good. Really good." She wet her lips, as if her honest confession wasn't temptation enough to withstand. He'd made her feel good. *Fuck yes.* If needed, he could live off that knowledge for the rest of his life. "I know that's not an excuse, though. I took advantage of you."

His pride took a nosedive. "All right," he scoffed. "Let's not get crazy."

Her nod was firm. "It's true."

"Abby, could you try not to completely crush my ego, here? I'm twice your size." He cracked his neck. "Not to mention, I—you *know* what I did."

"You called me angel. You've never called me that before."

"That's not what I was talking about." His throat hurt in a way he couldn't explain. He'd slapped her ass—left a goddamn mark—and she was fixated on his calling her a nickname. A secret nickname he never used out loud but one that fit her perfectly. It felt as if he'd been holding back something important from her. Just that one word.

The direction his thoughts were taking was dangerous. This was how mountains eroded. One tiny crack in the foundation, and the whole thing flattened in an epic dust cloud, obscuring what had been there in the first place. *You can't have this girl.* He'd known that since he'd laid eyes on her, since she'd opened her mouth, and beautiful innocence had floated out, so at odds with the freak show in his mind. The foggy yet brutal memories of his past, coupled with the surge of sexual dominance she brought to the surface. That had been before he'd found out about her endless supply of money, which had sealed the deal. He couldn't provide for Abby, and, therefore, he couldn't try.

Failure to make her happy would, quite simply, be the death of him. He'd failed once before. Watched a loved one fade while being incapable of stopping it. Unable to repair that person's discontent. He couldn't do it again.

Right now, this moment, when she was being so open with him, being so *Abby*, when most girls would be playing games or guilt-tripping him for that handprint on her backside and what he'd said—something he would fully deserve—Russell knew if he went to her, she'd open her arms. He could kiss her with every iota of feeling inside him, feeling he had only for her. But if he did that, there would be no coming up for air. He'd steal her virginity on her lily-white bedspread, and if that happened . . . God help them all. How could he let her go after that? She'd be unequivocally his—and before long, history would repeat itself, only this time, Abby could be the victim.

Russell couldn't do it. Couldn't steal her chance at the future that had been mapped out for a girl like Abby. A future that sure as shit wouldn't involve a blue-collar roughneck who didn't even attend college. He could see it now. His dirt-smudged contractor's license hanging next to her degree from Yale. Not happening. So this was where he stepped up for them both, chalked tonight up to a mistake brought on by too much tequila, and forced them back into normalcy.

She would thank him someday.

"I've never called you angel before? Pretty sure I call everyone that."

The expression that transformed her face after his pronouncement reminded him of someone's walking outside into freezing weather. Her eyes went glassy, and she sucked in a breath, her body withdrawing into itself as though trying to conserve warmth. If Russell hadn't been paralyzed by that reaction, he would have dropped to his knees and buried the nearest sharp object between his ribs. One moment of hurt was better than a lifetime of unhappiness, he reminded himself. Living paycheck to paycheck, clipping coupons. Why didn't he feel reassured?

"Oh. I guess I never noticed." She glanced down at the bed. "So you could have been sleeping next to anyone, and the same thing would have happened, I guess."

"Probably." The word was a sword being drawn from his throat. "I'm a guy, Abby. I woke up with you pressed against me, and I reacted. I'm sorry if you thought—"

"No. I didn't think." She came off the bed and disappeared into her closet, her limp slightly less pronounced than earlier. When she came back out, she had a robe wrapped around her. Like a shield. Against him. God, he wanted to die. Especially when she smiled that Abby smile at him because that was who she was. The girl who smiled when she should be screaming. "Honey should be home soon."

"Right." In other words, if her roommate came home and found them in Abby's bedroom, questions would be asked, and Abby wasn't even a half-decent liar. "Are you going to be okay?"

"Feels better already," she said in a rush. "Lesson learned."

Russell knew she wasn't talking about wearing high heels while running down stairs, but he couldn't comment on it. Had to just swallow it and leave.

"Bye, Abby."

She didn't say anything, merely nodded. Her bedroom door closed before he'd even left the apartment. It sounded like an explosion inside his head.

Russell collapsed into a booth at the Longshoreman across from Ben and Louis. At the moment, collapsing basically maxed out his capabilities. He felt like fire ants were making a permanent home inside his esophagus. He was either the noblest man on the planet or the biggest, dumbest clown ever born. A few blocks from here, a girl who lived to please people was feeling the opposite of special. *Unremarkable*, even. And it was on his fucking head. How? How did this happen when he'd only ever wanted the exact opposite?

I've never called you angel before? Pretty sure I call everyone that.

He slammed his forehead into the table, hard enough to leave a mark. If he didn't think insane behavior would get him hauled out of the bar and strapped to a bed for his own good, he would have kept going. Slamming and slamming until he passed out into blessed unconsciousness. Anything not to see Abby looking like she'd walked into an unexpected snowstorm.

"Hey, Russell," Ben said. "We're only a couple months into the regular season. I have every faith the Yankees are going to pull it together."

Since he was incapable of responding to jokes—probably forever—he reached into his pocket, pulled out a dollar bill, and slid it across the table toward Louis.

Louis held up both hands. "Whoa. What's going on here, man?"

"I'm hiring you."

"Why?"

"Attorney-client privilege."

"Ah, shit. What did you do?"

"Oh no." Ben finally broke in, taking a pull from his beer bottle. "As an English professor, I have no such privilege. If this is going to get me into trouble, tell me right now so I can opt out."

Russell crossed his arms and leaned back, waiting. One of them would crack eventually. Usually, Louis caved first, and Ben got dragged in by virtue of proximity.

As expected, Louis plowed a hand through his hair. "You're really not going to tell us unless I take this fucking dollar, is that right?"

Russell stayed quiet. It was easier than usual to hold his tongue since the last time he'd opened his mouth, he'd hurt the one person he'd sworn never to hurt. Did dentists wire mouths shut even if the patient wasn't injured? Something to look into.

"Don't cave," Ben warned Louis. "Think about it. If he's swearing us to secrecy, it has to do with one of the girls. He doesn't want us passing on this apparently monumental revelation to Honey and Roxy. And they'll find out. Girls always find out."

"Yeah," Louis murmured, clearly still on the fence. "But it doesn't have anything to do with Roxy because I've been keeping her well and truly occupied for the last forty-eight hours. And Honey has been in school, right? That leaves Abby."

That was when Ben joined Louis on the fence. Russell could tell from the way he adjusted his glasses and scrutinized him like he would one of his students. "Whatever it is, he's not happy about it."

"Exactly." Louis tapped a coaster on the table. "Knowledge is power, man. If he did something stupid that will piss off the girls, we need to know—"

"—so we can circumvent the fallout," Ben finished.

"Are you guys done?" Russell asked. "You're giving me a rash over here."

Louis snatched the dollar off the table. "Fine. It stays between us."

Ben groaned. "You're his attorney. What's going to be my reason for staying silent when this inevitably bites us in the ass?"

"The bro code," Louis and Russell answered at the same time.

"That's not a real thing." Ben split a look between them. "Stop pretending that's a real thing."

"I friend-zoned Abby," Russell forced past dry lips. "She almost got blown up today, for fuck sake. Her ankle was hurt, so I stayed and . . . *things* took place. Things of an adult nature. Tequila was involved."

"Finally."

"Took you long enough."

Russell glowered at his friends. "You know how I feel about

this. Nothing was ever supposed to happen with her. That's why I took care of it."

"Oh yeah?" Dread was written all over Louis's face. "How'd you do that?"

"Doesn't matter how." Pain sprung up at the back of Russell's skull, and he welcomed it. Hoped it spread and grew worse. "The result is Abby in the friend zone."

Ben leaned back in his chair, looking thoughtful. "Nope. I'm calling a foul. You're already in the friend zone. A friend zonee can't friend-zone the friend zoner."

Louis was nodding before Ben even finished. "He's right. To the best of my knowledge, it has never been attempted, nor accomplished."

"I concur. But I wouldn't mind consulting the rulebook to be safe."

Before Louis could respond to Ben, Russell held up a hand. "You two are a rare breed of shithead. You know that?"

"Why are you telling us this?" Ben leaned forward to ask. "This isn't merely to unburden yourself, is it?"

Russell wished that were all. If he were capable of keeping Abby at arm's length without their help, he would do it. But it wasn't a viable option now. He could still see her bare ass, feel it writhing against his groin. He knew she came with her whole body, shaking, sobbing, and twisting. For the love of God, he needed help staying away now. Serious help.

"Look, she's going to tell her roommates. They're probably having a three-way text party right now to plot my early demise."

It hurt just thinking about it. She'd laid her head on his shoulder so trustingly and fallen asleep today, but tonight? She probably wouldn't go near him if he begged, but he wasn't taking any chances. "When Honey and Roxy tell you guys what went down, just . . . assure them it was for the best. Tell them I'm an asshole, a liar . . . a cheater. Whatever you have to say. I just need it to get back to Abby so she stays away."

"Nope. Not lying to my girlfriend. That's where I draw the line." Louis slid the dollar back across the table. "You don't need a lawyer; you need a therapist."

"Again, I concur," Ben said, shifting in his seat. "Russell, we all know how you feel about Abby. You might as well have skywritten it the day you two met. Why are you trying to sabotage yourself?"

Russell arched an eyebrow. "Oh, hello, pot. Meet kettle."

"Yeah, I screwed up with Honey. Louis did the same with Roxy. Are you seeing a fucking pattern here?" Ben actually looked angry with him. *Get in line.* "How about learning from our mistakes?"

"This isn't the same thing." God, he hated talking about his insecurities. Knowing they were there was hard enough without dragging them out into the open. "You two have educations, long-term jobs, even the way you speak sounds different than me. I'd be a novelty to her, and eventually, the shine would wear off."

Louis let out a low whistle. "Way to give her credit, man."

Russell was done trying to explain his position. The definition of *useless* was trying to convince two assholes in love with their girlfriends that shit didn't always work out perfectly. Not every situation had a happy ending. "Right. I'll let you two get back to planning your double wedding. I'm calling it a night."

When he pushed back from the table and stood, Louis gripped his forearm. "Listen up. Whatever damage you've done is probably fixable at this stage. Don't heap so much shit on top of the situation that an apology won't be enough."

Russell walked out of the Longshoreman with those words ringing in his ears.

Chapter 6

*A*bby rubbed her blurry eyes and blinked a few times, hoping the laptop screen would come back into focus. No dice. She'd officially hit the wall. Problem these days was, even when she lay down and attempted to sleep, numbers streamed by on the inside of her eyelids. Important numbers. She used to love playing with formulas and manipulating values, but she never got a break anymore. Numbers had transformed into her enemy.

She could hear Honey and Roxy out in the living room, spoons clinking on bowls as they ate ice cream and watched *Finding Bigfoot*. They'd tried several times since Monday night to entice her into hanging out, but she'd continued to hide in her room, pretending work was the *only* thing keeping her there. *Coward.*

Two days had passed since she'd fallen asleep with Russell and woken to an orgasm to beat the band. Two days since she'd had her eyes opened and seen Russell in a new light. Two days since he'd held up a mirror, reflected the light straight back, and blinded her. Truthfully, she was embarrassed. For so many reasons, she couldn't even begin to enumerate them. Like a typical starry-eyed virgin, she'd projected feelings that weren't there. Seen and felt something from Russell that didn't exist, very likely damaging their friendship in the process.

If she were more confident where the opposite sex was concerned, she could just blow his rejection off. *So what? I'm not his type.* Then go find someone who could appreciate an awkward, small-breasted math geek still in possession of her cherry.

Abby slapped a hand to her forehead. More than anything, she wanted to tell Honey and Roxy what had happened and get their take, but she no longer felt sure of how they would react. After all, hadn't she been one hundred percent positive Russell would never hurt her feelings? He'd sure as heck torn that belief down the middle with a resounding *rip*. Roxy and Honey had faced obstacles at the outset of their relationships, but they'd definitely never had to deal with the man not finding them *attractive*. Yes, she had very little experience with men, but she was fairly certain that if Russell had found her appearance pleasing, he wouldn't have zoomed for the exit. Were men even capable of turning down a sexy, obviously willing woman? From what she'd been told, her roommates' boyfriends definitely hadn't.

Would Roxy and Honey react with pity? Or worse . . . maybe Abby's problem would be such a foreign concept to them, they wouldn't even know what to say. At twenty-four, with zero sexual experience to speak of, she felt enough like a freak already without the additional freakhood.

"Hey, Einstein." Roxy appeared at her door, rubbing one stocking-clad foot against the opposite leg. "Honey found *Weekend at Bernie's* in the ninety-nine-cent bin at Rite Aid. Get in on this."

"I made cupcakes, fool," Honey shouted from the living room. "Made them with strawberry frosting because it's your favorite, and being laid regularly has made me seriously philanthropic."

There was no way Abby couldn't laugh at that, so she did. "All right, fine. I need a break anyway. I'm starting to see in double vision."

Roxy bumped her with a sharp hip as they left Abby's bedroom. "When is this project going to be finished? You've been at it for weeks."

Project? Is that what she'd told them? "Uh . . . soon, I think. I need to weigh the risk of a few more investment opportunities—"

"Abby, you're making my head hurt. I'm an actress for a reason." Roxy winked at her. "What I *do* know is how to keep your body instrument fine-tuned, and yours looks tired. Whatever you're doing in there . . . I—we—think you need to scale it back."

When they reached the living room, Abby glanced over her shoulder to find Honey looking cross-armed and downright mean. Recognizing an ambush when she saw one, Abby started backing toward her bedroom. "Oh no. What is this? An intervention?"

Honey blocked her entrance to the hallway. "Roommate style, bitch."

"Come." Roxy grabbed her by the arm and dragged her back into the living room. "Cupcakes and a chat never killed anyone."

"There's no *Weekend at Bernie's* is there?" Abby groaned. "I really don't need to be . . . intervened. Interventioned. Is there a word for this?"

"Worried." Honey guided her down onto the couch. "We're

seriously worried, okay? You were already working too hard and not sleeping enough, but the last few days, it has gotten worse. Talk to us."

"Yeah," Roxy said. "You listen to us complain all the time. We want our turn to be good friends." Since Roxy was usually the most emotionally closed-off of their threesome, Abby was surprised to see a hint of vulnerability creep into her expression. "I only learned recently what *good friend* means, and it sure as hell isn't letting you waste away in your bedroom while we watch a music montage of a dead guy being carried around."

Abby swallowed a smile. "So . . . there is *Weekend at Bernie's* . . . ?"

"Oh, sure. Make jokes during my *Full House* moment."

"This intervention appears to be getting away from us," Honey broke in. "Tell us how we can help, Abby. Baked goods only go so far."

Abby reached for a pink-topped cupcake, letting her breath seep out. Opening up felt like the right thing to do. She was carrying around too many secrets, enough to eventually topple her if she continued in this vein. But when she opened her mouth to tell them about Russell, about the scary, new feelings for him that had popped up only to be shot down, something else entirely came out. Maybe she just wasn't ready to let their one-and-only moment fly away just yet. Or maybe it was her self-consciousness. Whatever the reason, she shoved it deep down into an inner cave for safe-keeping, allowing an even bigger secret to finally break free.

"My father isn't running the hedge fund anymore." As soon as the words passed her lips, a stack of wet newspapers slid from her shoulders. "He . . . can't. That's why I've been working so much."

Her friends were silent a moment before Honey spoke. "I don't understand. Why can't he run his own company?"

Abby bit into the cupcake and chewed slowly, so she'd have time to decide on the right words. She hadn't anticipated telling anyone about this tonight, so there was no ready explanation. There was only the truth. A truth she'd been warned to keep to herself. "A little over a month ago, my father went on a golfing trip to Scotland. Alone. It was really odd timing, but the first quarter had been stressful, so my stepmother and I didn't make an issue out of it."

Roxy and Abby traded a look. Obviously, this wasn't what they'd been expecting. Well, they could join the party because she hadn't expected it either.

"While he was in Scotland, he . . . locked himself in his hotel room and refused to come out." She grabbed a cushion and stuffed it behind her head, her neck suddenly too tired to function. "The staff eventually entered and found him . . . they found him huddled in the bathtub. He'd had some sort of mental breakdown. It was the pressure. It had gotten to him, and there were drugs involved, too. He couldn't cope."

"Oh, my God," Roxy said. "Abby . . ."

"My stepmother went over with a therapist and Mitchell, the company's lawyer, to bring him home. He's getting better—*much* better—but he needs more time." She reassured each of them with a look. "I'm just keeping things afloat until he comes back."

Honey appeared to be frozen in horror. "There's no one who can help you?"

"No one can know. Investors would pull their accounts, we'd

be bankrupt within a week." Although her legs felt liquefied, Abby stood, needing to stress the importance of keeping quiet to her roommates. "I've been acting as my father. Answering his correspondence, making decisions based on what he's done in the past. Mitchell has circulated a story about his pursuing investment possibilities overseas, and everything is operating as usual."

"Except you," Roxy pointed out. "You're dead on your feet."

"I'm fine." Her voice was firm. "I'm mainlining Red Bull, but I can quit any time."

"That's not funny," Honey said. "You're downplaying."

Yeah, she was. And she owed them better than that after all the happiness they'd brought into her life. God, had she even been *living* before they showed up? "Okay, I'm treading water." Their shoulders sagged. "But there are no other options. I'm not going to let my family's livelihood tank for eight hours of sleep."

"Does Russell know about this?" Roxy asked, effectively sending Abby's stomach dropping to the floor.

"W-why would Russell know?" Just saying his name made her lips feel numb. When Honey and Roxy sent each other an unreadable look, Abby frowned. "What?"

"Nothing," Honey said. "It's just . . . you two are close. And you know how Russell is . . . he's protective about you."

"He would flip out, is what Honey's trying to say."

"That's not true." Especially now. After she'd deceived him into giving her an orgasm while he hadn't been fully conscious then let her know that he had no desire for a physical relationship with her. Roxy and Honey were right about Russell's being protective, though. She thought of the way he'd carried her to the fireworks, how he always checked her window locks and killed spiders for her. How whenever the girls went out alone, he lectured her about not leaving her drink unattended. How he insisted on a clear, concise text message the second they walked into the apartment. Russell really *was* a good friend, and she'd lost sight of that in favor of physical release. No wonder she hadn't heard from him in two days. Somehow, starting tomorrow, she would repair this. She wasn't willing to lose him as a friend because of some silly, fleeting crush.

Even though it didn't feel like a simple crush. Not like the ones she'd had before on classmates or tutors. Crushes didn't make you shiver straight down to your private parts at the mere thought of their names. A crush didn't make you slap your own bottom late at night, trying to re-create the same wicked hot sensation he had made you feel with that one, beautiful strike, to no avail.

"You're thinking awfully hard over there." Honey looked almost hopeful. How odd. "Come to any conclusions?"

"Yeah." Abby smiled. "You were both right."

Roxy gathered her hands beneath her chin, eyes widening. "We were?"

"Yup. I need some sleep." Feeling better after having revealed her secret and having a plan to make Russell forgive her, Abby headed for the bedroom. "G'night."

Chapter 7

*U*sing power tools was probably the worst way to celebrate a hangover, but since Russell had been in this condition three days and counting, it was no longer a viable excuse. Mother Nature had sent rain New York City's way, so he and Alec had weatherproofed the Manhattan worksite that morning, giving him the remaining daylight hours to work on the Queens house.

Russell leaned over his worktable and noted a measurement, then checked his watch. Two fifteen. Jesus, he'd thought—hoped—it was later. Time seemed to be moving so slowly, creeping past like a slug after a storm. Or maybe that was him. The slug who was avoiding Abby. They hadn't spoken in three days—not so much as a text message—which was highly unusual for them. How was her ankle? Did she hate him? Enough never to fall asleep on him again?

Hoping to distract himself from the endless cycle of thoughts, Russell pushed away from the table and surveyed the room. He'd made some serious progress in the space of a year, since his father had moved to California, leaving their family home and the memories it represented behind. Since Alec was content to continue renting indefinitely, Russell had commenced renovations of the house, with the understanding that he would live there once they were completed. Funny, he'd never envisioned himself living in a house, but recently, fixing up the place had absorbed a huge chunk of his spare time. He'd gutted most of the rooms, put in new insulation and drywall, gotten crucial deals through loyal Hart Brothers Construction suppliers on new windows, roofing supplies, and lumber. It had taken some hustling to make it all come together, but seeing what his hard work had yielded, damn if he wasn't a little . . . proud.

Russell snorted at the hokey direction of his thoughts, reminding himself that a two-story pile of bricks in Queens was nothing to be proud of. His mother certainly hadn't been proud of the house at which his father had carried her over the threshold. She hadn't been proud of anything *inside* its walls, either, so different from the upper-middle-class home of her upbringing, followed by four years at a respectable university. She'd been engaged to a law student when she'd met their father and canceled the wedding. At one time, he'd been robust—a huge personality that was optimistic about moving higher in the ranks at his construction job . . . but over time, he'd stopped laughing under the weight of her disappointment. Stopped trying.

A memory of his mother crying at the kitchen table in a cloud of cigarette smoke forced him into another room. But there were visions waiting to play out in all of them. His parents fighting about money—never having enough of it, to be precise. His mother coming home tipsy from a block party and telling Russell and Alec about all the men she could have married if she hadn't settled. Settled. *Settled.* That word had never been far away growing up. He'd heard it so many times, the term defined his childhood.

Maybe attempting to live here had been a mistake. He'd thought the past would fade with new walls, new floors and fixtures, but lately, they'd gone from misty recollections to full-blown flashbacks.

When he heard a knock on the front door, he thought that's what was happening. Another vivid flashback, but the knock came again. While striding toward the door, Russell shoved the pencil behind his ear, assuming it was Alec. His brother hadn't taken much interest in the house, but there was a first time for everything.

He opened the door to reveal Abby.

If Derek Jeter had been standing there with a giant check from Publisher's Clearing House, he would have been less surprised. Abby in *his* neighborhood? She didn't even know about the house, so how had she found it? And then, oh God, after the initial shock wore off, all he saw was *her*. Abby in a yellow sundress and purple Wellingtons, holding an umbrella in one hand and motherfucking cupcakes in the other. Was he hallucinating? She looked so sweet and beautiful and *everything*, he wanted to drop to his knees and weep. Damn, he'd missed her.

Instead, he shouted at her. "*What are you doing here?*"

Where she would usually beam at him despite his less-than-gentlemanly greeting, she winced a little but kept her back ramrod straight. "I'm here to make friends again." She held out the clear Tupperware container. "I won't pretend like I made these cupcakes—that's Honey's thing—but I did carry them here on the 7 train. And why didn't you tell me you were building a house?"

"I'm not building a house. I'm renovating one."

"Oh." She wet her lips. "Is it safe for me to come inside?"

No. No, you're not safe around me looking like fresh-baked temptation. "If you don't mind your dress getting dirty," he said, stepping back.

"I don't," she murmured, moving past him, obviously making a concerted effort not to make any form of contact, even with her clothes.

He hated that. *Loathed* it. "There are tools everywhere. You're going to hurt your ankle even worse than it already is."

"My ankle is fine." Her eyes danced to each corner of the room. "It must have been a twist because it's only sensitive now."

Russell hummed in his throat, eyeing the ankle in question dubiously. "How did you find me?"

She shook out her umbrella and set it down inside the door. "I went to your brother's house, where I thought you were staying—"

"I am. I'm sleeping on the couch." *For now.* On the heels of reminding her of their vast economic differences, he felt a punch of nerves over her seeing what he'd accomplished. Two conflicting purposes, yet they were equally strong. Push her away while wondering if he might draw her closer. Maybe Louis was right, and he did need a therapist. "Uh, the kitchen is to the right. Family room to the left. There's a bedroom in back and two more upstairs, along with an office. It's a pretty standard layout. Most of the houses on this block are the same."

She propped the cupcakes on her hip and placed one hand on the staircase banister. "Maybe it was the same before, but you're doing all this great . . . stuff to it."

His lips twitched. "Stuff?"

"Yeah." Finally, a hint of her smile. "*Great* stuff." It went away just as fast as it had appeared. "Anyway, Darcy told me where you were. I'm glad she did. I can't believe no one knows about this place." Her gaze swept over the entryway. "You're going to live here?"

Russell nodded even though he wasn't sure of anything. "Since you're here, I might as well show you around. Head on up."

On the way up the stairs, he kept his head focused on her ankle. No higher. Just enough to make sure she wasn't limping. If he got an eyeful of her ass or a flash of thigh, he'd be showing her a lot more than the bedrooms upstairs. His cock had already grown heavy, recognizing her from a million fevered dreams. She was the fuel that had provided the guy downstairs with hours and hours of frantic stroking, and dude wanted to say a personal thank-you. But it would not be happening. This was a good thing. She'd come here wanting things back to normal. Russell wanted that, too. Right? *Right.*

When he reached the landing, her yellow dress beckoned him into the small office, adjacent to the master bedroom. "Office," he said, stating the obvious, like an asshole.

"Wow. Such great lighting in here." She went up on her toes to look out the window. "That's one thing my office at work is lacking. It could be nighttime, and I wouldn't even know if I didn't have a clock."

He felt his features arrange themselves in a scowl at the thought of her in an airless, windowless room, but remembering what she'd said Monday night about his always being mad at her, he erased the expression before she could turn around. "The jobs we've done, a lot of customers don't like too much light in their offices because it creates a glare off their computer screens."

"Oh. Not me. I'd want it to feel like I was working outside. Maybe even a big old skylight." She tucked a stray strand of rich, brown hair behind her ear. "Everyone has their own tastes, though. It's perfect the way it is." Still carrying the cupcakes, she passed him and left the room. Russell considered the small space a moment, ruminating on the merits of added sunlight, before following.

It was ridiculous, but he actually hesitated on the threshold of the master bedroom. At this point in time, it wasn't a bedroom just yet. He'd managed to put up Sheetrock on all four walls, but beyond that it was mainly sawdust, tools, and another worktable. Not the place he was possibly planning to sleep for the rest of his life. But once he saw Abby within those walls, would he be able to take it back? Or would she be there every time he fell asleep, even fifty years from now? Peeking out the window in her yellow sundress, outlined by the rain?

Russell took a steadying breath and entered the bedroom. Abby had set the cupcakes down on the worktable so she could pick up his hammer drill. Ah Jesus, Abby holding a power tool. His two favorite things in one. Code fucking red.

"Why aren't you at work?" he asked, kicking at some sawdust on the ground.

"I took an extended lunch break." She set the drill down on the windowsill, as if it had grown too heavy. "I have to go back later, though. I just—"

"What? You *just* what?" God, why couldn't he stop being such a jerk to her? Maybe because every second he spent breathing white-grape sunlight caused a buildup in his chest, crowding his insides and threatening to spill free. It wasn't so much being a jerk as trying to hide his panic.

Abby smoothed a hand down the skirt of her dress, big hazel eyes trained on him. "I *just* don't like that I've deleted about a hundred text messages to you since Monday, okay? Or not knowing if you'll want to hang out with me again." She rolled her right shoulder back. "I know I took advantage of you. But I apologized, Russell. And to be perfectly honest, I think you're taking this silent treatment a little too far. And now I find out you have this whole other life—"

"Back up." She'd written and deleted messages to him. Messages that would never reach his phone. That knowledge was a shotgun bullet right in the gut. "What was that first part, again?"

"I took advantage of—"

"Yeah. That part." His booted footsteps created an echo as he approached her. "Don't ever say or think that bullshit again. Are we clear?"

Her back pressed against the wall when he got close enough to touch, her brow wrinkling. "But it's true, I—"

Russell laid his palms flat above her head, pulses pounding wildly all over his body. His temples, his chest, below his belt. "I'm warning you, Abby."

That was the exact moment he showed his hand. And he didn't know if he held aces or a deuce-seven off-suit. He only knew based on Abby's curious expression that he'd just alerted her to the fact that a decision hung in the balance. It was hers to make, and the result was his backing off or going forward.

Or maybe there was no decision at all. Had it all been decided Monday night in her bedroom? The first time she'd walked out onto her building's stoop and he'd sunk like a stone beneath a crashing wave? He didn't know. But hearing her blame herself for their becoming physical simply wouldn't fly. Not when he'd wrung his dick out nightly for the last six months, pretending like she was watching it happen, gasping in approval, and kissing his neck. Christ. His Abby had been defiled by him so many times, a number didn't exist. She would take the blame for what happened between them over his dead body.

Long seconds of Abby's studying his face had passed, as if she could discern what was taking place in his head when even *he* didn't have a fucking clue. Those eyes were obscured a moment by her eyelashes, and Russell could feel that gaze move over his erect cock where it tented his jeans, then shoot back up. He expected surprise, maybe more confusion. Instead, he got relief and *excitement*. No. Not that. He couldn't handle that.

Her sweet, ripe tits rose and fell on a shudder. "I'm sorry I used the situation to my advantage, Russell. It was wrong of m—"

He kissed Abby. Abby. He . . . kissed *Abby*. Sensation exploded in his head like an atom bomb, incinerating everything in its path. No, not everything. Only the *negative*, replacing it with optimism, *relief*, elevating him above anything that could touch him beside her. That was how good—how *right*—she tasted. Like a beast that had been chained for centuries, and the second those imaginary chains fell away, he attacked without hesitation. Stopping now was a hysterical notion because her arms were around his neck, her body flattened against the wall . . . by him. Yeah, that was *him* grinding every inch of himself to her, branding her, imprinting the pattern of his muscles and flesh on Abby. He was kissing *Abby*.

The resonance of her name cut a path through the ringing in his skull. If he continued kissing her like this, her virginity would be as good as gone. Even now, her inexperience showed, her tongue testing itself against his. A tentative lick that almost sent him ejaculating against the fly of his jeans. He moaned into her mouth, telling himself *one more minute, just one more.*

Better make it count. Russell gripped a fistful of her hair and rotated it, wrapping the long strands tight and forcing her head back. With his other hand, he urged her chin lower so he could invade her mouth deeper, get another one of those self-conscious touches of her tongue because *fuck* they were perfection and misery all rolled into one. She gave one to him—*yes, God*—and he felt the stroke in his dick, as if that pulsing part of him were inside her mouth, rather than his tongue. A vision of Abby on her knees gave him no choice but to press her harder against the wall, lest he urge her to the floor. Goner . . . he was a goner.

He felt her hand flatten against his chest and push, then *pat pat pat.* Breathe. *Shit*, she needed to breathe. Alarm managed to break through Russell's lust, and he broke away on a harsh groan, scanning her face to make sure he hadn't killed her.

Just one look and she killed *him* instead. Damp, swollen lips, face flushed pink . . . achingly beautiful. Like some untouched maiden sent into the woods to pick apples who had found herself ravaged by a wolf instead. That settled it. He'd have to sleep in the other bedroom. Abby, this moment, would never fade.

She shifted, and her belly dragged over his hard cock, ripping a growl from his throat. Her mouth fell open as if stunned by his reaction, making him frantic to kiss her again, so he banged his forehead against the wall and kept it there.

"You *are* attracted to me," she murmured, voice husky in a way he'd never heard it . . . and tinged with that same relief he'd glimpsed in her expression before. Why the hell was she surprised by his wanting her? Didn't she realize he'd walked out of her bedroom because it was for the best? Slapping her ass hadn't been enough of a hint that he didn't know a damn thing about being with a virgin? Or . . . making love? He wasn't the kind of man she deserved. His tastes in bed were only *one* part of why he couldn't make her happy. So maybe she needed a reminder. One that would leave no question unanswered.

"Abby, attraction is a weak-ass term for what's going on here. It doesn't begin to describe what I'd like to do to you."

"Wh-which is?"

He placed his mouth against her ear, the truth coming out on a rush of breath. "I'd like to bang your little virgin brains out."

Chapter 8

*O*h. *Oh, boy.*

Longing moved like smoke in Abby's middle, wafting lower and growing dense. She should have slapped him across his face for saying those words, but some female intuition that had been sorely lacking in her life until this point stayed her hand, telling her a slap was exactly what Russell wanted. He expected her to be horrified and run from the house like a scandalized church girl. Too bad she wasn't budging. Because the same way she'd always appreciated Russell's rough-around-the-edges attitude toward her—the way he treated her like no one had ever dared—she *liked* the way he'd just spoken to her. *A lot.*

The evidence that Russell wanted her dug into her belly, no less big and swollen than when they'd been kissing. Seriously, could what they'd just done even be termed a kiss? *Mouths* participated in a kiss, whereas Russell had made it into a full-contact sport, rubbing their bodies together like he meant to start a fire with the friction, exploring her mouth as if he'd been starved for it.

Had he? His hot, rapid breaths against her neck told her . . . yes. This man she had so many confusing but exciting feelings for wanted her back. A wealth of shiny bubbles sailed through her chest. This was *good* news, right? Why had he stopped kissing her? She'd caught her breath and wanted more, darn it. But his posture was that of someone heading for the gallows. If he needed encouragement, she was all too ready to provide it. When he'd left her Monday night, her body hadn't been ready to say good-bye. Neither had her mind. Both were tired of being in the dark about the unknown, so much that the unfulfilled ache worsened with each passing day.

So, encourage she would. And if Russell thought he was the only one who could shock someone, he had another think coming.

"Russell." Abby ran a hand down his back, let it mold to the tight swell of his ass, the bold act ratcheting up her excitement another ten degrees. "Do you want to bang my little, virgin brains out on the floor or against the wall?"

His breathing cut off—he didn't move—for what felt like hours. His erection remained ridged between them, though, so she didn't give in to the urge to start rambling. No taking it back now, was there? Good. She didn't want to.

Finally, he pulled back and drilled her with a look. "You sure as hell better not let me off the hook for saying that to you, Abby. You better get pissed, or else—"

"Or else what?" His gaze darkened in a way she'd never seen. It didn't alarm her, though. No, they were on the edge of breaking past something, and she wanted to race straight into the eye of the storm. "What are you going to do? Frown me to death?"

She deliberately let her attention fall to his mouth. "Or something more interesting?"

His fists thumped the wall above her head. "You're getting yourself into trouble here, angel."

The nickname sent another shot of bubbles twirling inside her, but she squashed each one to nothingness. It wasn't special. She was an adult with realistic expectations, and this encounter didn't have to be a fairy tale. Right now, her only wish was for Russell to stop holding back. "What does *trouble* mean? Show me—" Her words ended in a gasp when Russell dropped a hand from the wall and reached under her dress. The feel of his big, work-roughened touch squeezing her bottom—*tight, so tight*—burned away any remaining doubts that she wanted to take it further, but Russell's dark expression told Abby she had work to do.

"You deserve a man who will ask permission before he does this." He pulled the material of her thong tight against her center, teeth sinking into his bottom lip as he performed the breath-stealing move. "This, too."

"I gave it to you." Her voice shook, thighs clenching as moisture rushed between them. "Stop treating me like I don't know my own mind."

Something resembling panic glimmered in his expression before it was gone. "Look. What we did the other night, what you're asking me for now . . . you'll do that with your husband. Or . . . or a boyfriend someday. Not me. Not now."

She reached up and ran her nails over his shaved head, feeling encouraged by the shiver that passed through him, his eyes closing. "Russell—"

"*No*." He snagged her wrists and pinned them to the wall but seemed to realize immediately the new position had been a mistake because it only brought their bodies more flush. Determined to use every advantage, she pushed her breasts higher, tilted her hips, and absorbed the groan that rumbled in his chest. "Abby, please. I like things you're not used to." His gaze strayed to her breasts, and they swelled beneath his attention. "You'll end up with someone who knows what a girl like you needs. Someone who treats you right."

"No one treats me better than you," she whispered against his mouth. "You only pretend otherwise. I trust you."

A broken sound left him, but still he shook his head. "Think about it. You want to introduce *me* to you father? Huh?"

The one thing she hadn't been prepared for him to say impacted her like a snowball in the face. Not because she would feel an ounce of shame introducing Russell to her family—how *dare* he even suggest it—but because for the last half hour, she'd forgotten about the difficult situation with her family, the responsibility on her shoulders. God, she couldn't introduce anyone to her father even if she wanted to. An image of her desk, her overflowing in-box popped in to say hello and polarized her. Stress stomped through her stomach like a college marching band.

"That's what I thought," Russell said, pulling away, his face grave. "It's a good thing, all right? Believe me, the last thing I'm in the market for is a girlfriend."

Abby sagged against the wall in the absence of his weight, her mind performing a frantic dance to catch up. Did Russell actually think her reaction had been over the thought of his meeting her father? A knot twisted in her stomach at the realization. He was walking away without giving her a chance to explain—and suddenly she didn't *want* to. This friend who knew her better than *anyone* thought her nothing more than a materialistic rich girl who cared about appearances. Just like everyone at the office.

For the second time that afternoon, she probably should have run from the house without so much as a backward glance. But that would have been too easy. She wanted—*needed*—to regain this sense of loss that multiplied every step Russell took away from her. More than that, though, she was tired of being controlled by the expectations of others. *You'll end up with someone who knows what a girl like you needs.* How could he spout such nonsense when *she* didn't even know?

Well. She knew *one* thing. Her body felt . . . hot and neglected. Even after he'd reduced her to a petty rich girl, she *still* wanted him to touch her. Enough to make her flesh heat over the way his body moved. Shoulder muscles bunched, backside outlined by his faded jeans. Swaggering. Always swaggering. She wanted to rid him of that self-assurance—that assurance of *everything*—and turn him as needy as she felt.

When Russell reached the door, he laid a big hand on the jamb and turned, features tight as he looked everywhere but at her.

"Come on, I'll walk you to the train."

Sti cazza. In another, more appropriate term, *screw this.* With a silent prayer for courage, Abby found the hem of her sundress and peeled the garment over her head, letting it fall to the floor. "I'm not ready to leave yet."

There was a split second where she almost scooped her dress

off the floor and covered herself back up. Russell might have seen her bare butt Monday night, but she'd never been seen in less than a bathing suit. Not by a man. Thanks to the pale color of her strapless dress, she'd worn a white, strapless bra and matching thong and—*crap*—was that even sexy? She had no earthly idea.

Doubts fell from her consciousness like a cup of overturned paper clips when Russell stalked forward, prowling across the room and shifting the air around her. This impulsive disrobing had started as an act of rebellion, but now a furnace blast hit her head to toe. The raindrops pelted the window in time with her jumping pulse. The fierceness in his eyes told her to expect being pinned against the wall again, but it never happened. Instead, he fell to his knees in front of her, gripped her bottom . . .

And buried his face between her thighs.

A multitude of new sensations overwhelmed Abby, sending her falling back against the wall. His stubble rasped over her smooth skin, his rough hands yanking her hips closer so he could rub his mouth back and forth over her most sensitive spot. Cursing over and over under his breath, he pressed his forehead tight against her core, nudged and dragged, all through her cotton panties. There wasn't a part of his face that didn't touch her, burn her through the material.

Very slowly, he stood, trailing his tongue up her belly until he reached her breasts. As he stared, his gaze voracious, her nipples went so tight, it hurt to keep them contained. Before she could remove her bra, Russell's voice grated along her firing nerve endings. "All that, everything I said, and you still want it, angel?" The hint of pain in his tone had her reaching for him, but he grabbed her wrists. "You'll be sorry."

"Stop acting like you'll hurt me. You couldn't."

Russell released a shaky exhale. "You've misplaced your faith in me." He freed her hands, only to flick open the front snap of her bra. "I should be zipping you back into your girl-next-door dress and sending you home with those cupcakes." Both sides of her bra were shoved aside, exposing her peaked breasts. Russell muttered something that sounded like *little peaches*, before his hands closed around them and lifted, squeezed, massaged. "Instead of sending you home, I'm going to find out what a virgin tastes like."

Her feet left the floor as Russell swung her into his arms, turned, and placed her on the worktable. Despite the abrasive surface, Abby could only replay his words. Could only experience the massive anticipation as Russell peeled off his T-shirt to reveal the tattooed, hair-covered chest she'd been fantasizing about since Monday night.

"You like the way I look?" Hands braced on either side of her hips, he leaned down and sucked her left nipple into his mouth. "That's good, angel. You're looking at the first man to tongue-fuck your uptown pussy."

Blood roared in her ears, keeping time with the storm outside. A burst of irritation tried to wend its way through her need, but she fought it off. So close. She was so close to feeling something she'd always wondered about. "I love the way you look," she said. "I wish I could see all of you."

His jaw flexed. "If I *showed* you all of me right now, I'd have to *give* you all of me." He licked across to her right breast and flicked her nipple with his tongue. "And if you want to know the truth, I haven't stroked myself off since last night. It would be too hard and too fast. You'd walk funny for a week."

"Oh. That wouldn't be good," she murmured, her words ending in a sob as he pushed her knees wider. As if he was mad at her for not taking him to task over his blunt speech. Even now, was he hoping she would call it off? She didn't understand the sudden pang of tenderness for him, only knew she'd missed something along the way. Something he was experiencing alone. Before she could check the impulse, Abby reached out and cupped his stubbled face. "I haven't stroked myself off since last night, either, if it makes you feel better."

A laugh boomed out of him before he cut it off with a single shake of his head. "Fuck, Abby," he said, his voice hoarse. "I shouldn't be doing this, but I'm not good enough to stop now. You're my fucking wet dream sitting there in those white panties."

"You dream about me?"

This time, his laugh was all pain, no humor. By way of response, he curled his fingers around the crotch of her panties, nudging her clit in the process, and stripped them down her body. "Get on your damn back, Abby."

She hadn't even finished reclining onto the coarse surface when Russell's mouth found her. At first, just the explicitness of having another person touching her so intimately sent a thrill blasting up her spine. Like before, when she'd worn her panties, he chafed her center with his face. Cheeks, chin, mouth. Making her feel cherished in a way maybe he didn't know how to vocalize? No. Stop thinking. Focus on the—

Pleasure. Abby's body convulsed on a moan. Holy *shit*. Her hands scrambled for something to anchor her to the table as the physical equivalent of a scream went off below her belly button. Her belly bottomed out like she'd just flipped upside down on a roller coaster. She'd touched herself in the same place many times, but the smooth glide of Russell's tongue would forever ruin self-pleasure for her. With his left hand, he traced a pattern up her arched torso to palm her breast, his tongue busy on her clit. Automatically, she rushed to cup the other one, rub a thumb over her aching nipple so she could experience the answering tug between her legs.

Russell broke away on a growl to scoop her backside into his hands. Abby stared in awe at the transformation in him. His eyes were bright, as if he was running a fever. "If you weren't a virgin, I'd have two fingers nice and deep." He laid a kiss on top of her clit. "We're going to keep this baby innocent today, though. Mostly. Nothing innocent about your legs wrapped around my head, is there?"

Abby double-checked through hazy vision and saw her legs were still spread. "L-legs wrapped around—" He sucked her clit into his mouth and Abby screamed, legs closing around him, thighs pressing against his ears. "Oh my God. *Oh my God.*"

The hands on her bottom tightened, punishing her flesh with bruising strength as he sucked and released, flicked his tongue against her tortured bud, then sucked again. She loved the mix of pleasure and pain so much, she begged for his hands back when they suddenly disappeared. In the far-off distance, she heard the metallic zing of a zipper and the grunt that followed. His lips shook around her clit a moment, before they firmed again and gave one final pull, shooting Abby over the finish line.

"*Russell,*" she cried, reaching out to tug his head closer, without shame. She had no capacity to feel anything but beautiful, blazing relief as every muscle she possessed clenched like an iron fist. "I can't breathe."

Abby didn't realize her eyes were closed until they opened to find Russell standing over her . . . with his erection in his hand. It looked heavy and painful as his touch moved base to tip in hurried movements, his ridged abdomen flexing as he stroked. "Jesus, I'm sorry. It's too much. You know how fucking sweet you taste?"

"What do you need?" The words tumbled out before she knew what they meant. Russell's agonized groan hit her with a brutal punch, forcing her into a sitting position. "Do you want me to—"

He let go of his erection. Abby only had a second to watch in fascination as it bobbed against his belly, before he yanked her off the table, spun her around and bent her forward. "Say what you were going to say," he demanded, laying his arousal on her backside and pumping his fist around it once more. "Do I want you to *what?*"

A mixture of shock and renewed heat coursed through her. She focused on the latter, marveling over how desired it made her feel. How *bad*. "Do you want me to suck it, Russell?"

Her name sounded strangled as he shouted it, just before she felt warm moisture coating her bottom. "Ah, Christ. *Christ*. That ass has been teasing me for months. I'd love to give it a good fucking *smack*."

"Do it," she gasped, craving the new, the unexpected. Wanting to ease the misery she'd seen etched into his face even if she didn't fully understand how it would help. "Please."

Abby's body jolted against the table, hips bumping the hard edge as Russell's palm connected with her offered bottom. Her mouth fell open in a silent cry, fingers scratching at the table's surface. *Oh. I-I want more of that.* A new, almost stickier pleasure ticked the inside of her thighs, feathered the inside of her belly. She wanted Russell to do it again so she could explore the new development, but her backside was covered with soft material—a T-shirt?—the evidence of what they'd done being wiped away.

When Russell finished, she turned to find him facing the other direction, refastening his jeans. His shoulder and back muscles were tense, movements jerky. Abby's self-consciousness didn't just creep in—it *roared*—until he glanced at her over his shoulder and she saw shame in his gaze as it moved over her.

"God*dammit*." His hands found his hips, head falling forward. "I told you, Abby. I told you, and you wouldn't *listen*." Then quieter, "I'm sorry, angel."

Abby crossed to her discarded dress and stepped inside, pulling it back up around her, feeling as though she was preparing for battle. No . . . there *was* a battle there, right in front of her. Intuition wouldn't let her deny it. The battle might not end today or in the near future. She didn't know what the outcome would be should she lose or win. But she had no choice but to fight. Starting now. "I'm not sorry."

"Oh, yeah?" His boots scraped on the floor as he turned, visibly pissed off. "Do you have any idea where these . . . things I want to do to you end? I don't. I don't *know*." His Adam's apple rose and fell. "How can I want to protect you and want to do them at the same time?"

Abby's heart lurched. "Do you only want to do them to me?"

His breath whooshed out. An answer seemed to be on the tip of his tongue, but he turned away and wouldn't meet her eyes. "This can't be permanent, Abby. I'm sorry if that's what you expected, but—"

"You're not in the market for a girlfriend. I remember that part." Pain and embarrassment threatened, but she kept her features schooled. Again, she experienced the feeling that something was eluding her. Sure, her physical relationships with men had been limited to awkward high-school dances and the rare kiss, but she couldn't remember any of them behaving like Russell did when they touched. Would he treat *any* girl the same way? Her intuition said no, but if she pushed and turned out to be wrong, the resulting humiliation would be awful.

So he didn't want a girlfriend. Did she want Russell to be her *boyfriend*? She hadn't allowed herself to consider it, but now that her mind had presented the question?

Yes. Yes, if that meant spending more time with him. Having him touch her whenever she wanted. At the very least, she wanted to *try*, but only if Russell wanted it, too. He didn't. Should she leave, then? Forget today ever happened? Or trust her gut, trust him, and have faith the missing puzzle piece would eventually fall into place? The alternative was leaving now, letting Russell go on believing she deserved someone better and losing her chance to explore this daring, new side of herself. And wow, it had felt good letting her inhibitions go and just *feeling*.

"I don't need a boyfriend," she said, even though it felt dishonest. Even though it made her throat tighten. So she tempered it with honesty. "But I need this."

Russell paled. "Please, don't do this to me."

"What am I doing to you?" Abby waited, but he didn't answer, merely watched her like she'd just buried an ice pick in his chest. It made no sense. He was attracted to her but didn't want a relationship. Shouldn't her offer make him happy? "You, uh . . . you don't have to answer now. I need to get back to work, anyway. So . . ." She headed in the direction of the door, having to bypass Russell to get there. His tense energy warned her to give him space, but she didn't want to get used to avoiding him, so she stopped and planted a kiss on his cheek. "Bye, Russell."

He didn't say a word or move a muscle as she left the room.

Chapter 9

Russell made sure no one was watching as he cracked open the beat-up paperback book and continued reading. If Alec caught him reading a romance novel on his lunch break, the ball-breaking he'd receive would be the stuff of nightmares. Honestly, he would deserve every painful second of it, but nothing could force him to put the goddamn thing down. It had started as a guilty exploration, or possibly his newly revealed masochistic streak, but when he'd noticed Darcy reading *The Dark Duke's Virgin Bride* over breakfast, he'd pocketed it without a second thought. Unfortunately, the more Russell read, the certainty that he was screwed with Abby only amplified.

With another furtive glance over his shoulder, he read on.

Dreading the inevitable pain he would cause Violet, Sebastian paused at the barrier of her virginity, sucking in a breath at the loveliness of her naked body. The way her breasts shook with excited breaths, even though her eyes held a touch of nerves.

Right. Okay. Russell was with the duke so far. Hot virgin. Check. Shaking breasts. Double check.

Violet bit her lip as Sebastian pushed forward, speaking of discomfort that couldn't be avoided. He tried to console himself with the knowledge her pain would only be temporary. That she would finally be his.

This is where the head shaking started. The duke was one selfish motherfucker, wasn't he? As far as Russell could tell, Violet hadn't wanted any part of the marriage to some weird-ass recluse in the first place. She'd only agreed to wed the dude to save her disgraced family from bankruptcy. Didn't the duke give a shit that he was taking away her freedom? She'd be stuck with him for *life*.

Sebastian braced his hands on either side of Violet's hips and whispered a heartfelt apology beside her temple. With a single, measured drive, he claimed his bride as his wife in every sense of the word. Her body tensed beneath his much larger one, a cry of surprise passing her lips. "I'm sorry," Sebastian rasped, sweat beginning to dot his brow. "The pain will pass in but a moment. I won't move until then, but . . . ah, you feel so perfect, Violet."

Russell shoved the book into his glove compartment, wondering why the hell he'd waited to read the sex scene while at work. Operating a buzz saw with a hard-on probably wasn't the wisest move.

"Damn books should come with a warning," he muttered, adjusting his cock through his work pants. Nothing could stop him from replacing himself with the duke and the lip-biting Violet with Abby, however. Which was completely out of bounds. Before yesterday, he'd only dreamed of going all the way with Abby in moments of total weakness. Since she'd shown up with cupcakes and offered to get on her knees for him? He'd mentally fucked sweet, little Abby up one side and down the other, in several positions, in every room in his house. Immediately after he came—every single time—he would renew his vow never to sleep with her in real life. *Never.* He could *not* let it happen. But nothing short of a lobotomy could stop him from picturing it. Over and over and *fuuuuuck*.

Would Abby cry out in pain like that when he got inside her? The duke was a class-A prick in Russell's estimation, but man, the way he'd just stayed still while Violet got used to him? Admirable. Russell was pretty sure he'd fail then and there. When he got physical with Abby, something inside him took over. He'd never been gentle in bed, but he'd never spanked a girl. He'd never wanted to pin a girl down and never let her up, the impulse so intense it choked him. *Scared* him. If he hurt Abby, going on with his life would be torture. Every waking minute would hurt.

But that was exactly what he was considering, wasn't it? *I don't need a boyfriend, but I need this.* Need. Abby *needed* something from him, and his every instinct, at all times, demanded he give her anything and everything she needed. It was a compulsion. An honor. His intention yesterday had been to drive her away, show her how unworthy he was, what an asshole he could be. Instead of cursing at him in Italian as he'd expected, she . . . she'd kissed his cheek.

Russell realized his palm was pressed to the side of his face and forced his hand to drop. If she'd only stormed out, calling him every name in the book. *That* he might have been able to handle. But she'd offered him no-strings-attached sex, and he didn't know if enough nobility in the world existed for him to pass that up. Not with Abby. Maybe he could say no at that moment, but put her in front of him with her dress off again? He'd be a fucking goner.

Having a physical relationship with Abby without labeling her as his girlfriend was low. *So* damn low. Move over Duke Sebastian, there's a new dickhead in town. But Russell had woken up this morning with a glimmer of hope lodged in his rib cage, refusing to budge. *What if. What if. What if.* He had the bank meeting next week. If by some miracle he secured the loan, Hart Brothers Construction could go to the next level. It would take a shit ton of hard work, but it would be enough to give a comfortable life to Abby. More comfortable than the one his father had provided his mother. And if Russell could have Abby in his life, he'd work fifteen jobs and still take side gigs.

So, as of now, he had a plan. A plan to be with Abby if everything went exactly right. If he managed to put on a suit and convince the loan officer he was a responsible man with a vision to expand his business, he'd ask her to be patient while he built it into the best damn construction company in New York City. He couldn't believe he was allowing himself to even consider a future with her, but after yesterday, resistance was futile. He *needed* Abby.

Now he just had to avoid her until then, so he didn't fuck everything up. He couldn't allow them to become friends with benefits, something that would be beneath her. God, did she really believe that was all he wanted to offer her? Thought he didn't feel enough to give her the real thing? Knowing that hurt after how close they'd become, but he'd fix it. He'd fix everything soon.

A knock on his truck window sent him shooting up in the

driver's seat, his head hitting the ceiling with a bang. "What the—" He turned to find Ben staring back at him through the window, sipping a paper cup of coffee and looking highly amused. He stepped back when Russell pushed the door open. "What are you on a field trip or something, professor?"

"Nope." Ben surveyed the construction site. "Although, I have no doubt my English students would learn some colorful language here."

"Fucking-a." Russell shut the driver's side door and leaned against the sun-heated side. "What brings you and those shiny loafers to this neck of the woods?"

"You didn't answer your cell phone, and I need a head count."

"For?"

"A road trip to the Hamptons. Tomorrow through Sunday." Ben shrugged and tossed his now-empty cup into the nearby trash can. "Honey and Roxy came up with the idea, and since I don't have a death wish, here I stand."

Russell frowned. "*Death* wish?"

"Take Abby out of town without telling you? I'd like to keep my anatomy intact."

"Abby." Russell stood up straighter. Of course she was going. Those three girls didn't do anything apart anymore. Except for surprise trips to Queens, apparently. And while he wanted to laugh off Ben's assumption that he'd blow his top if she went out of town without his knowledge . . . it had been accurate. For the million and first time that day, he wondered where the hell this protectiveness with Abby ended. *Did* it end? Would it grow? The back of his neck had already started to sweat, just envisioning her in a car driving farther and farther away. "Where did they come up with this idea?"

The way Ben eyed him made Russell nervous about what was coming. "Between you and me, Honey mentioned that Abby's been stressed. They thought the trip might help—"

"*Stressed about what?*" Based on Ben's raised eyebrow, Russell knew he'd shouted the question. Christ, please don't let it be because of him. It couldn't be. Could it? She'd seemed tired yesterday, but no more than she had been for the last month. But that was due to work. Right? She'd been working too hard. Why hadn't *he* thought of getting her out of town?

Ben gave his shoulder a shove. "I assume from the smoke coming out of your ears that you've decided to join?"

He was supposed to be avoiding her, dammit. The timing couldn't have been worse. When he noticed Ben watching him curiously, he stalled. "Uh. Where is everyone staying?" *Where will Abby be staying? Will she be safe?*

"That's kind of the crazy part." Ben adjusted his glasses. "Honey was all set to book some affordable motel until Abby casually mentioned her family owns an estate in Southampton. A big one. We're staying there."

Russell's stomach sank to the ground. An estate in Southampton. He could work seven days a week for the rest of his life and never give her that. Was there even a point in trying? Yeah. Fuck yeah there was . . . it was Abby. But he needed more time. He'd had a damn plan up until a minute ago. Now he was facing two days of being in the same house with Abby, knowing she was sleeping down the hall and wanting to continue what they'd started. A nightmare and a dream come true, rolled together in a ball of total mindfuckery.

"Look, I checked, and there are enough bedrooms for you to keep Abby in the friend zone. If that's what you want." When Russell only stayed quiet, Ben laughed. "I don't know what's going on with you, man, but if Honey was going to be in a bikini on the beach, the only single girl in the bunch, I'd be shitting a brick."

"*I'll go*," Russell grated. "I'm going."

It was Saturday morning. Abby should have been packing her travel case for a lazy, sunshine-laced weekend with her friends. Instead, she was staring over the top of her Mac computer screen at the company's lawyer, Mitchell, and one visibly irritated stepmother. *Her* stepmother, to be exact.

Abby had woken early, thinking to drop into the office to tie up some loose ends so she could relax over the weekend, but she'd stumbled upon a meeting between her stepmother and Mitchell, who were less than enthused about her impromptu vacation. Oh, they were trying to hide it, but her stepmother's tell had always been rummaging through her purse. And the Balenciaga bag had been rummaged within an inch of its three-thousand-dollar life.

"You'll be on call, though, won't you?" her stepmother asked, pulling out her wallet and replacing it seconds later. "Don't get me wrong, I'm thrilled you're finally taking advantage of the estate. I've been begging you to accompany me for a visit for years. But, Abigail—"

"The situation here is minute to minute," Mitchell interjected.

"We appreciate the time and effort you're putting in, as does your father."

Abby didn't look up from her keyboard. "How would I know that when he won't see me?"

"Sweetheart, he doesn't want you to see him this way. You know what a proud man your father is. Soon, I promise. Everything will be back to normal."

Abby inhaled deeply, reminding herself to stay calm. They weren't in Southampton just yet, but she'd resolved to breathe this weekend. Over the last week, the pressure had mounted to the point where, not only was this trip meant for fun, it might even be necessary for her health. A thought that terrified her, knowing what her father had gone through at the helm of the company. "Yes, I know. And I have everything under control. If it makes you feel better, I'll have my phone and laptop with me while I'm there." Her fingers flew over the keyboard, entering reminders into next week's calendar before switching screens to respond to a client email. "It's not unusual for Father to be unreachable by phone over the weekend. Our clients know they can communicate with him via email, and I'll be there to handle any concerns."

"There is a conference call with Venezuela on Monday morning," Mitchell said, consulting the datebook in his hand. "You'll be back by then, won't you? It's your father's account, and no one else is familiar with it."

"Yes. I'll be back Sunday night." She spun in her chair and opened a file-cabinet drawer, slipping out the client's information. "I'll take the file with me, so I'm up to speed. Is there anything else?"

Her stepmother started to speak, but a familiar voice shouting in the hallway interrupted her. "Mayday, Mayday. We're down one party girl. I repeat, party girl has gone rogue. Must recover." Roxy.

"Roger, that, chopper one." Honey. "We've got our eyes peeled for an off-the-grid party girl. We've been advised her killer legs are registered weapons and will proceed with caution. Over and out."

When Roxy and Honey sailed into her office wearing goggles and duck-shaped flotation devices around their waists, Abby burst into laughter, ignoring her stepmother's mask of horror. Not exactly a traditional way to introduce your best friends to your stepmother, but she wouldn't have had it any other way. Dang. There was a tight welling in her chest telling her this weekend might be more in order than originally thought.

Last night, she'd been lying in her bed, formulas and risk evaluations overflowing from every crevice of her brain, when Roxy and Honey had burst into her room like a pair of Tasmanian devils. As soon as she'd stopped screaming from the shock, Honey had pounced on her, holding her shoulders down as Roxy straddled her waist.

"Thought this intervention was over, didn't you?" Honey crooned.

Every inch the actress, Roxy released a truly chilling, haunted-house cackle. "Oh, it has only just begun. We're taking a road trip, baby."

Abby tried to get up, but Honey held fast. "Have you guys been hanging out with Louis's twin sisters or something?"

"Say what you will, but the terror twins get shit done," Roxy responded.

"Just like we're about to." Honey's face was poised inches above Abby's. *"We're getting out of this city for the weekend. You're going to relax if we have to tie you down and have a shirtless pool boy force-feed you Vienna sausages and chocolate."*

"Honey Perribow, you are a straight-up natural at this," Roxy praised.

"It's all in the delivery."

Abby had put up a token protest because her workload only seemed to triple every time she blinked, but her friends had feigned actual deafness until she said yes. And the minute she had, the sharpest edges of her anxiety started to ebb. Anxiety brought on not only by her workload but Russell's radio silence. Maybe it was naïve on her part, but she'd expected him to stop her before she'd even gotten on the subway after leaving his house yesterday. Then again, when she returned home, she had been positive he would call, tell her he wanted to pursue the physical relationship she'd proposed. But . . . nothing. *Nada.* Suddenly, the one person who had always seemed hell-bent on her not getting hurt was doing the hurting. As a result, her confidence was taking a significant dip at a time when she really didn't need any additional crappiness heaped on top of her.

"Earth to Abby," Roxy said, waving a hand in front of her face, reminding her four other people stood in the office. Staring at her. How long had she been zoned out?

"Sorry." Abby tucked some stray hair behind her ear and stood, shoving a handful of essential files into her laptop case. "Um. Mother, meet Honey and Roxy. My roommates and best friends."

Her stepmother's smile was strained as she shook hands with

the girls. "Are you planning to wear those . . . *ducks* while in Southampton?"

"Don't worry, we promise not to let your daughter be seen in one." Roxy winked at Abby's stepmother. "We brought her a frog."

Mitchell broke the horrified silence with a nervous laugh. "I hope there's a pocket for your cell phone on that frog."

When Honey and Roxy both opened their mouths—no doubt to inform Mitchell and her stepmother that no work would be attempted or completed over the weekend—Abby jumped to intercede. "Come on. We don't want to keep the guys waiting."

Her stepmother's knuckles went white as she clutched her purse. "*Guys?*"

Abby didn't break stride as she sailed toward the door. "Yes. *Guys*. I'm twenty-four years old, and it's about frickin' time."

And holy hell. Not doing what was expected of her felt *really* good. She needed to make a habit of it. Starting this weekend.

Chapter 10

When Abby came into view on Ninth Avenue, Russell paused in his stride, hefting his duffel bag higher against his shoulder. That first eyeful of her always packed a punch, but it had the effect of a full-on knockout round now. She sat outside her building, perched on a designer suitcase that could probably pay his brother's rent for six months. Honey and Roxy sat on either side of her, sipping from Starbucks cups in between conversation and bouts of laughter. Abby had this habit of laying her hand on someone's shoulder and giggling when they said something funny, and she did it just then to Honey, making his throat hurt.

God help him this weekend when it came to keeping his hands off her. She looked angelic, with her thin, white T-shirt tucked into a short, flowery skirt. What did it say about him that he only wanted to get that angel on her ever-loving back? Naked and moaning, the way she'd been Thursday afternoon in Queens.

No. Maybe his logic was twisted, but he *needed* to keep Abby . . . untouched. At least in the final way that mattered. If he could manage that Herculean feat a while longer, just until he knew a future between them was even possible, that he could give her a happy life, he'd be a candidate for sainthood.

Russell tipped his head back and breathed through his nose. "I am not my dick. My dick does not make decisions for me."

A passing woman started walking faster, and Russell sighed. Best to keep his new mantra internal the next time he felt the need to repeat it in public. And he had a feeling he'd be chanting it like a motherfucker before the weekend was over.

"*Russell*," Roxy yelled from across the street. "Did you forget where we live?"

"Hint," Honey chimed in, gesturing with her coffee cup. "We're sitting *right* in front of it."

Russell smirked at them as he crossed Ninth Avenue, sufficiently reminded that although his dick would be having a rough weekend, the rest of him would have fun. While his focus was always on Abby, he'd developed a pretty serious soft spot for his buddies' girlfriends. Not that he was insane enough to let them know it. Once women knew they could smile and get a favor out of you, they turned into loaded weapons. *Some* women, at least. Abby waited until he offered, *then* smiled.

One of the first warning signs that he was lost over Abby had been one month into their friendship. Louis threw a surprise party for Roxy one night after she'd landed her first big acting role. He'd noticed Abby walking into the apartment with liquor bottles, setting them on the counter and heading back out into the hallway. Twice she'd done it before he'd gotten frustrated enough to ask her if she needed help carrying something. Turned out, there'd been three heavy cases of liquor for the party sitting downstairs, and she'd planned on carrying the contents up, two bottles at a time. Instead of asking for help.

Russell had stacked the three boxes on top of one another and brought them to the apartment, grumbling about stubborn women the entire way. But when he'd set them down in the kitchen, he'd turned to find Abby beaming at him like a certified hero. God, if she'd asked him to jump out the window at that moment, he would have leapt without a thought.

As he approached the girls, however, Abby wasn't looking at him like a hero. She wasn't looking at him *at all*, and it instantly fucked him up. If he didn't suspect it would show his hand, Russell would have flung himself down on the sidewalk and begged Abby to ask him for a favor. Anything. Anything in the world so he could go get it for her. A pink armadillo. A flower from the highest peak in the Swiss Alps. A baby goat. Whatever. He just wanted her to *look* at him the way she always had. Before he'd slapped her ass and sent her back to Manhattan. Jesus, he was a prize asshole.

You're going to fix it. Just hang in there.

"Hey," he said, his voice reminding him of sawdust. "Where's your old ball and chains?"

Roxy appeared to register Abby's lack of greeting but didn't comment, thanks be to God. "Louis is picking up the Zipcar—or Zip*van*, really. Ben is—"

"Right here," Ben said from behind Russell, opening his arms just in time for Honey to fling herself into them. He kissed his girlfriend's forehead and tucked her against his side with a smile that had *contentment* written all over it. "Louis is en route. Roxy? Try not to freak out."

"Why?" the actress tilted her head, but Ben stayed quiet. "Shit. What did he—"

A series of three loud beeps interrupted Roxy, her face not even bothering to register shock as a white, stretch limousine glided to a stop at the curb. Louis popped out through the sunroof and spread his arms wide. "Did someone call for a ride?"

"Louis McNally II." Roxy stomped her foot. "You did *not*."

"I did." When Roxy crossed her arms and made no move to enter the limo, Louis sighed. "I'd rather hold my girl than a steering wheel for three hours. Don't be mad at me, Rox. I got overexcited at the prospect of seeing you in a bathing suit."

When Roxy's lips twitched, Russell knew the fight would end the way all fights ended between his ex-playboy best friend and Roxy. A shit ton of PDA. So he tuned out and let his gaze roam over the limousine, wondering how much Louis had dropped on the damn thing. More than he could afford to chip in on, probably, which left a bad taste in his mouth. He didn't fault his friend—the guy was generous to a fault—but Russell preferred to pay his way.

Abby rolled her suitcase to the back of the limo, as if she'd done the same hundreds of times. Well versed in this world of limousines and weekend trips to the Hamptons. The driver appeared, presumably to help Abby lift her luggage into the trunk, but before Russell registered his own movement, he'd lunged forward to perform the task himself.

Well, at least she's looking at you now, dumb-ass.

"Thank you," she murmured.

Russell swallowed a baseball-sized lump. "I bet you packed a bunch of high heels just to drive me crazy."

Her expression warmed. "Someone has to do it."

"Excuse me," the driver said from behind them, forcing Russell to step away from Abby so the guy could load the other suitcases. Frankly, he wasn't thrilled over the fact that some stranger was going to be responsible for Abby's safety for the next three hours, but he figured everyone would give him shit if he asked to see a license.

Abby seemed to remember something at the last second, reaching into the trunk to pull an item out of her suitcase before climbing into the running vehicle. Russell finished helping the driver load the luggage and followed. As he ducked through the entrance, he kept his face neutral, so no one would realize it was his first time in a limo. Jesus, the inside was huge. They could have fit another eight people comfortably. Ben and Honey were cozied up just inside the door, Roxy and Louis making out, as expected, a few feet down the middle row.

Abby sat closest to the driver, trying not to look uncomfortable over being alone. Of course, everyone assumed *he* would sit beside her. And why wouldn't they? That was where he always sat. At her apartment. In the bar. Everywhere. This time should be no different.

It was, though. After what they'd done together, sitting in the darkness on smooth, expensive leather was a temptation he didn't need. Nor did he need Ben, Louis, or their sharper-than-hell girlfriends questioning him.

Who the hell was he kidding? There was no choice. A mere ten seconds of seeing her all alone was turning him into a certified mental patient. Russell walked in a crouch toward Abby and dropped into the seat beside her, just as the limo started to move. "I'll give it ten minutes before you fall asleep."

She looked affronted, but he caught a note of relief, too. "I'm wide-awake. I even brought an activity."

"An activity."

"Flash cards." She dangled a Ziploc baggie in front of her. "You said I could help with your business-loan meeting at the bank. Did you think I'd forget a chance to discuss numbers?"

Was it possible for a heart to burst through a man's chest cavity? "You, uh. You still want to help me with that?"

"Of course," she said, too quickly. "Why wouldn't I?"

I've been an asshole, and she's too sweet to punish me for it. What he wouldn't have given at that moment to have the same freedom as his friends. To pull Abby onto his lap and kiss her however long he wanted. To turn off the blinding awareness that he felt like a poseur in this giant car on steroids, while everyone else appeared completely comfortable. Too bad the fancy ride and apparently free liquor that came with it only made the divide between him and Abby feel more pronounced. He hated it. *Hated* it. But there it was, like one of those neon lasers in a spy movie that would set off an alarm. "What's on these cards?"

Her shoulders relaxed. "There are eight questions a loan officer typically—"

Music began pumping from speakers all around them—slow and bass-heavy—drowning out Abby's voice. Russell threw an irritated look toward the opposite end of the car, but Ben merely gave him a thumbs-up and went back to staring at Honey. It took Russell a second to grasp why the loud music presented more of a problem than simply not being able to hear Abby speak. When her breath feathered his ear and lust spread to his groin, however, the clouds cleared and revealed the mind fuck.

"Um." Jesus, she was talking an inch from his neck, having scooted closer on the seat. "The first thing any bank officer will want to know is how you'll use the loan proceeds, where exactly the funds will be allocated to help them make their money back the fastest." She paused to lick her lips, and he almost died. "Some officers suggest a ten-year business model, but most would rather see a strong five-year plan than a thin, long-term one."

Huh. He'd been using the ten-year model in the meetings, but maybe he should reevaluate. This was Russell's opening to inform her he'd been working on bank presentations for months. Presentations that had ultimately failed. She had no way of knowing how important securing the loan was to him—he'd never shared it with her or any of his friends for a good reason. If no one knew his ideal future hinged on being approved, no one could pity him if the bank stamped a big, red DENIED on his forehead.

Furthermore, if he revealed any of that to Abby, she wouldn't feel the need to coach him. And right now, with her bare thighs angled toward him, giving him hope of a panty flash, he was keeping his mouth shut. To his detriment. Because he was an Abby masochist. An Abbychist.

Russell turned his head, so their cheeks were pressed together, giving him a lungful of white-grape sunshine. "We've got office space picked out over in Hollis. It's small, but there's a lot out back for storing equipment and supplies." Voicing his plan, even partially, felt odd. But *good*. "Instead of paying rent to a landlord, we'd use half the loan to purchase the building. We'd rent out the top two floors to cover the mortgage, so most of our profit will go back into the business."

"That's great," she breathed, shifting against his side. "Will you hire more employees?"

"Some." Jesus, it was hot as hell in there and she smelled so good and that skirt had ridden up a little too high. "Mostly, we want to give our part-time guys a full-time gig. We'll probably hire a secretary to search for jobs soliciting bids and submitting them for us. Alec and I would rather get our hands dirty than sit at a computer."

"A secretary?" Abby tilted her head back and met his gaze. "Like a girl?"

"Now who's the chauvinist?" Her eyes sparkled up at him in the darkness, and breathing became a challenge. "I'll put you in charge of hiring the secretary. How's that?"

Her mouth curved into a smile. "I'm thinking a cheerful grandmother of ten named Martha. Or Deloris."

"Does Martha or Deloris bake?"

"Oh, yes. She's a retired pastry chef."

"Hire the woman."

Abby laughed, and Russell felt it against his lips, but she sobered before he got his fill. "You liked baked goods so much, yet you completely ignored the cupcakes I brought over on Thursday." He barely had time to register surprise that she'd brought up their afternoon together, before she continued. "I know. Abby doesn't make people uncomfortable or discuss sore subjects. But I just defied my stepmother for the first time since I was a teenager, so I'm kind of on a roll. I guess . . . you just have to deal with it."

"Okay," he murmured, pride battling his shock. Somehow, this new development signaled impending disaster, but the determination on her face was so breathtaking, he couldn't gather enough motivation to throw up a roadblock. "I never realized you were holding back."

Her gaze dropped a moment before lifting again. "I don't want to anymore."

The husky change to her voice made his dick feel heavy. He felt like the coyote waiting for the anvil to fall on his head. Only Abby was way hotter than the roadrunner, with her tits rising and falling on shallow breaths. "Say what you want to say, angel."

Something flickered in her eyes at the nickname. Fuck, he needed to be careful here, but the darkness and pulsing music had wrapped them in a fleece blanket where reality couldn't intrude. The absorbent sound swallowed his groan when she wet her lips, her adorable ass shifting on the seat. "I want you to fuck me, Russell."

"*Goddammit*," he breathed, feeling like he'd just run fifteen miles in the blistering sun. Barbed wire damaged his insides, neck to stomach. But Jesus, below the sharp pain, his cock had hardened to the point of agony. His hands punished the leather seat, so he wouldn't reach for her, settle her on his lap, and enter her pussy beneath that flimsy skirt. Would she whimper and twist around, trying to get off? Or would she let him talk her through her first time? What if he damaged the trust she'd placed in him by causing her pain? God, that would kill him. Just the act of sitting there beside her, knowing what she wanted and not acting, was a torture he could barely withstand. He wanted to end the torture. Wanted so badly to show her what the word *fucking* really meant . . . What it meant to *him*. . .

"Say something," she said beside his ear, distress evident in her voice, slicing him to ribbons. "I can never tell what you're thinking anymore."

"You don't want to know."

"Yes." Her voice was firm. "I do."

The part of Russell that craved self-preservation encouraged him to tell her. It would push her away until he could sort his life out, sort these *urges* out. But would he ever get her back if she knew? There were no guarantees. Still, didn't she deserve to know whom she wanted to gift with her virginity? "Abby, I . . ." He swallowed a handful of nails. "Did you like it when I spanked you?"

She pressed her lips right up against his ear. "I liked it a lot."

Christ. She couldn't realize what she was saying. Didn't *know* any better. "There are other things I think about doing. I'm not sure . . . a normal guy, a good guy would want to do those things to you, Abby."

"What does normal mean? Some people would say a twenty-four-year-old virgin isn't normal." For a moment, he swore she was going to kiss him. Her lips were less than an inch from his, her eyelids at half-mast. He would have let her, too. Wouldn't have had the willpower to stop her. "Whatever *you* are, Russell. That's what I want." His heart was pounding so violently, a response was out of the question. His love would have just poured out like water from a fire hose. He was grateful that she continued, until her words fully registered. "I know you don't want anything serious, and that's okay. We were friends before . . ." Her spine straightened in degrees. " . . . and we'll be friends after."

Chapter 11

Maybe bravery came in fragments. Back at the office and in the limousine, she'd had a bright burst of independence. She still couldn't quite believe what she'd said to Russell. Or what he'd said in response. What was done was done, though. It couldn't be taken back, and she didn't *want* it to be. Rather, she couldn't wait to assert herself *again*. Perhaps that explained why she'd feigned sleep promptly after propositioning her best friend and remained that way the duration of the trip. She'd been resting up for more speaking her mind. Right.

Or it might have been an attempt to ignore the phone calls and emails she could already feel clocking in on her phone, vibrating the device in her purse. She didn't have to check the screen to know it was her mother. Mitchell. But she wasn't playing ball today.

Abby tugged the key to the estate out of her purse, unable to resist smiling over her friends' animated chatter as they wheeled their suitcases behind her on the driveway. Most of them were animated, anyway. Russell's expression was carved from stone as he looked up at the thirty-thousand-square-foot vacation home Abby's father had bought as a wedding present to her stepmother.

Many of her childhood memories had been formed inside these walls, although they weren't all pleasant. If she could project them against a blank wall, an observer would say the memories were *pretty*. Beautiful, even. White, billowing curtains. Beautiful women in pastel dresses, their summer tans glowing. Glasses of sparkling, gold liquid being passed around. Drifting piano music. The fragrant smell of the Atlantic lifting the hair from her neck.

Abby pushed open the front door and stepped aside to let everyone pile into the house. Louis threw a laughing Roxy over his shoulder and strode into the white-marble foyer, his expression one of familiarity, since his family's money was on par with her own. They'd spoken about their summers in Southampton only briefly, but had laughed over the fact that they might have been at some of the same parties as children. Honey stepped inside, her jaw dropping. Ben pushed it back up with a single finger and leaned in to kiss the back of her neck. Abby turned to find Russell hovering just outside the door, as if deciding whether or not to come inside.

Unease swarmed in her belly. Russell had never voiced discomfort over her family's abundance of money, but she'd always sensed it beneath the surface, seen him tense up when someone else picked up the tab at dinner. Now, though, seeing his hesitancy even to step past the threshold, she wondered how deep it ran. Over the last week, she'd started to question just how *much* Russell kept hidden.

Seeing him so indecisive to take that single step toward her was hard, so Abby turned away and followed her friends into the kitchen. True to form, Louis and Roxy were already taking stock of the liquor in every cabinet, lining the bottles up on the counter. Ben had his arms wrapped around Honey as they stared out at the ocean view.

Their excitement gave Abby a moment to get her bearings. She hadn't ventured to Southampton since high school for a reason. The time she'd spent here growing up had been lonely. Blending into the colorless walls while parties swirled through the rooms. Not knowing how to include herself in conversations or even feel-ing interesting enough to do so.

Then "the incident" had taken place.

Something had felt different when she'd woken up that morn-ing. She'd had a dream where she'd run screaming down the pristine Southampton beach, everyone staring at her and whis-pering behind their hands. She'd twirled and twirled and kicked up sand, not caring a single bit. Enjoying their criticism and that of her parents. When she woke from the vivid dream, her pulse had still been racing with the thrill. She hadn't wanted to let go, wanted to hold on as long as possible. If she called the image of rebellious Abby to mind, she found she could breathe in the giant mausoleum of a house.

So when her stepmother demanded she attend a stuffy, all-adult luncheon at the local country club—an activity where she would be prodded about her future, her weight, her clothing—she'd nearly broken out in hives. Her stepmother's face when she said no was still perfectly detailed in her mind. And how it had looked afterward, when Abby started flinging breakfast plates across the kitchen, crushing china beneath her sensible ballet flats, shouting in a voice she couldn't recognize, but it had felt so *good*.

Until the following morning, when she'd woken to find her parents gone. A vacation from their vacation, which she'd known meant they'd needed a break from her. It was that morning she realized how easily people left. Summer-camp friends, classmates, parents. Once you cracked and revealed a nonfunctioning part, they bailed.

Days had passed during those summers where she hadn't been required to speak a single word. Silence had been a running theme that followed her into adulthood. Until recently. No more, though. When she spoke now, her friends listened. Her mother. Russell. She wasn't that shy, awkward girl who'd learned to keep her opinion or any form of protest to herself. This weekend, she would replace the beige memories inside these walls with ones she could be proud of.

Abby pushed the handle of her suitcase down and tossed the house key onto the counter. "So. Are we walking to the beach or hanging at the pool out back today?"

"Can we drink at the beach?" Roxy asked over her shoulder.

"Nope."

"Poolside gets *this* girl's vote."

Honey hopped onto one of the stools surrounding the breakfast bar. "Seconded. I just have to change into my bathing suit."

"And I just have to assist her," Ben deadpanned.

"You're such a giver, man." Louis flipped a stack of red Solo cups in his hand. "Who's having a margarita?"

Five hands went up just as Russell walked into the kitchen. "What are we voting on?"

Abby tried not to let her relief over his appearance show. "Alcohol. What else?"

"Count me in, but make it light. Wouldn't want to get lost in this place."

There was just enough of an edge to Russell's voice to give everyone pause. Abby watched a silent communication pass between Ben and Louis, but it happened so fast, Abby wondered if it had been inside her head. It made her mad; the feeling that she wasn't involved in some secret. She didn't appreciate being left out. Not inside this house, of all places.

And there was more to her anger. A lot more. She'd been alienated by her coworkers for being the boss's daughter. Been the rich girl whose silence was mistaken for superiority. It had sucked all those times, but to have Russell edging toward that same ridicule when she'd never been anyone but herself around him? The pain knocked the wind right out of her. Or tried to, anyway.

Abby sauntered toward Louis, plucked a cup out of his hand, and poured herself three fingers' worth of tequila. "If you're so worried about getting lost, leave a trail of breadcrumbs, Hansel." She tossed back a mouthful of liquor, her nose burning as it went down. "There are two rooms upstairs, three downstairs, and one in the pool house. Take your pick." Down went the remaining tequila. "See you at the pool."

Abby stared down at the selection of bathing suits on her bed, hands on hips. Gold, sparkly bikini, or black, modest one-piece?

The corner of her mouth edged up as she let her floral skirt drop and stripped the T-shirt over her head. Gold sparkly. No question. It might be a little outrageous for her—okay, *way* outrageous— but she'd seen what Roxy and Honey had packed, so at least she wouldn't be alone in her daring. She murmured a thank-you to whichever past visitor had left the garment behind in the guest- room bureau and put on the bikini.

A look in the full-length mirror had her wincing, though. Had this thing belonged to a ten-year-old? It barely covered . . . anything. The thin triangles plumped her breasts, separated and pushed them high. The gold between her legs peeked out, cover- ing only where necessary. Oh boy, no way could she wear this thing in public.

Her gaze swung back to the basic, black bathing suit mocking her from the bed. Putting it on would feel like giving in. But her mother's room was across the hall. Maybe she had a sarong or wrap she could wear over the gold bikini . . . kind of a modesty ca- veat? Abby gave her reflection an encouraging nod and headed for the door, hoping to sneak into the other room unseen and perform a quick search. But when she opened the door and poked her head out, Russell stood at the opposite door, one foot already inside.

"You okay?" he asked, one eyebrow dipping low.

"Fine." She started to duck back into her room, intending to wait until Russell left for the pool before rooting through the closet.

"Look . . . downstairs. I didn't mean to—" He cut himself off. "Why are you hiding behind the door?"

"I'm not dressed."

"Mmm."

Hot, neediness stoked the fire beneath Abby's belly button. The one that never seemed to stop blazing anymore. And yeah, something about wearing the explicit bikini was only amplifying the sexual warmth. The material cupping her between the legs felt like a caress, but didn't have the satisfying friction of Russell's work-roughened hands. Abby was so busy processing her insane desire to be touched—*now, please*—she didn't notice Russell staring at something beyond her shoulder. She followed his line of sight and gasped, catching her reflection in the mirror. Oh Lord, she hadn't even seen how little the bikini covered her bottom. The answer was, almost none of it.

Abby turned back to find Russell's eyes glassy, his voice a mere rasp when he spoke. "You aren't wearing that. You'll have to kill me first."

There were times when Russell's proprietary attitude toward her was a turn-on. This was not one of those times. "Oh yes, I am."

He tossed his duffel bag to the floor. "The *fuck* you are."

Blistering need blazed a path right down to her toes, her irritation doing nothing to cool it. In a confusing twist, however, she tried to shut the door when Russell stalked toward the entrance. None of her actions made sense to her, but she didn't care. Rebelling felt good. Tempting consequences felt even better.

His forearm blocked the door, preventing its closure with ease. Abby had no choice but to step back and expose herself or get swept aside by the heavy wood. Russell made a dark noise and ran a hand over his open mouth. "Jesus Christ." His hands flexed at his sides. "I don't think you understand. Wearing that *thing* around anyone but me . . . I'd lose my shit, Abby. It would be a scary thing."

She was shaken by his intensity but refused to lose ground. "That's too bad. I'm not taking it off and being boring old Abby just so you'll feel better."

He pinched the skin between his eyes. "Please. Please, angel. Go change."

Abby didn't understand the sympathy that crept past her defiance. He looked on the verge of imploding all because of some stupid bathing suit. His broad shoulders shook as he inhaled a deep breath. *On the edge.* She'd put him on the precipice of breaking, and although she had no idea what would happen when they crossed the line, the inferno licking at her thighs and stomach needed an answer. "Make me," she forced past trembling lips.

Her words sucked all oxygen from the room. Dread warred with sexual drive on Russell's face for a moment, but sex won, and it won *hard.* His features became a granite carving as he cracked his neck once . . . and stormed toward her. A wave of yearning crashed into Abby, so concentrated that she could only watch as Russell's hands fisted the front of her bikini top and ripped the string between her breasts in two. *Snap.* The release of material sent her stumbling back a step, her bottom meeting the mattress, but their proximity to the bed only registered in a vague, faraway manner because Russell's gaze raking over her breasts was suddenly *everything.*

"You want to show off your pretty tits, you show them off to *me.*" He planted his fists on either side of her hips. Leaned in so close she had no choice but to recline. "Go ahead, then, stubborn girl. Give them a shake. Give me something to think about while I stroke off tonight across the hall."

Infused with indignation, Abby pushed up, got right in his face. "Oh, you're calling *me* stubborn? I told you on the way here—"

"Do *not* say it again." His eyes strayed to the gold triangle between her legs. "God, you were just going to walk around with that scrap of nothing over your pussy?" He used his knees to shove her thighs wider, growling as the fabric stretched over her center. "No man's ever licked it but *me*. No one looks at it but *me*." His head dropped, his mouth hovering just above her nipples. "That goes for all of you. Every fucking inch of this dick-tease body."

"I'm not a tease," Abby breathed, absorbing his every word like a greedy sponge but refusing to accept them completely. She'd been nothing but honest with him and resented his playing head games. Tell her to stay away one minute, claiming ownership the next. "*You* are the tease, and I'm tired of it. Put your money where your mouth is or *get off* me."

When Russell only squeezed his eyes shut and released her name through clenched teeth, Abby had experienced enough. Tears burned inside her throat as she shoved him away and escaped off the bed. Desperate for a distraction from the sharp pain in her side, Abby stooped down and snatched up the torn bikini top. With shaking fingers, she attempted to tie it back together.

"What are you doing?"

"I'm wearing it."

The top was snatched out of Abby's hands from behind, but when she spun on a heel to give Russell hell, the words died on her lips. No shirt. He'd taken off his shirt and those muscles moved with every step in her direction. With his free hand, he flicked the button open on his jeans and drew the zipper down with a wince. "You calling me a tease, Abby? Look what you do. What you always do." He reached into his fly and brought out his fisted erection. *So big.* "Six months of your sitting on my lap. Wiggling around and laughing, no idea I wanted to fuck you through a wall. Don't you *dare* call me a tease. *I've* been teased. I'm so fucked up, I can't hear your name without getting hard."

The flesh between Abby's thighs felt heavy . . . *ready.* An electric line sizzled, connecting her nipples to that sensitive spot Russell had once licked so expertly. She wanted him to do it again . . . but some untapped piece of her was stricken by his pain. More so than she wanted pleasure, she wanted to *give* it. The closer he came, the more her anger at him fell into a distant second place behind eagerness to relieve him. Had he really been so miserable in her presence for so long?

Russell brushed up against her, looming so large, she felt intimidated . . . and liked it? No, she *loved* his staring down from above, deciding what to do with her. *To* her. Loved knowing that Russell would decide her fate. Through the burning anticipation, though, she saw worry simmering behind his fierce expression. Knew he'd need to be pushed. Just a little more.

He leaned down and spoke, his lips moving on her forehead. "Apologize for teasing me."

I'm sorry. So sorry. "No."

His growl vibrated against her skull. "I don't know what you're waking up here." The torture lacing his tone ripped at her heart, but she stayed silent, waiting for him to speak. "What if it scares you, angel?"

Abby tilted her head back to meet his blazing eyes. "What if it doesn't?"

A muscle jumped in his cheek, and she witnessed a change come over him. Saw his energy shift and change shape, hardening in some places, softening in others. It didn't alarm her, though.

No, it felt like she'd been waiting for this side of him to arrive.

Moving so fast, Abby barely had time to register what was happening, Russell grabbed her wrists, positioned them at the small of her back, and—*oh God*—tied them together with the mangled bikini top. His lack of gentleness and absolute focus on the task turned Abby's need on its head, whipping the already raging inferno into a frenzied, five-alarm barn burner. *Need this. Love this.*

"You've done it now." He jerked one of the ties, making the material tighten around her wrists. "I might have been able to handle it, too. Go forever just letting you tease me. So long as I could look at you, talk to you, watch you sleep. Now I hurt everywhere. It's everywhere, and it'll never go away."

"I'll fix it." Logic didn't apply to this conversation, only intuition. A unique communication that only flowed between her and Russell. "Show me how."

Finished with the task of securing her hands, Russell's touch found his erection again and gripped the base. "Fucking hell, Abby. *Look* at you. I'm done being noble." He sucked his bottom lip into his mouth, let it go with a slow pop. "The ache is down low. If you want to fix it, get on your knees and go find it."

As if her strings had been cut, Abby dropped to her knees, thrusting out her breasts for him to look at. A rush of excitement and power suffocated any remaining nerves. This was her secret fantasy come to life . . . and she could admit now that Russell's face had always been obscured in those daydreams. But she'd known it would be him. She'd *known*.

He eased closer, held the tip of his arousal just above her mouth. "What do I want to hear?"

"I'm sorry for teasing you," she whispered.

His left hand threaded its way into her hair, the action uneven and desperate. "You know there's absolutely nothing you could do that would be wrong, don't you?" Biting his lip, he ran the smooth head across the seam of her lips. "You could lap at it like a kitten, and I'd come like the dirty motherfucker I am."

Okay. Abby hadn't lived with two sex-crazed roommates for half a year without hearing a few things. She knew how to give head even if she hadn't physically performed the act. *Deep. Deeper. All of it. Please.* She'd heard those very words being growled through closed doors in the apartment when she shouldn't have been listening beyond the initial groan. But those frantic instructions had clued her in on the right way to please a man. And she planned on doing it right the first time.

Abby rubbed her cheek against Russell's grip. When even that simple action almost buckled his knees, liquid warmth gathered between her thighs. A beating started all over her body. A simultaneous, rhythmic pumping of blood. Unable to wait another second, Abby pushed forward on her knees, took Russell between her lips, and sucked the thick, round head. Inched lower with an easy glide. Then descended as far as she could take him.

"*Abby.*" The hand in her hair turned to a fist. "*Goddamn.* That mouth isn't a tease, is it? Wants to satisfy me. *Good.* Good little mouth."

Knowing her mouth had fostered that reaction, those rasped words, sent her slipping into a place of blurred reality. The harder he pulled the strands of her hair, the more pronounced the tug in her belly became, forcing Abby to rub her thighs together, seeking friction. Oh God, was it possible to have an orgasm from hearing a man moan your name? Not just any man. *Russell.*

"I kept it for you, Abby. All for you." His hand started to stroke in time with Abby's mouth and impossibly, his erection thickened even more. The added girth only made her more determined to take him deeper. So she did, forcing her throat to relax and allow him entry. "Ahhh, fuck. You making up for lost time, angel? All that teasing you did?" He slipped deeper and let out a low growl. "Damn right, you are. It was worth the pain, wasn't it? Worth it to see your cheeks hollowing out, feel that purr at the back of your throat. I'm going to love sexing up that virgin mouth."

His voice cracked on the final word, his hard length jerking in her mouth. She had no time to prepare as Russell pulled out, dropped to the floor, and spun her around. After what happened in his house that afternoon during the week, she expected him to release on her backside, but he didn't. Instead, one strong arm banded around her shoulders and yanked her backward, into a prone position, so she lay on top of him, with her back to his chest, tied hands flattened between their bodies.

"R-Russell—"

"Open your legs," he grated.

Her body moved to obey his command, heels digging into the floor on either side of him. She felt his forearm flexing beneath her right thigh as it moved between his legs, working the erection she'd so recently pleasured with her mouth. Up and down in a blurred motion until liquid warmth landed on her belly, lower. Beneath her, she could feel Russell's muscles bulging against her back and bottom, his breaths catching and rasping at her ear.

"You sucked it so good, Abby. Made me come so fucking hard. *All over you.*" His hips bucked beneath hers. "Let anyone but me see your body? I can't. I can't."

"Okay . . . it's okay," she gasped, attempting to catch her breath. She never got the chance. Russell's fingers delved between her thighs, using the moisture from his own body to coat her center, make her slippery. Abby's back arched on a muffled scream, the sensation of coarse touching smooth blowing her mind. She'd been so focused on Russell's pleasure, she'd lost sight of her own needs, but they wouldn't be ignored now. Her feet scraped on the floor as two rough fingers became her entire universe. They circled her clitoris, pressed and held, slid down the sides and pinched, circled again. Faster.

Abby's body writhed on top of Russell's stronger, more powerful one, but the arm banding her shoulders only tightened to keep her still.

"Ahhh. Now I know, don't I?" His voice rumbled at her neck,

making her shiver. "I know when you mouth off and push me, you need your pussy taken care of. That's *my* job. My privilege. Next time just *ask* like a good girl."

Her climax was blinding, the buildup of frustration she'd only been aware of peripherally, rolled off her in a tidal wave. Flesh quaked, hands scrambled for purchase, as the tension within her was obliterated. "Russell, Russell, Russell . . ."

"I'm here," he murmured. "If you're coming, angel, it's a foregone conclusion that I'm there every fucking time. Understood?"

"Yes," she sobbed, collapsing back onto his chest. "Every time."

Russell kissed the side of her face, holding her close as he moved them into a sitting position, Abby between his outstretched legs. His heart thundered against her back, bringing a drowsy smile to her face. Whatever questions lay between them, wasn't their equally erratic heartbeats the most important answer? Russell had a dominant side—was that the reason he'd been keeping her at arm's length? She couldn't wait to tell him how ridiculous that was. It had all become clear since he'd entered the room. Since the beginning, that part of him—the gruff, commanding, often angry part—had attracted her. His stern manner, his protective nature. All of it. Knowing it was darker and even more demanding didn't repel her in the least. Oh no. On the contrary. She wanted to be drawn into the eye of his storm and spun madly. The counterpoint to his nature had been right there inside her, she'd just been waiting for him to act. Waiting to put a name to the urges and sensual imagery in her head but not knowing if they were normal. They were. And Russell's own needs intersected them. Thank God, she didn't have to wait any more for answers.

"Russell—"

A knock sounded on the door, followed by Honey's muffled voice. "Hey, Abby. You fall asleep or something? Wouldn't be surprised after that belt of tequila." A beat passed. "Have you seen Russell? Ben says he's touring the perimeter, looking for Abby-specific hazards." Another round of silence, this one infinitely more uncomfortable than the prior one. "Okay, last chance to get decent, I'm coming in."

Abby started to call out that there was no need, she'd be down in a second. But Russell started to untie her hands, his movements jerky. When the task was completed, he surged to his feet and strode toward the bathroom, the sudden distance she felt yawning between them catching her off guard. As he closed the door behind him without even looking back or making an iota of sound, Abby could only sit huddled on the floor, positive her heart had just been ironed flat.

Chapter 12

Russell balled his fists on the white-marble sink and breathed through the compulsion to shatter the bathroom mirror. Looking at his reflection was unbearable, but it was a laughable degree of misery compared to what followed when Abby's soft voice drifted through the door, telling Honey she was fine and would be downstairs in a few minutes. She sounded anything but fine, and it was on his head. Sat there like an eight-ton elephant.

An image of Abby sitting on the bedroom floor by herself assaulted his mind, and Russell dry heaved, deflating onto the sink. He'd panicked out there. Just panicked. He'd heard Honey outside the door and thought, *This is it, once our friends know, she'll be stuck.* He still believed that with his whole heart. Abby was so loyal. She would never leave his side once their relationship was acknowledged even if it was the right thing to do.

There was an even more sickening scenario, though, and it had propelled him toward the bathroom like a man shot from a cannon. If he didn't get the business loan, if the officer took one look at his no–college degree, no–accomplishment, no–savings account ass and laughed in his face, he would do the right thing and walk away from Abby. No way in hell would he leave her scorned in the eyes of her best friends. Jesus, walking away would be hard enough without embarrassing her in the process.

And for Chrissakes, the pressure to succeed once they were officially boyfriend and girlfriend might kill him. He already felt halfway to dead, just knowing she sat a few yards away, probably wondering if she'd done something wrong, when she'd done everything so fucking right. But his feet were leaden, refusing to carry him those few yards to permanently claim the future he couldn't have but had come too close to stealing. He'd never make it a day for the rest of his life without replaying what they'd done. Abby, hands tied behind her back, that enthusiastic mouth perfect on him. So perfect. Big, hazel eyes glued on him, back arched, tits swaying as she moved. Sucked. Ruined him.

The way she'd accepted his impulses without question, the way she'd seemed turned on by them . . . resisting the compulsion to explore became harder by the minute.

What if it scares you, angel?

What if it doesn't?

Was he corrupting her *and* hurting her at the same time? Was there an end to the damage he was capable of here?

He had memories of his parents' marriage, going back to when he'd been a small child. His mother laying her head on his father's shoulder at the dinner table. His parents leaving them with a babysitter for a few hours, then coming back through the front door laughing. But somewhere along the line, it had all gone to shit. He remembered it perfectly. There had been a tangible shift in the air, sometime around his ninth birthday. Remodeling work had slowed down for his father. His mother had started drinking. Lines formed around her mouth. Angry lines. The family had stopped having dinner together, eating whatever they could scavenge individually from the refrigerator. Sometimes his mother didn't come home at all, sending his father on a drinking binge.

A sharp pain hit Russell right between the eyes at the mere thought of Abby's being with him but wishing for someone better. Abby could never be unfaithful; she simply didn't have it in her blood. But she had the potential to marry someone who wouldn't need to work at all. Ever. Someone just like her, who didn't need to work unless he damn well felt like it. Abby and this rich, imaginary dickwad could travel and have nannies. Gifted children. Parties in fucking Southampton. Until he'd seen the estate, Abby's wealth had been like an open umbrella he'd been carrying around, but walking into this house had snapped it closed around his head. He couldn't even see where he was going now, it was so in his face.

What the hell did she need with *him*? A dirt-poor, uncultured asshole from Queens who—in a delightful twist—also liked to tie her up. Hold her down. Make her beg. Things he'd only ever wanted to do with Abby. Before the day she'd walked out onto her building's stoop, he'd been with girls and never felt the desire for more than hard, fast sex. There'd been no need for control— not like the kind Abby made him crave. The goodness in her, the total trust when she looked up at him, had roused something powerful, and it continued to grow and strengthen. He wanted that trust *everywhere*. In bed and out. Always focused on him. It surprised him beyond belief that now she seemed to enjoy what they did, but she might stop one day. Realize she deserved to be cherished. Not manhandled or sent to her knees to *find the ache*.

Russell pushed away from the sink with a sound of disgust. One thing was for sure. They needed to talk. He needed to find a way to assure Abby that he was the fucked-up one in this situation. Not her. Never her. Yeah . . . she needed to know that *now*.

He took a breath to brace himself, just in case he found her still sitting on the floor. But when he opened the door, the room was empty.

"Fuck."

A part of Russell he wasn't proud of calmed somewhat when he spotted the shredded gold bikini in the wastebasket, but an urgency still existed to get eyes on Abby. Make her look him in the eye when he apologized for walking away without a word. After the trust she'd given him, his behavior was a ten on the shitty meter.

Soon. She'll understand soon.

Russell went across the hall and changed quickly into an old pair of board shorts and a Yankees T-shirt, snorting at his choice of attire in the Hamptons. He wouldn't be winning any fashion contests today, thank God.

After pausing several times on the way down the staircase to stare at pictures of Abby growing up, Russell finally walked out onto the back patio, where Louis was already barbecuing hot dogs. His gaze sought out Abby where she lounged beside the adjacent pool with Honey and Roxy, taking in every detail about her in a sweeping head-to-toe check. Her hair was more mussed than usual, her lips slightly swollen. Gorgeous. It pained him when she didn't look up, didn't acknowledge him, but he'd more than earned that treatment.

"You hungry?" Louis asked, looking completely at home in a pair of Ray-Bans and some deck shoes. "How about a well-done wiener?"

"*What?*" Russell heard his defensive tone and reeled back his attitude. Something about grilled-wiener talk right on the heels of a blow job didn't sit right with a man. "Uh. Yeah . . . well-done."

Ben managed to pry his attention away from a bathing-suit-clad Honey. "Find any booby traps around the estate?"

"Pretty sure I'm not the one who's fallen into a booby trap, bro."

"Guilty as charged," Ben said, and went back to staring at his girlfriend.

Feeling Louis's perceptive-lawyer antenna pointed in his direction, Russell managed not to devour the sight of Abby in a sexy, black one-piece. Modest by most people's standards but not by his. His hands itched with the need to bundle her up in a beach towel and carry her back upstairs, but he forced himself to relax as much as possible. His friends weren't capable of looking anywhere but at their girlfriends, so they were on neutral ground. Now, should the super group decide on the beach as their destination tomorrow, he'd have a shiny, new battle on his hands, wouldn't he?

"Hey, uh. Russell—"

"I just want to preempt whatever you're going to say with this," Russell said to Louis. "You look like an Abercrombie & Fitch advertisement. In a very real way."

Louis gestured with his tongs. "You're being defensive. That means you did something stupid. Tell me what it is while we're alone."

"I'm here, too," Ben chimed in.

"That's debatable." Louis turned his back to the girls and lowered his voice. "As your attorney, I'll do my best to advise you."

"And protect your own ass," Russell added. "Anyway, you gave me a refund, in case you forgot."

"That was a symbolic refund. I can claim plausible deniability if push comes to shove, but we're still protected by the bro code." Louis gave him a meaningful look. "Has push come to . . . shove?"

"I don't know what we're talking about anymore."

"Me either." Ben threw an exhale toward the sky. "Just tell us why Abby came out here looking like someone ran over her puppy."

"She did?" Russell wheezed the question, feeling as though he'd been slugged in the stomach by a giant. "Ah Jesus, this weekend was a bad idea. I just needed until Wednesday. Less than a fucking *week*."

His friends traded a baffled look. "What?"

"Never mind," Russell muttered. They wouldn't understand. Both of them came from money. Louis had embraced his role as heir apparent to the McNally fortune. Ben might have shunned his status, but his bank account had been there all along to fall back on. Russell Hart had nothing. No padding to cushion him. Not for the first time, Russell questioned his role in the group. He was the oldest, the least successful, the one without a defined life path. Shit, here he was, hours from everything he knew, making sure no one looked sideways at Abby. A girl he had no business wanting. What the fuck was wrong with him?

"Hey, man." Louis handed him a hot dog on a plastic plate. "I'd rather you were defensive than quiet."

Ben leaned back against the railing and crossed his arms. "Russell, I'm going to talk in my professor voice. Are you listening?" Russell raised an eyebrow, refusing to admit Ben's stern tone had just sent him back to the middle-school principal's office banked in his memory. "Louis and I complain about your often outlandish advice, but the truth is, it has helped us in the past realize we were being shitheads. Mostly by listening to your erstwhile wisdom and doing the opposite."

"Thanks," Russell stretched out. "I think?"

"Just go with it, man," Louis said, while sending a wink toward Roxy.

"Do you know of the sirens from Greek mythology?" Ben asked, removing his glasses to polish them with the hem of his black T-shirt. "They sent sailors crashing against the rocks, having lured them with beautiful singing voices."

"I'm with you so far," Russell said, wondering where the hell this lesson was going. Had his friends always been this weird? "Hurry up, though, Professor. I'm late for health class."

"Here's the lesson they don't teach you in school." Ben replaced his glasses. "The sirens were trying to tell the sailors something, and the fuck-ups wouldn't listen. Find out what that something is, Russell, and don't crash into the rocks."

ABBY TOOK A healthy slug of her third margarita, hoping this one might have some effect. Maybe she was already too numb for the tequila to do its job. Evening had started making advances, darkening the sky by long-drawn-out degrees. She sat on a deck chair beside Honey and Roxy, listening to them trade summer-vacation horror stories, laughing when it seemed appropriate. It wasn't right. She should have been enjoying herself, soaking up every second with her best friends, erasing the negative memories lingering in the house. It was impossible, though, when her cell phone continued to vibrate where she'd shoved it beneath her thigh. Mitchell. Her stepmother. She'd stopped checking. One weekend. She'd only wanted one weekend.

Abby sensed Russell watching her steadily from the deck, where the guys were cleaning up after their foray into grilling. Really, he hadn't stopped watching her since coming downstairs—and the urge to flip him the bird was so intense, it actually alarmed her. She didn't make rude gestures. Didn't ignore phone calls. It was taking a massive effort just to sit there and look *normal*. Every time she felt the vibration against her thigh, a gnarled tree root grew inside her throat, extending deeper until it reached her stomach.

Is this what her father had gone through? This stress that stole your ability to function? Upon discovering that they'd found her father huddled in a bathtub, she'd been horrified by the image. Her capable, forward-thinking father shutting out the people surrounding him, unable to face the outside world. Now? Yeah, she could see herself hiding in a bathtub. If the damn phone would just *leave her alone*. If Russell would just stop *looking at her*. On top of the workload she could feel piling up by the minute, trying to discern Russell's thoughts and intentions, analyzing his actions, was starting to feel like the straw that would snap the math geek's back. She didn't feel like herself, and that scared her.

Everything hurt, her muscles protesting at being tensed for so long. Worst of all, her heart tripped over every beat, as if performing its job on an empty tank of gas. For a really long time, she'd had feelings for Russell; she simply hadn't known how to define them. The horrible way she missed him when he wasn't around. The utter joy and relief that exploded in her chest when she saw him coming. Upstairs, everything had come into focus, only to be made blurry again. In every aspect of her life, succeeding didn't seem possible. For each piece of work she completed, it divided into two. Every time she swore that she and Russell were on the same page, he turned it. Well, she was done. *Done.*

Abby started when Louis plopped down beside her on the chair, throwing a brotherly arm around her shoulders. It was only then she realized Ben and Russell had joined them, too, taking up the surrounding chairs. How long had they been sitting there? She refused to look at Russell but could feel his displeasure cloaking her from two chairs away. Or maybe it was directed at Louis. Thankfully, her ability to care had disappeared along with her third margarita. Which—praise the Lord—had finally gone to her head.

"Hey, there," Louis said, shaking her a little. "We haven't heard your shitty-summer-vacation story yet."

She felt a rush of gratefulness toward Louis for including her in the conversation and redirecting her thoughts from Russell to where it should be. Her friends. This weekend away from work. Making new memories. "Um." She took a calming breath. "I spent my summers here, so I don't think they can be classified as shitty."

"Come on." Honey smiled at her. "Everyone has something. Bad kisses, a wave stealing your bikini top. Camping outside the box office for Garth Brooks tickets only to find out he's playing the next town over." She patted her blond hair. "Not that *I* ever did that last one."

Shitty-summer-vacation story. Maybe purging the old memories would make it easier for new ones to take their place. "One summer, my parents left me here with the nanny and went to Italy for a month. Does that count?"

No one said anything. She heard Russell curse behind her and frowned. Not the reaction she'd been going for. Honestly, her story hadn't been as bad as the others, had it? Their expressions told Abby they felt bad for her, and it really didn't sit well. Not when she already felt bad enough for *herself* to sink an oil tanker. Not when she desperately wanted to move on from those memories.

"Sorry, Abby," Louis muttered. "I shouldn't have—"

"Actually," she interrupted, striving for a bright tone, "it was a lot of fun. The nanny brought her daughter over, and we made up dances. I still remember it." Reaching to the very bottom of her liquid courage, Abby stood, dislodging Louis's arm. "Want to see it? I actually have the song on my phone."

Roxy whooped. Honey put two fingers in her mouth and whistled loud enough to echo around the pool area. "Hell yeah, we want to see it. DJ, drop that beat."

"I can't believe I'm doing this," Abby murmured, positioning herself in an open space that faced her ring of friends. Again, she felt Russell staring but swatted his attention away like a bug. Her nerves were mysteriously absent. Any kind of public speaking or performing—which had been proven during a disastrous piano recital in fourth grade—typically broke her out in hives. But right now? Recapturing some of the bravado she'd discovered this morning at the office felt like the only course of action. *That* Abby had started to slip away, and she needed to grab on with both hands, yank her back.

She found the song in her phone, hit Play, and tossed the phone to Ben, who placed the device in the portable Bose speaker and cranked the volume, sending "Everybody Dance Now" blasting through the speakers. Simply hearing which song she would dance to sent her friends into a laughing fit, but the laughter did nothing to detract from her courage. No, she was laughing, too, as she broke into the running man, keeping time to the beat. When the male voice started to rap, she somehow recalled every word from her childhood, closed her eyes, and lip-synced with over-the-top enthusiasm. When she opened her eyes again and saw how entertained and happy everyone looked, satisfaction lifted her spirits.

Then she looked at Russell, witnessed his broken smile, and those raised spirits went plummeting beneath the pool's surface. He looked happy . . . but the happiness was causing him pain. It refreshed her anger. Screw him for confusing her. For sending her mixed signals. Abby stopped dancing, words rising in her throat that she would surely regret, but wasn't capable of holding back. *What do you want from me? You wreck me and then get sad when I pick my pieces back up?* Those words died in their inception when Russell's attention left her and landed on her lit-up cell phone, vibrating where it was connecting to the speaker, a call interrupting the song.

When Russell stood and reached for Abby's phone, she lunged for it, but he got there before her, disconnecting it and picking it up before the blaring song could start to play again. "Who is Mitchell, and why do you have forty-two missed calls from him?"

"Give me the phone," Abby demanded, not caring for his cold tone. Not at all. There was a counterpart to her distress, though. She hadn't told Russell about her father and the subsequent workload, but she wasn't entirely sure of the reason for omission. Now, as he waited stubbornly for an answer, phone clutched in his hand, Abby knew. She'd wanted Russell—*at least*, Russell—to see her as more than a dutiful worker bee. Was it so much to ask? To be desirable instead of reliable? That chance was gone now. Maybe it had never really existed. Not the way she wanted it to.

Russell stepped into her space. "Answer me."

"*Sti cazza. A fanabla!*"

"Uh-oh . . . she's breaking out the Italian," Roxy whispered.

Riding the surge of defiance and irritation, Abby plucked the cell phone from Russell's hand and chucked it—still ringing—into the pool. The reduction of pressure pushing down on her chest was so *extreme*, she bent at the waist, planting her hands on her knees. "Oh my God." Oxygen seeped from her lungs. "That felt really good."

Abby's voice broke on the last word. She felt her friends come up beside her, resting their hands on her back. "Hey, let's go upstairs," Roxy said. "I'll send Louis out for some ice cream."

"Someone needs to tell me what's going on here." Russell's voice came from behind Abby, harder than she'd ever heard it. "*Now*, please."

She straightened and turned on a heel, started to tell Russell that no explanations were owed to him, but his expression stopped her. After what he continued to put her through, she shouldn't care that he looked haunted. Shouldn't care that his face had gone ghost white. When would she stop? "I—"

"*Abby.*"

The new male voice brought all six of them up short. Abby's pulse went dull for a few beats, then turned erratic along with her breathing. Mitchell, the firm's lawyer, stood on the deck, looking down at them. She blinked, hoping he would vanish, but there he remained, dressed as though he'd just walked out of a boardroom.

"What are you doing here?" Roxy asked, her obvious recognition of the lawyer drawing questioning looks from the guys.

"I've been calling Abby nonstop, and she wouldn't answer. I had no choice but to make the drive." Mitchell squinted into the pool, which was still rippling from the tossed cell phone. "I guess I know why my calls were ignored."

Abby's vision was cut off when Russell removed his shirt and pulled it down over her head. The worn-in material dropped to her knees. Until then, she'd forgotten all about her lack of clothing, save the bathing suit, but apparently Russell hadn't. His arm banded around her waist, dragging her up against his side, before addressing Mitchell. "Who the hell are you?"

Mitchell coughed into his fist. "I'm Mitchell. Abby and I work together. There's a business matter that couldn't wait until Monday." He nodded toward the house. "It won't take long."

Russell gave a humorless laugh. "I don't care what this is about. She's not going anywhere." He shook his head. "Wasn't her father available for this?"

The lawyer's chin went up a notch. "I'm not in a position to discuss that with you. Although, I'm surprised Abby hasn't. You appear to be her . . ."

When Mitchell let the question dangle, Russell spoke up, discomfort transforming his features. "I'm her . . ."

Silence fell. Until Abby started to laugh. The hysterical sound bubbled from her mouth, impossible to control. There was nothing funny about any of it. Not the fact that work had followed her to the Hamptons. Or Russell—someone so important in her life—not even knowing what to call her. But the alternative was to sob and sob and never stop. So she laughed.

"I'll be inside when you're ready," Mitchell called before escaping the awkwardness she'd created by striding back into the house.

"Should we give you two a minute?" Ben asked, clearly aware that it would take a bulldozer to move Russell. His arm was wrapped around her so tightly, drawing breath was a challenge, especially after her laughing jag.

"Yeah," was all Russell said, his breath lifting the hair on her forehead.

"Screw that." Honey crossed her arms. "How about asking what Abby wants?"

"It's fine," Abby forced past numb lips. "Really. Go inside and get comfortable. I'll be in soon, sign whatever paperwork Mitchell needs signed, and we'll get back to relaxing."

Roxy looked inclined to argue further but didn't. "You've got some killer moves, roomie. You've been holding out on us."

Abby managed a smile that solidified when she heard Honey whispering on the way back into the house, "Did you know that Russell had chest hair?" Ben narrowed his eyes at his girlfriend as she passed, but the blonde only held up her hands. "Just seems like something we should have known."

Then she and Russell were alone, and the smile on her face flickered before collapsing. It was hard to muster optimism when a discussion with one very pissed-off construction worker was on the horizon. And it wasted no time getting under way. Good thing she'd never felt more prepared.

Chapter 13

Russell paced the edge of the pool, feeling raw, caged in. Like he'd woken up from a two-year coma, and everything he'd known no longer held true. Something was wrong with Abby—*his* Abby—and he'd fucking missed it. That was all he knew. Flickers of memories from the last few weeks bombarded him, cursing him with perfect hindsight. Now he couldn't look at her without seeing the fatigue on her gorgeous features. Where the hell had his head been? He'd failed her. Even without knowing the full story, that much was obvious. Not only had he failed her, he might have made whatever she was going through worse.

All this time he'd been trying to prevent his worst nightmare from becoming a reality when it had already been happening right under his nose. The sparkle she used to have in her eyes when looking at him was gone. Vanished, the way his mother's had over time. History had repeated itself. Maybe there had never really been a way to avoid it. Dammit. *Dammit.*

A jackhammer drilled into his skull, and he massaged the spot so he could think clearly, but it didn't help, so he hit it with a closed fist. Once, twice.

"Russell, stop."

God, he was such a bastard. Abby looked ready to drop, and his mind kept turning to the lawyer who'd driven all the way from Manhattan to see her. Did a man do that just for some bullshit paperwork? Could anyone spend time with Abby and not covet her? *No.* That was who he'd always pictured her ending up with, wasn't it? Some suit and tie wearing chump? The image of her dancing and laughing sprung to his mind, making his throat close up. *Jesus.* His unbelievable girl could end up with someone else.

Russell's entire being rioted at the possibility. "Tell me he's *only* a coworker." He braced his head in both hands, positive it was about to burst into fragments. His question was irrational, and somewhere within the chaos, he knew it. This was Abby. She wouldn't date someone else and let him touch her at the same time. But even the idea of lawyer man asking her out broke him out in a cold sweat. "Tell me. Please, angel."

"That's your foremost concern?"

"It's the one I need cleared up so I can think straight." He dropped his hands and took a few steps in her direction. "Believe me there's more."

She stared off toward the beach for a minute, sixty seconds that stretched into the longest of his life, as if debating whether or not he deserved to know the truth. And he'd earned every second of agony that came before her answer. They weren't together. Their relationship was murky and undefined. He'd made sure of it. Finally, she answered. "He's only a coworker, Russell. I don't even like him." She tugged at the hem of the Yankees T-shirt he'd covered her in. "He's just a mouthpiece for my stepmother, delivering bad news so she doesn't have to feel guilty."

"Okay." He breathed the word, relief showering down on him like an epic rainstorm. He was selfish for being relieved when her problems still existed, but seeing her with another man would have broken him, rendering him useless to help her. At least now he could breathe. "Tell me the rest."

She dropped onto one of the deck chairs, wrapping two arms around her raised legs. "My father is undergoing psychiatric treatment. The stress caught up with him about a month ago, and he's unable to run the company right now." She lifted her shoulders in a weary shrug. "I'm just stepping in until he gets back on his feet."

It took a moment for Russell to process the implications of that. "You're running a multimillion-dollar hedge fund?"

"No, I'm running a billion-dollar hedge fund."

"You're making light of this?"

"No." Her brows drew together. "No, I'm not making light of it. My father isn't well. I don't really know to what extent because he won't even *see* me. I'm one computer keystroke away from losing millions of dollars every second of the day. So, no. Not making light."

"Why didn't you tell me?" His voice was hoarse from holding back a shout. Not at Abby but into the ether. A general shout of *what the fuck* that would echo for a year. He wanted to level self-disgust at himself for underestimating her, for thinking she'd been working some cushy office job that catered lunch and over-paid their employees for sitting on their asses in air-conditioning all day. He'd always known Abby had a brilliant mind, but he assumed working was optional for her. It appeared to be anything but. "You tell me everything. What was different this time? I would have found a way to help."

Abby pushed to her feet with a soft laugh. "You just answered your own question. You can't help this time around. And it would have driven you crazy."

"Don't worry, I'm making up for lost time in the crazy department."

She glanced toward the house. "Look what happened when I told Roxy and Honey. Now *my* problem is *theirs*. Now none of us can enjoy the weekend. I was fine with its just being me."

"Of *course*, they're worried, Abby." He closed the gap between them and grabbed her shoulders, shaking her a little. "You're worthy of everyone's worry. If the same thing that happened to your father happened to you, I'd . . ."

"You'd what? Get mad at me? Stomp around and shout at everyone? Do you think that would *help*?" She jerked away from his grip, temper making her eyes glow in the partial darkness. "And I'm *worthy*? Worthy of what? Getting on my knees for you . . . but not actually being your girlfriend. Right?" Her words dug into his chest like a round of bullets. "*Manache!* Your words mean *nothing* to me right now."

Russell had no idea how long he stood there, staring at the spot where Abby had been standing, her outline still visible. A chain saw had been swiped across his midsection, sending his vital organs falling to the ground. His legs didn't want to hold him up, but collapsing would require movement, and he hurt too much to attempt that.

Abby thought he'd been using her. That was the sick truth his dishonesty had bred. This girl he dreamed of making his wife thought he wanted a temporary hookup—and why not? *I'm not in the market for a girlfriend.* Hadn't he said those words, possibly even more than once? She'd stuck around anyway, and the only reason he could come up with was . . . she'd trusted him to do the right thing by her. And in fucktastic fashion, he'd fulfilled the prophecy originated by his father and done the opposite.

Could he tell her the truth? That he'd only wanted to be *sure*, positive that he could provide for her before taking that major step he was dying to take. Asking her, *begging* her, to be his forever. Right now, forever with Abby sounded like even more of a long shot than it had this morning. Now he was working against more than his couch-surfing status. He had to overcome the wound he'd inflicted by letting her feel used.

Russell cursed, the jackhammer in his head revving once again, ready to finish the job. Right now, he could only follow his instincts. They were telling him to get inside and do *something* to help her. And yeah, maybe it made him a bastard, but Abby around another man didn't sit right. Never would. But when he walked inside, he found Mitchell sitting alone at the kitchen table, stuffing documents back into a briefcase.

"Where's Abby?"

When the guy eyeballed him, Russell remembered his lack of a shirt. *Deal with it, man.* "She headed out the front door. Said she wanted some fresh air." The lawyer's smile was tight. "Maybe you should let her get it."

"Maybe you shouldn't talk to me about Abby. Ever. How's that sound?"

Mitchell laughed, and it sounded phony as hell. "Mrs. Sullivan will be interested to know whom Abby decided to bring into their home." He snapped his briefcase shut. "Of course, the others seem perfectly fine."

Russell refused to show an ounce of self-consciousness. But it stung. Maybe this guy wasn't the corporate drone he appeared to be. There was a sharpness to Mitchell that hadn't been apparent when he spoke to Abby outside.

But he'd think about it later. Right now, he wanted to go find Abby. He didn't like the idea of her walking around alone in the dark. Was she still only wearing a damn bathing suit and his T-shirt? Russell shouldered past the lawyer and left the kitchen. He could hear everyone upstairs, speaking in hushed tones, but he didn't hear Abby. The front door was slightly ajar, making him think Mitchell had been telling the truth about where she'd gone.

The night was warm, but he only registered the temperature dimly, totally focused on figuring out where Abby had gone. When he caught up with her, he would apologize until his voice was gone. He'd be as honest as possible without completely tipping his hand. If she knew everything hinged on one bank meeting, she'd tell him he was being ridiculous. That was Abby. But she hadn't seen what the future could look like yet without the benefit of financial security. He *had*. He remembered every second, and she wouldn't be subjected to it.

A short staircase to his left led down to the beach. Since there was no sign of Abby on the pathway, he took it, refusing to indulge the foreboding prickling the back of his neck. *Calm down*.

Waves washed up onto the beach, white surf spreading until it soaked into the sand. Every fifteen feet sat a green-and-white-striped cabana for beachgoers to escape the sun. What ever happened to good old-fashioned umbrellas? He'd only ever been to Rockaway Beach in Queens, but he would appreciate the vast difference between the two locations tomorrow. Right now, he—

Russell stopped short, an alarm blaring in his head. Cold blasted him. His T-shirt had been discarded in the sand, right at the edge of the water. Moving on autopilot, he bent down to retrieve it and noticed the footprints leading right into the ocean.

ABBY SAT ON top of a flat rock, knees pulled to her chest, staring out at the water. The paperwork Mitchell had brought had been fairly straightforward, authorizing the moving of funds, overseas transfers. One new hire contract. And shuffled in between them all, a power-of-attorney document, giving her permission to make decisions on her father's behalf.

She'd signed something similar when her father was first incapacitated, to cover them if word got out that he wasn't actively running the company, but it hadn't been nearly as extensive. Mitchell continued to say her father's condition was stable, but she didn't know what to believe. One thing was for certain. She wouldn't sit around anymore and wait for her father to request her presence. As soon as she got back to New York, she would see his condition for herself.

Another interesting detail had snagged her eye while reviewing the paperwork. She personally owned a 2 percent stake in the company. Something she hadn't been aware of until tonight and wasn't even sure she was *supposed* to know. Why had she never been made aware? The discovery had sparked an idea. An idea that required more thought. One that snowballed the more she entertained it.

Abby's racing thoughts were interrupted when Russell appeared on the beach. Her initial reaction at the sight of him, as always, was a mixture of warmth and contentment. But it was tempered with disappointment now. Sadness. And unfortunately, some significant sexual awareness that probably would never fade, now that she knew what their bodies could do together.

She watched as he picked up the T-shirt she'd thrown off in what had been an admittedly childish move. Just because she was angry with him and didn't know where they stood, didn't mean she should ditch his clothes in random spots. She hated feeling guilty for her parting shot by the pool. Really, she should own the statement she'd made because she'd *meant* it. Right now, though, she couldn't help but crave their closeness from before. Before they'd been intimate. When she could lay her head on his shoulder and tell him everything on her mind.

Abby's insides jolted when Russell shouted her name. Had he seen her? He wasn't even looking in her direction. When he charged headfirst into the water, her confusion sunk into the yawning pit in her stomach. His voice sounded strangled as he called her name over and over, diving beneath the surface. Looking for her? Yes. He thought she'd gone into the water. As quickly as possible, Abby gained her footing and leapt from the rock onto the sand. Her still-sensitive ankle protested, but she paid it no attention, sprinting toward the water.

"Russell."

The sound of waves crashing half swallowed her voice, but he would have heard her, had he not just dived below the surface once more. Abby had just reached the shoreline and splashed into the ocean when Russell rose with a strangled curse, water coursing down his back. He spun in a circle, obviously still searching the dark waves, hands moving furiously in the water as if he could peel it back and find her.

"*Goddammit!*" he shouted. "Angel, *please.*"

"Russell," she said again, out of breath. He heard her this time—*thank God*—his entire body stiffening, before slowly turning to face her. The turmoil on his face made Abby stumble in her awkward attempts to reach him, but she pushed forward and threw herself at him without thinking. His big body was an unmoving block of ice, so she grabbed his shoulders and climbed, wrapping her legs around his waist and holding tight. "I'm sorry. I was on the beach. I'm sorry."

Still, he made no attempt to hold her back. Tremors began to move through him, shaking them both where they stood in the churning water.

Abby buried her face in his neck. "Say something. You're scaring me."

"I'm scaring you." The words were toneless, but she could feel his pulse thundering against her lips. "You were under the water."

"No, I wasn't."

Russell's entire body heaved a shuddering breath, then two powerful arms were crushing her against his chest. It didn't matter that she couldn't inhale; at least he'd come back to her from wherever he'd gone. "You keep doing this to me." His whisper was furious in her hair. "Keep almost taking yourself away. What would I have done, Abby? *What?*"

Another shudder passed through Russell, and it sent realization coursing through Abby. An understanding that this man had made mistakes, maybe he would make even more, but his feelings for her were real. As real as hers for him. There was no room for a barrier between them at that moment, and she needed to take advantage. Find out why Russell would charge into an ocean for her but didn't want a serious relationship. For crying out loud, from where she was standing, their relationship was more serious than most marriages she'd encountered among her parents and their friends.

"You don't call anyone else angel." She leaned back to meet his gaze. "I thought all the way back to our first hang out. Not a waitress, not my roommates. No one. You only call me that."

She'd caught him at a weak moment, when he was still coming down off the imagined tragedy. It was evident in the way his eyes closed, his head tipped forward to rest against hers. "Yeah. I know."

"Why would you tell me otherwise?" She swallowed what felt like a handful of pebbles. "Do you want to push me away?"

"You think there's an easy answer to that?" The question burst out of him with the force of a gale wind, warming her face. "Yes and no. There's your answer."

"Why *yes*?"

Russell didn't speak for a long stretch, just continuing to hold her so tightly, as if she might try and escape. They breathed together, bodies moving as one in a way that felt natural. How it was supposed to be. Abby didn't realize she'd closed her eyes until Russell finally spoke, forcing them open. "Look at me, angel." She leaned back and did as he asked, gulping in the face of such intensity. "Look at how fucked-up I am. You can't even go for a walk without my being convinced the world is going to swallow you up. It's not normal."

Abby tried to interject—with *what*, she wasn't sure—but he cut her off.

"There's a reason." His muscles tensed against her. "It's not good enough. Nothing excuses the way I act when it comes to you. Remember that, okay?" He sucked in a breath. "I lost someone. My mother. She . . . died. It was a long time ago, but I remember what it felt like. It could have been prevented if we'd just found a way to make her feel better. And it's not right, Abby, it's not right, but I have to make sure I don't feel that way ever again. You're the only one who could make me. The *only* one."

The taste of salt invaded Abby's mouth, a mixture of tears and the surrounding ocean. Russell's pain harpooned past her ribs and struck deep. She hadn't been the only one keeping a secret, and it killed her. Killed her knowing he'd been harboring it on his own. She wanted to ask how his mother died, but the hurt radiating from him was already so profound, she couldn't find the words. Instead, she clung to him like her life depended on it, laying kisses on his collarbone and neck, whispering comfort that only made sense to them.

"There's more, Abby. She—my mother—would still be around if . . . if maybe she'd had a hero. I don't know . . ."

Russell trailed off, and Abby waited, but he didn't finish his thought. She didn't want him to. She could practically feel the wounds gaping on his flesh where it pressed against her. He'd opened up enough for one night. The need to heal and distract rising within her was so powerful, it was almost visible in the air surrounding them.

She had the ability to make him forget his pain tonight. *Always*, if he'd let her. Hadn't every secret shared, every touch exchanged, been leading to this moment? Heat tickled her belly, thinking of how Russell had been in the guest room, how in control he'd been . . . and all the while, just a hint *out* of control. Craving the experience again, needing to soothe the memories they'd dug up, Abby didn't second-guess herself as she trailed her tongue up the side of Russell's neck, breathing against his ear.

"Now tell me why you *don't* want to push me away."

Chapter 14

*R*ussell slipped a hand down Abby's back, over her slick bathing suit. He wanted to peel off the tight nylon and see his girl naked in the moonlight, feel her bare ass in his grip, but he forced his hand into a fist at the base of her spine. And breathed. Which was a mistake because she smelled like white grapes with a hint of tequila. Naughty and nice, wrapped around his body, ready to give him everything.

She was giving him an out, this sweet, beautiful girl he loved. He really shouldn't take it. Should come clean about everything. His insecurity over her money, his failed attempts to close that financial gap, his plan to try one final time. The reality of his family life . . . how that family had broken apart. Hell, he'd already chipped away at the dam, telling her something he hadn't even told his friends. It had felt good. Right. Would he feel better for spilling everything?

"Russell," she murmured at his mouth, obliterating his concentration. "Tell me the reason you can't push me away."

His heart drummed faster and faster, matching his breath.

Jesus Christ. He knew what was coming, knew she would offer herself to him tonight. On a regular basis, he felt unworthy of Abby, but right now? Right now, she looked like some exotic mermaid, glowing under the night sky, the ocean as her backdrop. She wasn't something a man like him was allowed to experience. A painfully sexy virgin, tempting him to fuck her on some rich man's beach. It was like a pornographic postcard. Or it would be if he wasn't prepared to die for this girl at the prompting of one, single word from her mouth.

"You know why I can't stay away, angel. Work your hips up, and you'll feel it." Eyes sparking with excitement, Abby flexed her thighs around his waist, lifted, and rolled her body, gasping at the pronounced thickness inside his wet board shorts. *Shiiiit.* When had she started to move like that? She knew right where he needed to feel her pussy, knew to give a tight, little buck that conjured thoughts of his own hips doing the same. Only she'd be beneath him with her thighs spread. Christ, he needed to take this slow. Needed to make an *attempt* to deserve this. Deserve *her.* "Hey. Let me see your eyes, Abby." Her hazel gaze was foggy as it lifted, snagged on him. It was a moment before he could speak normally. "I want your body. Want it bad as fuck. But I can't stay away from you, Abby, because you're *you.* Okay?"

"Okay," Abby breathed. She went for his mouth with such unexpected eagerness, the impact of her taste sent him back a step in the water. Her moan as their tongues met had the effect of a smooth hand wrapping around his dick. The familiar voice that growled *mine* whenever he touched Abby increased in volume, competing with the ocean. Her thighs started moving restlessly on either side of him, climbing his waist and grinding down, all the while making these head-wrecking, whimpering noises when her sweet spot met his cock. Their mouths were competing for the best taste of one another, lips greedy and desperate.

Closer. Need her as close as possible. With one arm wedged beneath her ass, Russell used the opposite hand to yank down the straps of her bathing suit. As soon as he got the stretchy material around her waist, he kissed down her neck and sucked each of her nipples in turn. "I can't believe you're going to let me inside this body. So hot . . . so smooth. I don't belong there, but it's mine all the same. Isn't it?"

Her fingernails dug into his shoulders as she leaned back to give him a perfect view of her tits. "I don't want anyone but you. How many ways can I say it?"

Goddamn. If he didn't get her out of the water and into someplace private, he would fuck her standing up. Which sounded *awesome* to his Abby-starved brain, but no way in hell would he cause her more pain than necessary. Keeping a tight hold on her, Russell began wading toward the shore, pausing every few feet to get his mouth on her nipples or kiss a whimper out of her. In the dark, pressed so close to the girl he craved, secrets contained inside his head so long made for the exit. "What I said . . . about how I worry about you. There's a huge part of me that loves it, Abby." His hands found her ass and kneaded. "I love covering your body up with my clothes. Being the one who gets you home safe. I love it. It's *my* job."

She brushed her lips over his ear, making him shiver. "I was mad at you earlier for ripping my bathing suit . . . but I wasn't mad, too."

"What do you mean?"

They reached the shore as she answered, Russell's footsteps eating up the sand on his way to the closest cabana. "I'm still figuring it out. But . . . I know when you tied me up, I realized that's what I'd wanted all along." She rested her forehead against his. "Does that make sense?"

His heart squeezed, then boomed louder. Faster. Some part of him had known all along she was made for him. These unfamiliar impulses she'd woken inside him corresponded to hers. They couldn't be wrong if she needed them, too, right? "Yes . . . I think it does make sense, angel. I hope like hell it does."

They reached the cabana, and Russell shouldered past the hanging canvas that kept the inside private. Side-by-side beach chairs, reclined to their flat position, were just inside, and he quickly picked the left one, laying Abby down. When she kept her arms wrapped around him, he had no choice but to descend with her. Their positions stayed the same, but when laid vertical, his dick shoved between her thighs with five times the pressure and friction.

"Ahhh, fuck." He captured her wrists and locked them over her head, giving her a tight twist of his hips. "I'm not a duke, Abby."

Her eyes popped open on a moan. "W-what?"

No way. No way he'd just said that *out loud*. Russell dropped his head into the crook of her neck, using the opportunity to feel her pulse against his lips. Because any second now, she'd realize she'd entrusted her virginity to a guy who took pointers from imaginary noblemen. "I, uh." She ran her fingertips up his spine, and nothing had ever felt so amazing in his life. "My brother's wife leaves these books lying around. Romance novels. And this duke—his name is Sebastian, but that's not important—he . . . it was his girl's first time. He went so slow, letting her get used to his . . . manhood." Russell reached between their bodies and palmed Abby's breasts. "I don't know if I can do that."

"Manhood?" Her body vibrated with laughter. "You read a romance novel for me?"

Slowly, he shook his head. "I'd *kill* for you, Abby."

When her smile vanished, Russell wished he could snatch back the words, bury them back down where they belonged. At least, he wished it until she pushed up on her elbows and kissed him. Her tongue licked against his, slow and sweet, the teasing action making his dick thicken, an effect she felt right between her thighs, if the sexy purr she let out was any indication. "Russell," she said, in a shaky whisper, "there might also be such a thing as going *too* slow."

"I'll remind you of that in a few minutes." He slipped his hands down her rib cage, snagging the edges of her bathing suit. "I need a hit of that pussy first. It's had me on edge all fucking day, wondering when I'm going to get a lick." Russell moved to a kneeling position, growling at the way her bathing suit's material hugged her core. Was it possible to be jealous of a piece of clothing? Yeah. When it came to her, anything was possible. Russell stripped the black suit down her legs and tossed it aside, every ounce of his blood rushing south at the site of her. Bare and waiting. "Come on, angel. I want those knees pointed at opposite ends of the beach."

His harsh speech started her tits rising and falling with deep gulps of breath. A naked, beautiful, goddamn sight he could feel branding itself in his memory bank. But she hesitated. "I'm . . . are you supposed to put your mouth there when I'm already so wet?"

Praying like hell he wouldn't come in his board shorts, Russell pushed her thighs open and fell on her with a groan. A groan that didn't stop as he lapped at Abby, delved his tongue inside her heat and worshipped that tiny bud with his lips. He swore he could taste her shyness, and it cranked his lust to a fevered state, giving him no choice but to release his cock, the hungry weight of it dropping down onto the reclined chair. "*Damn.* Maybe I shouldn't have gone down on you." He licked up her belly, over the taut flesh between her tits. When he reached Abby's neck, he scraped his teeth up and down the sensitive skin, his way of comforting her while his knuckles dragged over her pussy. "How am I going to hold off on fucking you hard when I can taste how much you want it?"

"I don't know." She arched her back. "P-please keep doing that."

Russell braced himself to have his fingers inside Abby for the first time. "You know how many times I've fantasized about slipping my hand into your panties and giving you an orgasm?" He rotated his finger and added another, pushing into her tight entrance with a curse. "The one that always gets me off is picturing you on my lap in the bar, while I stroke your clit under the table." He followed through on his words with a rough thumb, gritting his teeth as she jolted on the chair. "Would you have played along, Abby? Let me finger-fuck you beneath one of those loose skirts?"

"*Yes.*" Her belly hollowed and shook, her hands grabbing at his wrist, pressing his touch closer. "I would have done anything. I'll do *anything.*"

"Do anything for what?"

Like she'd been transported straight from his filthiest subconscious, she threw both arms over her head and begged him beneath heavy eyelids. "You know what I need, Russell. You always know."

That was the end of going slow. He slid both fingers from inside her, using them to circle her clit, faster and faster. "Come. *Come* so I can give you the real thing."

As always when she climaxed, her heels dug in, hips lifting. He fucking *loved* knowing that about her. Loved knowing that no one else would ever know but him. Dampness met his fingers as she twisted on the chair. "*Russell.* Feels so *good.*"

A drumbeat ricocheted around his skull. He didn't even register positioning himself between her thighs until he was there, running the head of his dick through her wetness. *Need need need.* With one hand, he shoved the confining shorts down and felt a hard slap against his thigh. His wallet. Condom. *Condom.* Jesus, what if he'd forgotten? Hoping Abby hadn't noticed his almost slip, Russell drew out the leather wallet and ripped out the single condom, opening it with his teeth.

She shifted beneath him. "Do you always carry those with you?"

He marveled over the touch of self-consciousness in her voice.

Had he not made it clear as crystal that other girls might as well be invisible for all the attention he paid them? If she hadn't gotten the message, they weren't moving forward until she did. "Give me your hand," he demanded, rising up over her. When she did as he asked without question, he curled her fingers around his dick. "I bought them the night you hurt your ankle." He watched that sink in. "I knew I'd never be able to say no if we got here. And what is my job, angel?"

"Worrying about me," she murmured into the near darkness. "Protecting me."

"That's right." Slowly, he thrust his cock into her grip. "*Abby's.* That's Abby's."

Eyes unfocused, she grazed his sides with her knees. "Show me."

Russell rolled on the latex, then fisted his hardness. He pushed the tip inside her, stopping when a shudder wracked him. "I'm afraid to hear you scream. I don't want to know what a bad scream sounds like from you." He aligned their bodies, both of their skin having grown slick in the summer heat. "If you need to, do it into my shoulder."

Abby nodded and placed her lips where he'd indicated. They plumped against his shoulder, reminding him they'd been on his dick just hours earlier. *Don't even think about a replay, or you'll never last.* The anticipation, the excitement in her eyes, the churning need for release clawing to get out became too much, and he shoved deeper, wincing at the tight fit. Something else was happening, too. A bone-deep impulse to ram himself home and lay claim to her in an irreversible way. Dammit, this is what he'd been terrified of. This ever-present conflict when it came to Abby. Never—ever—wanting to harm her while experiencing the sense that she wanted an unknown amount of . . . force.

"Russell, more plea—"

He drove his remaining inches inside Abby, her choked cry splitting the air between them. His instincts propelled him forward to cut it off with his mouth. Comforting words tried to find their way up his throat, but the pleasure choked him, made it impossible to speak. He hadn't been ready. Never would have been ready for the tight clutch of her pussy, the sensation of her feet digging into his ass. Was she struggling or attempting to move, to get closer? He couldn't hear or discern a goddamn thing over the rushing between his ears. *Wake up, asshole.*

"I won't move. I won't. Just tell me when—"

"Now. *Now*, please."

"Thank fuck," he growled, rearing back with his hips and fucking into her with a satisfying slap of damp flesh. "*Ahhh God.* Am I hurting you?" How would he stop if he *was*? It would be worse than losing a limb. Getting impatient for a response, he pushed her knees up toward her elbows and bore down. "An answer, Abby."

"A little. It hurts a little." Her teeth raked over her bottom lip. "But if you stop, it'll hurt worse. *Please.*"

Not helping. She was as conflicted as him. "I waited too long. Let it build up too much. All this fucking *want*." Another tether inside him snapped loose, setting free the enveloping need to shake the confusion out of them both, force a decision. Russell lost his grip on control, or maybe he did it voluntarily. In one hand, he pinned Abby's wrists over her head, bringing them face-to-face. A flicker of relief and encouragement made her eyes sparkle. *Please don't let me be imagining it.* With the opposite hand, he gripped her jaw and tilted her head back in a single, rough movement. When he spoke, it was right up against her ear. "What did I tell you in my house that day, Abby? What do I want to do to you?"

He could feel the pulse in her neck racing, beating against the base of his hand. Trapped. He had her trapped, but she liked it. Her hips moved in restless figure eights beneath him, entreating him to thrust. Those heels were doing their thing, trying to find purchase on the backs of his thighs. "You . . ." She sucked in a breath, pushing her pointed tits into his chest. "You said you want to bang my little virgin brains out."

"*I meant it.*" Attempting to bring himself down from the insane high of hearing those forbidden words out of Abby's innocent mouth, Russell licked past her lips for a searing kiss. It didn't work. All he could feel was the hot sensation of her pussy contracting around him. Pulse. Pulse. "Are you doing that? Are you . . . *stop.*"

"No." Her swallow was audible because of the angle he still held her jaw. "You're thinking too hard. We both know what . . . what you need. I need to be the one who gives it to you. Don't take that away from me." She writhed on the chair, gasping when he tightened his hold automatically.

"*Stay still.*"

He hated the almost total darkness and loved it simultaneously. Wanted to see her face in the light but didn't want her to see *his.* As he released her jaw and used both hands to pin her, he had to look like an animal. He felt like one. He jerked his hips back and slammed forward, groaning at the welcoming slickness. The narrow perfection of her. Abby's cry was absorbed by his chest, and fuck, he loved that. Loved looking down and seeing her beneath him, feeling the vibration of his name as it passed her lips.

"*Yes,*" she moaned. "Again."

If any remaining reservations still had a foothold, they slipped down the slope on which he'd been desperately attempting to balance. He didn't recognize the words or sounds that left his mouth as he fucked Abby, the girl he loved. Their bodies slid up and down against one another, moving in a frantic rhythm. His cock felt so full already, ready to spill, and Abby did nothing to help postpone the inevitable, wrapping her long legs around him and begging, *begging*. God, she was so gorgeous he couldn't stand it. Couldn't deal with her beauty on top of the driving demand to claim her body. Satisfy her. Himself.

Knowing he only had a small window to get her off, Russell released her manacled hands and wedged a forearm beneath her hips. "Tilt them up, angel. Same way you did when I used my mouth. We're going to find that sweet spot, aren't we? I might be banging my little virgin, but I'm going to make her come, too. Always. That's another one of my jobs, and I love it. Your come is mine."

He broke off into a groan as Abby angled her hips with the aid of his lifting forearm. The new angle brought the base of his length into contact with her clit, and fuck . . . the unsteady whimper of his name almost made him bust. She threw her head back on the chair and started to roll her body, meeting his pumps with incredible accuracy.

Meant to be with her. This was all part of some plan. His thoughts collided with his heart, sending it speeding out of control.

Abby buried her fingernails into his ass, her thighs beginning to tremble around him. "I'm going to . . . oh my God, don't stop. I'm . . ."

Russell dropped his head forward and closed his eyes, putting all his focus into staying right where the fuck he was, not deviating from what was pushing her toward a climax. Just a little longer. Just a little—

"*Russell.*"

Holy shit. His eyes flew open in time to witness Abby's tits shaking between them, her teeth buried into her bottom lip as she arched on the chair. Her heels had a firm hold at the small of his back as she rode it out, her pussy squeezing him in tiny spasms that he would crave like air for the rest of his time on earth.

He was aching and swollen inside her, seconds from going off. There was no explanation for what he did next, only knew that it felt like a travesty to release into a condom. A waste of what she'd done to him. He wanted to mark her, brand her in a way that she might not understand or might find confusing, but as he pulled out of her still-convulsing body, tore off the condom, and expelled his pleasure on her tits, his brain registered it as something beautiful. Seeing Abby wearing the evidence of how much he'd wanted her for so long, how much he'd want her forever.

After that, his muscles would no longer support him. He went down on an elbow beside Abby, kissing her shoulder until she turned on her side. His eyes searched in the darkness for something to clean her, making out a stack of towels just over their heads. He grabbed the terry-cloth material and ran it down Abby's front, neck to belly, all the while rubbing his lips over her heated skin.

"Russell?" Her sweet voice glittered in the darkness.

He draped the towel over her body. "What is it, angel?"

For long moment, he could only count her breaths. "We have a lot to talk about, don't we?"

His pulse tripped as he pulled her close, curved his body around her smaller one. *I'm going to sleep with my girl next to me.* "Yeah. I guess we do."

Understatement of the year. The list of things they needed to discuss seemed endless. The status of their relationship. Why he'd been pushing her away. How he planned to stop doing that and never let her go. Ever. There was also the nature of their sexual attraction, how they acted on it. He felt an urgency to ensure that his need to . . . *dominate* Abby was always done safely, because if he hurt her—

No. He would never hurt her again.

Not if he could help it.

Chapter 15

*A*bby woke up feeling a little sticky. And *a lot* amazing.

She lay still without opening her eyes for long minutes, trapping all the sounds and sensations inside a net of coveted recollections. Russell warmed her back, one heavy arm thrown over her hips. Of course, he snored. Like his having chest hair, snoring seemed like something she should have known. But hadn't *she* always been the one to fall asleep on *him*? Maybe *she* snored and didn't even know it. She'd have to ask him when he woke up.

Anticipation purred in her bloodstream at the idea of talking to Russell while they were both naked. Hearing what his voice sounded like upon waking.

The smell of ocean and suntan lotion filled her nose as the events of last night projected themselves on the backs of her eyelids. Each image was sharp, their outlines carved out with a box cutter. And each one had the subtitle, *I love Russell.* She did. She'd loved him in different ways for a long time. But *acknowledging* it—defining what she'd been harboring for him all along—made the feeling expand like a fleet of balloons. Big, colorful ones with the ability to carry her across the beach and ocean . . . anywhere she wanted to go.

Abby pressed her fingers against her lips, felt the smile there. Her mouth parted on an intake of breath when the sensitivity between her thighs registered. Finally, her eyes opened and immediately fell upon the light bruises circling her wrists. Why did seeing the shaded marks send a feather tickling down the center of her belly? No, she *knew* now. Knew the reason imagining gentle, straightforward sex had never excited her. Why she'd always felt safer with her confusing fantasies of being taken *hard*. Restrained. They weren't confusing anymore. At least, they were beginning to define themselves with every experience between her and Russell.

Were his sexual preferences the reason he'd been keeping her at a distance? Abby brushed her lips over a thumb-sized bruise on her wrist. Of course, this man who spent an inordinate amount of time worrying for her safety would hate the idea of being aggressive with her. Or, hate the idea that he *liked* it, more accurately. Abby let out a relieved breath. Now that she knew what he'd been battling, she could play defense.

Testing her well-used muscles, Abby felt a flush infuse her neck as she encountered the sticky feeling once again. Another, larger feather licked down her middle. *Russell looming above her, growling as he marked her.* She couldn't wait to do it again. Today. This morning. Now.

She lifted Russell's arm off her body and sat up, noticing traces of blood on her inner thighs. Before they talked or touched each other again, she needed a shower. Maybe it was ridiculous to feel self-conscious around the man who'd been present for the cause.

She'd have to work on that but felt no pressure to accomplish any more milestones at the moment, having reached a huge one last night.

Abby laid the towel over Russell, muffling a laugh when his snoring amplified. She picked up another towel and wrapped it around herself, hoping no one would spy her on the short trek back to the house. Southampton residents typically didn't rise this early, so she was probably safe. She'd shower, change, grab a set of clothes for Russell, and be back with coffee before he even woke up.

Refusing to dim the wattage of her smile, Abby fairly danced out of the cabana and speed-walked along the beach, ascending the staircase like she had springs on her feet. She would have to be quiet in the house. Her friends were no doubt still asleep, preparing to wake up with hangovers in a couple hours. A large part of her was glad she'd have a chance to talk with Russell before seeing Honey or Roxy again. They would no doubt have questions, and she couldn't wait to have answers, for once.

She reached the gate at the estate's edge, swung it open and stepped onto the paved driveway, but drew up short when she saw Mitchell, leaning against the trunk of his car. The towel around her suddenly felt flimsy, transparent. There was nothing sexual about the way he perused her, only businesslike. Practical. But it didn't make her feel any less exposed.

"What are you still doing here?" She was pleased at the strength in her voice, despite the awkward situation. "Did I miss a signature page?"

When he remained tight-lipped, she thought he wasn't going

to answer. Finally, his lips lifted into a smile that didn't go near his eyes. "Car trouble, actually. The repair company just left. I was about to head back to Manhattan."

She shook her head, eyeing the brand-spanking-new Mercedes. "Car trouble." Her fingers curled into the top of the towel, grateful it covered her past the knee. "Did you sleep in your car?"

"Yes." He sauntered toward her. "I had a funny feeling your friends weren't going to let me into the house."

"You're probably right." A ditch formed in her stomach when Mitchell's attention caught on her wrists. "I'm going to head in now."

That creepy smile of his stayed in place as he nodded. "That's probably a good idea." He inclined his head. "We'll keep this between you and me. No need to worry your mother, right?"

A sour taste permeated Abby's mouth. She wanted to curse him straight to hell, but getting into the house was the more desirable outcome. A back-and-forth between them would prevent that. God, she hated that he'd ruined her morning. She just wanted to forget this encounter had ever happened and get back down to the beach. "Thanks, Mitchell," she muttered, skirting past him toward the house.

She waited just inside the front door until she heard his car pull away before tiptoeing up the stairs.

RUSSELL SHOT FORWARD in a panic, searching the cabana with frantic eyes. He shouldn't be by himself. Abby's sweet, warm body had been tucked up against him all night. He knew that because he'd woken up several times, convinced he'd been dreaming. But no. No, she'd been there, sighing in her sleep, letting him smell her hair, run hands up and down her thighs, shoulders, and belly. It had been the best night of his twenty-seven years, and he had *not* goddamn imagined it.

When he spied her bathing suit on the ground, he pressed two fingers against his forehead and breathed. Where had she gone? Why hadn't she woken him up? Didn't she know how he'd react to her disappearing?

Calm down and go find her. This fear that threatened wasn't just a product of his panic. Abby hadn't been hurt last night. If she had, could she have slept beside him so trusting and peaceful? The memory of her feet tucked between his calves sent warmth soaring into his chest, saving it from freezing into a block of ice. Okay. As soon as he saw her, kissed her forehead, everything would be fine. They would talk about everything. There was no room for secrets when he felt so close to her. She'd set his fears to rest about his physical urges, but the money issue would be no different. And he would believe her when she inevitably told him their future was *theirs* to decide because she believed in him. She'd trusted him with her body, and he'd beg that she do the same with her heart.

Crazy how one night could change everything. But it had. A clarity had stormed into his consciousness, wrought by his con-nection to Abby. Nothing was insurmountable as long as they could make each other feel as alive as they'd been last night. He'd live his life to make that happen.

Russell whipped the discarded board shorts off the ground, gained his feet, and pulled them on, halfway out of the cabana before he'd fully tied them. He saw the Yankees shirt, crumpled in the sand and decided to leave it there, liking the reminder of what had ultimately brought them together staying right where it was. When he reached the top of the staircase, his mind was already on what he'd make Abby for breakfast. She liked sweet stuff, like French toast—

"Mr. Hart."

Russell came to a halt on the road, so immersed in thoughts of Abby, it took him a moment to place the man, standing inside the door of his running Mercedes. Mitchell, the lawyer. What the hell was he still doing here?

He must have asked the question out loud because the guy smirked. "You know why the Sullivan family pays me so well?" He drummed his fingers on the car's roof. "I make sure problems don't present themselves. And when they do, I make them go away. I'm really fucking good at it, too."

Showing no outward reaction, Russell couldn't help being surprised at the expletive coming from the polished lawyer. Or maybe he shouldn't be surprised at all. "Is there a reason you think I give a shit?"

"There's a good reason for everything I say and do."

Russell almost looked up, positive he would see an axe materialize in the air. Intuition was like spikes flowing through his veins. He glanced over Mitchell's shoulder toward the house, praying he'd see Abby, but there was no one. Jesus, where had she gone? "If what you have to say is so important, get to it."

The look that crossed the lawyer's face said he was enjoying this. "Ran into Abby a few minutes ago." With those words, Russell's dread shifted and escalated into rage. She'd gone to that beach last night dressed in nothing but a swimsuit. A swimsuit he'd seen on the floor of the cabana. Meaning this fucker had seen her in . . . what? The possibilities made his eyes burn.

Russell struggled for a modicum of composure, but the effort was useless. "If you even spoke to her, I'd be worried."

"I did. Speak to her." A too-long pause ensued. "You bruise up a lot of girls, Hart?"

He was instantly winded, unable to catch a breath. That axe above him didn't just drop, it hacked away at him. *Hacked, hacked, hacked*, severing internal organs without mercy. Somehow, the guy knew his last name, but it was only a dim realization, swallowed up in the earlier statement. "What . . . what are you talking about?"

"Look, buddy." Mitchell held up both hands, like they could have an honest exchange after the bomb he'd just dropped on Russell's very existence. "I'm here as the fixer. As understandably upset as she was, Abby obviously needs one—"

"She was upset?" The words fell out of Russell's mouth and splintered into fragments on the ground, alongside his heart. Had he been wrong about the connection . . . the understanding between them? She'd enjoyed what they'd done, hadn't she? He wracked his mind, attempting to remember what she'd said in the darkness, before they fell asleep. *We have a lot to talk about, don't we?* Christ, that could mean *anything*. Images assaulted him. Abby's jaw in his grip. Her hands imprisoned over her head. The way he'd pulled out and bathed her in his release.

His knees felt weak with the need to give out. Was there a

man of sound mind on this planet that would do those things to a virgin? No. *No* . . . he'd done it all wrong. He'd hurt her. Hurt Abby. *God, oh God, oh God.*

"Where did she go?" Russell managed.

"Probably somewhere you can't hurt her again." Mitchell rounded the car at a casual pace, reaching into his pocket and removing a wallet. "And I'm going to make sure it stays that way."

Russell felt the horror down to his toes when the man presented him with a fist full of what looked like hundred-dollar bills. "What the fuck is that?"

Mitchell attempted to look sympathetic, but satisfaction was written all over his face. "We both know Abby is a good person. She wanted you to have this. For that construction company you're trying to get off the ground." The green bills were thrust in his direction. As if he would take them. Christ, he could barely stand the sight of them. Or the knowledge that he'd lost. He hadn't been good enough for her. No, it was worse than that. He'd . . . injured her. Ruined a night that should have been special. Maybe traumatized her forever. He deserved to feel like his stomach was being stomped on by baseball cleats. Deserved *far* worse.

True to form, she was *still* trying her best to help him, trying to help him succeed even thought he'd wronged her. That's why she was the best. That's what made her Abby. And he needed to get as far away from her as possible, for her sake. It was what the man who loved her should do—and he loved her so much he was struggling not to lie down in the road and demand this asshole drive over him with that fucking Mercedes. The symbol of everything he'd never be able to give Abby.

"I don't want your money," Russell choked out. "Or Abby's money, for Chrissakes."

The other man shrugged. "Fair enough." He pocketed the bills. "How about a ride back to the city?"

"Go fuck yourself. I'll take the bus."

Russell stood frozen on the road until the Mercedes drove out of sight. Then he bent at the waist and dry heaved over the sandy road.

ABBY BOUNDED DOWN the stairs, taking them two at a time. In the space of twenty minutes, she'd showered, changed, and answered five emails. Wonder of wonders, they hadn't even stressed her out. Would anything ever stress her out again? Her body felt so deliciously utilized, her vocal cords just raw enough to give her a smoky sex voice, a discovery she'd made while attempting to sing in the shower. A long-sleeved swim cover-up handily concealed the bruising on her wrists, but she liked knowing they were there. Like a naughty secret, reminding her how much she'd been wanted. She'd never had one of those before.

Her progress came to an abrupt stop at the base of the staircase. Having snuck in as quietly as possible, she'd expected everyone to still be sleeping. But there was the super group, standing in the living room, looking as if they'd been caught talking about something uncomfortable. Most of them, anyway. Honey and Roxy were still in their pajamas, hair unbrushed. Ben and Louis wouldn't even look at her. Trying to ignore the beginnings of alarm, Abby ran a hand down her ponytail and scanned the space for Russell but didn't see him.

"Hey." Abby headed toward the kitchen, well aware she was making an escape. From what, though, she didn't know. Didn't want to. "I was just about to make some coffee."

Honey followed her into the sunlit room, Roxy close behind. The guys were nowhere in sight, which only spurred her worry. Ben and Louis didn't go two feet without the girls if they could help it, meaning her roommates wanted privacy.

Honey climbed onto one of the breakfast stools. "Where did you sleep last night?"

"Um." She wanted to tell them everything. Maybe not every detail of her night with Russell but enough to reciprocate for all the secrets they'd spilled over the last six months. Something held her back, though. Whether it was the identical sympathetic expressions on her friends' faces or the fact that she hadn't spoken to Russell yet, but holding back suddenly felt conducive to survival. "I had some work to do and knew you two would give me a hard time, so I took my laptop out to the pool house. I fell asleep there."

They were both silent a moment until Roxy finally broke the tension Abby's lie had created. "Did . . . did Russell sleep there, too?"

When goose bumps broke out along her skin, she was twice as grateful for the long sleeves. "Why are you asking?"

Roxy took the can of Maxwell House from Abby's hand and performed the task of making coffee since Abby's had stalled out before even starting. "We're just trying to figure out why Russell left in such a hurry." Her friend's tone was softer than usual, but it detonated like a bomb in the silent kitchen. Not to mention,

Abby's stomach. "He wouldn't even come inside. Louis had to bring his bag out."

"He was acting really strange. Even for Russell." Honey's joke fell flat along with her attempt at a smile. "We thought maybe you two had a fight."

"No. We didn't."

Abby tried to bring her tone down a few octaves, but it was impossible. Her heart was flattening like a sand castle in a rainstorm. *He left?* She created a mental list of reasons he would leave after the night they'd had, the trust they'd shared, but nothing was good enough. Nothing made sense.

She reached into the cabinet for three coffee cups, indulging the urge to hide her face. "Was there an emergency at the construction site or something?" Even as she asked the hopeful question, she discarded the possibility. He'd left without saying good-bye, and that meant something infinitely worse.

"Ben said he wasn't in a talking mood." Honey traded a heavy glance with Roxy, nodded, and dug into her pocket. "He left you a note."

Abby tried not to lunge across the nook to snatch the note from Honey's fingers. Instead, she carefully arranged the mugs and casually reached for the folded piece of paper. She could feel her roommates staring at her, so she braced herself to give zero reaction. An almost impossible feat when the note contained only two words.

I'm sorry.

She dropped the note like it was on fire but stooped down quickly to pick it back up, shoving it into the back pocket of her jean shorts. It seemed like someone else was performing the menial tasks. It definitely couldn't be her when she felt paralyzed. A crater was opening in her chest, burning at the edges, but she couldn't lift her arms to put out the fire. Russell was sorry. Russell was gone. He regretted last night . . . being with her. What they'd done.

Was there any other explanation? His absence spoke louder than any note ever could. He'd told her, hadn't he? Since the beginning, he'd told her he wasn't looking for a permanent relationship, but she hadn't listened, plugging along like a naïve idiot and trusting everything would work out right. After what he'd said last night in the water, she knew he cared about her, but obviously it ended there. Oh God, had Russell given her a *pity lay*? She wanted to crawl into a small space and never emerge. At least it would keep the fractured organ in her chest in one place instead of spilling out onto the floor like it was attempting to do now.

"Abby." Honey had moved across the room to lay a hand on Abby's back. "You know you can talk to us about *anything*, right? We can help with whatever is going on."

"The way you helped with this weekend away? Because it *didn't*." The anger burst from her mouth before she could control it, but guilt had her wanting to stuff it all back in. "I'm sorry. I didn't mean that."

Roxy laid her head on Abby's shoulder. "Hey, it's okay to get pissed once in a while. And you're right, we forced this weekend on you without considering it might make things worse."

"No. It was sweet. *Really* sweet." Abby tried to swallow away the tightness in her throat. These were her best friends. The normal behavior here was to have a good old-fashioned girl talk. There was even a chance she would feel marginally better afterward if such a thing were possible when it felt like a war had been fought inside her rib cage. And there it was again, that faithful fear of humiliation. She'd been *ditched*. How could they relate to something so painful? Their boyfriends probably already missed them, while Russell couldn't get away from her fast enough. "I don't want to talk about it," she finished in a whisper.

"Okay," Honey said, rubbing circles into Abby's back. "We'll be here when you're ready, though."

I'll never be ready. I'll never forget how horrible I feel right now, in this moment.

And in this moment, I never want to see Russell again.

Chapter 16

*R*ussell felt like an imposter. Not because he was wearing a monkey suit and loafers, waiting for his appointment with the loan officer, scheduled to begin in fifteen minutes. And not because he'd put on his father's best watch for the first time since it had been bestowed on him. No, he felt like an imposter for functioning. Eating breakfast, driving his truck, inhaling. It was all a giant, fucking sham because he wanted to die.

Since Sunday morning, he'd been alternating between self-loathing and numbness, interspersed with bouts of misery, mostly because he wanted to see Abby. Wanted to kiss any marks he'd left on her body and apologize until his vocal cords gave out. Then he'd remember she very likely hated him and wanted him out of her life, which would inevitably send him back to numbness.

Why was he even bothering with this goddamn bank meeting? Why had he spent the last couple days revamping his entire ten-year business plan, whittling it down to a solid five like Abby had suggested? What did any of his goals matter now that the ultimate one had been removed from his grasp? It was possibly the worst punishment he could devise for himself because if heaven smiled on him, and he was granted the business loan, he still couldn't have Abby, yet he'd know how *close* he'd come. And that would fuck him up for the rest of his life. *Good.* At least the pain would remind him of her. Now that he wouldn't see her anymore, he needed all the reminders he could get.

Russell frowned when—out of nowhere—Alec dropped into the chair beside him, tugging at the neck of his dress shirt. "Who the hell designs a shirt with cardboard tucked into the collar? Would you please tell me?"

"You're supposed to take it out," Russell answered, barely recognizing his own voice. "What are you doing here? I thought you were in Vegas filming the ninja show."

"*American Ninja Warrior,*" his brother enunciated. "And a man has to have priorities, right? I got all the way to Vegas, suited up for the obstacle course and everything. But in the end, I couldn't leave you to do this alone. I knew where I needed to be. Right here. With my not-so-little bro."

"Really?"

Alec blew a sigh at the ceiling. "Nah, man. I got knocked out in the first round."

Russell wanted to laugh. Or smack Alec on the back. Anything, but he didn't have the energy. Might never have it again. "Sorry to hear that."

"Ah, no big deal. Vegas was . . . too big or something." Alec planted both elbows on his knees and leaned forward. "New York is bigger, but I *know* it. It knows me." He looked uncomfortable having voiced his feelings. "I couldn't get back here fast enough, you know?"

Funny enough, Russell did know. He'd felt the same way on the bus ride home from Southampton. Only there'd been a conflicting pull the farther he got from Abby, relentless in its reminder that home was in the other direction. *She* was home. Russell rubbed at his eyes. "Believe it or not, I'm glad you're here. I didn't exactly bring my A game."

"No shit. You didn't even break my balls over getting knocked out in round one."

"A lot of men finish prematurely, man. Happens all the time."

"Fuck you," Alec said on a hearty laugh, earning him a scowl from the closest bank employee. "Seriously, though. You didn't sleep on my couch while I was gone, so where've you been?" When Russell shook his head in lieu of answering, Alec pressed. "Heard a pretty girl stopped by the apartment looking for you last week."

Something wrenched in his gut at the mention of that day. Jesus, she'd been so beautiful on his front porch, holding cupcakes. So sweet and unblemished until he'd ruined her. "I've been sleeping at the house," Russell said hoarsely. Which wasn't a total lie even if he'd been working almost nonstop since returning from the Hamptons. Just another form of self-inflicted torture. Building the house, securing the loan. All for nothing, apart from guaranteeing his misery.

"You think I'm going to let you skip the pretty-girl part?"

Denying her existence seemed infinitely wrong. So did telling one more lie where Abby was concerned. "I lost the pretty girl."

Bafflement showed on Alec's face. "So what have you done to get her back?"

"I can't." It hurt saying the words. Beyond belief. "There's no getting her back."

"What?" Alec appeared to be praying for patience. "Do you have any idea how many times Darcy told me to take a hike when we were dating? If I'd listened to her, I would have hiked to Europe and back by now."

"This is different." *I acted like an animal. I didn't treat her the way she deserves.* "She wouldn't have been happy with me, anyway. It would have been like—"

"Like Mom. Is that what this is about?" Uncharacteristic sympathy crept into his brother's eyes. "You think no one has a chance because of what happened? Come on, Russell. You're supposed to be the smart brother."

It felt good to experience irritation. At least it was something other than desolation. "You see this bank we're sitting in? She could walk in here and withdraw enough cash to match the Yankees salary cap."

Alec sat back in his chair. "Wow. We're talking four zeroes here?"

"*Four* zer—" Russell pinched the bridge of his nose. "Let me do the talking in this meeting, okay? Seriously."

"Fine by me." Alec slid the cardboard insert from inside his collar and tossed it into the small, metal trash can. "Listen, Russell. I, uh . . ."

"What?"

"How was I supposed to know this thing with Mom was mess-ing you up? You never say anything about it." Alec lowered his voice. "You were the one who was home with her most, you were the one who found her. It makes sense that it would be on your mind more. But you can't let it change your destiny, man. Your fate is divine."

Russell sighed. "You're not an *actual* ninja, Alec."

Dammit, there was a reason they never spoke about it. There was never a good time to remember the day his mother—already addicted to prescription painkillers—had washed them back with a little too much gin. An accident, they'd called it. But Russell knew the truth. Had witnessed her depression, day in and day out. Brought her the tissue box in whatever room she'd chosen to cry in. The accident wouldn't have happened if her marriage had been happy. If she'd been content with her house in Queens. Her children.

Russell.

He took a deep breath, working through the memory in stages. Only now, the disturbing images he'd harbored since childhood were laced with visions of Abby, fleeing from him. The realization on her face that she'd gotten into bed with the wrong man. One who could never make her happy. Leaving her alone had been the right thing to do.

But God, it felt wrong. Everything felt *wrong*.

"Mr. Hart?" A female secretary approached the waiting area. "Follow me, please."

ABBY STOOD OUTSIDE the door of her parents' Park Avenue high-rise residence, the heels of her sandals sinking into the plush hallway carpeting. It was Friday morning, and she should have been at the office, but that would have been a waste of the full head of steam she'd woken up with. Late last night, she'd finally reached a solution that would make her father's life work amount to something. *A lot* of something. Not to mention, her idea would save her own sanity in the process. The thought of sitting behind her desk in the silent office made her stomach turn. No, it was time to go see her father.

Her confidence had wavered slightly downstairs when the doorman hadn't even recognized her face. Or name. Rightly so, since she'd only been to the co-op once for a housewarming party. But it wasn't normal to feel like a stranger going to see your own parents. Since returning from the Hamptons, she'd felt like a stranger wherever she went. Even in her own apartment, despite Honey's and Roxy's attempts to raise her spirits. She'd found herself on the beach in Southampton—found her voice—and now she felt stripped of it.

Like it had never existed at all.

Today, she would get it back, albeit in different manner. She wouldn't be the footstool propping up her father's company anymore. A footstool who'd already been divested of one leg, thanks to Russell. The remaining ones were starting to creak, the fabric wearing thin. If she didn't do something proactive now, she wasn't sure how long those legs would hold her.

She raised her hand to knock, wondering why her stepmother hadn't opened the door yet, being that the doorman had rung the apartment to check if Abby was welcome. But it dropped by her side. Why had she gone and thought of Russell? She'd managed to cast him out for the entire morning, sending him to a far corner of her mind, where he couldn't be as effective. Every time she broke free for a few minutes, a reminder of him would drag her back into the trap. Getting ready for bed last night, she'd refused to go through her nightly routine of checking all the locks. The way Russell always reminded her to do. Then she'd lain there wide-awake for hours, until some responsibility forced her out of bed to complete the task, hearing his voice the entire time. *Pull the latch, angel. It only takes a second. Do it for me, would you?*

How could someone who cared so much leave her stranded in hurt like this? She hated him for it even as her mind attempted to pin a reason on why she hadn't been enough. Why *they* hadn't been enough to make him happy.

Today, she would be enough for *herself.* She might have an ingrained need to please others, but she'd become a hazard to her own peace of mind. No more. This was her life, and she was done living it for other people. People who were supposed to care about her. Love her.

Abby rapped on the door, the sound echoing in the posh hallway. A few seconds later, a woman in a maid's uniform opened the door. "Hello. Miss Sullivan?"

"Yes." The woman stepped aside, and Abby entered the apartment, marveling over how little she recognized in the space. Not one familiar piece of furniture or family photo to be seen. "Is my mother home?"

"Abby." She turned in time to see her stepmother breeze into the room, elegantly dressed as usual and in the process of ending a cell-phone call. "I didn't know you were coming."

"I'm sorry, Mrs. Sullivan," the maid said, looking between mother and daughter. "The doorman rang, but you didn't want to be disturbed. I just thought—"

"She just thought since I'm your daughter, my showing up wouldn't make you look like you've seen a ghost. Although that just about sums up how I feel." Abby swallowed the weakness in her voice. "I came to see my father."

The older woman smoothed her skirt. "You know his wishes, Abby."

"Respectfully, Mother? Every moment of my time this past month has been dedicated to his company. Our *family's* company. So maybe he doesn't want to see me, but I'm done giving a shit."

Satisfied with her stepmother's dropped jaw, Abby strode toward the staircase, taking them two at a time, not even sure in which room she'd find her father. She'd never even been upstairs. How pathetic was that? The sad realization only reinforced how much of a real home she'd made with Roxy and Honey, unconventional though it might be. It was *hers*. Guilt for not confiding in her roommates clawed its way up her determination, but she set it aside for now. Fix one thing at a time.

She could hear her stepmother downstairs on another phone call, so she started pushing doors open. Empty bedroom. Bathroom. At the final door, her fingers paused on the knob a beat as she braced herself, before nudging it open. And there was her father, sitting at his computerless desk, playing solitaire . . . with actual cards. He didn't look up as she entered, quietly finishing his game and gathering the cards together in a neat stack. He didn't meet her gaze until he'd replaced them in the box, tucking the top into the slot with careful hands.

"Haven't been able to look at the computer screen," he said, his usually robust voice reminding her of a deflated balloon. "It takes longer this way, but you appreciate the wins more. The doctor says it's important to recognize small victories. Learn to be content with them."

Abby fell into the chair opposite her father, noticing not-so-subtle changes in him. He'd lost weight. Let his hair grow past his collar. But the stress that was usually visible around his eyes and mouth was gone. "That's good. Is it working?"

"Sometimes."

She nodded, but he didn't continue. "Why didn't you want to see me?"

Her question skipped like a stone in the still room, disrupting the air. Last week, she would have apologized for being so indelicate and taken back the blurted words, but she didn't have the energy or desire for avoidance any longer. Of any kind.

Her father tapped the box of playing cards against the desk's surface. "I'm embarrassed, Abby. Every day I wake up and get dressed, positive today will be the day I stop relying on my daughter. Putting her through what I went through." He dropped the card box and folded his hands. "The truth is, I'm too scared. It's not an easy thing for a man to admit."

"Thank you for being honest." A lump formed in her throat. "It's okay to be scared."

He turned his attention toward the window. "Not when it's hurting your family, the way I'm doing." His breath came out in a slow exhale. "If there was another way to keep the motor running while I figure out how to cope . . . I would do it. None of this is fair to you, Abby, but . . ."

"But you and Mother have equal shares in the company." She waited for him to meet her gaze. "She wants to keep me in your seat because it keeps the company in the family. Bringing in help might jeopardize that."

Her father leaned back in his chair. "Weeks passed where I could barely decide what I wanted for breakfast. It was hard to gain back the ground I'd lost after that."

Sympathy had significantly dampened the fire she'd woken with this morning, but she pushed forward, hoping her gut had guided her in the right direction. "Forget about all the pressure and expectations. Forget about what everyone else wants." She lifted one shoulder. "Do you *want* to go back to work?

"No." He closed his eyes. "No."

"Good." Abby reached into her purse and removed copies of the documents she'd signed in the Hamptons. The ones she'd asked Mitchell's assistant for, claiming he needed her to review them for a meeting. She'd spent the last week poring over them in her free time. "I wasn't aware of this until recently, but I have a two percent stake in the company. You never told me."

Some of the shrewdness he'd been known for crept into her father's expression. It was a relief to see a hint of the man she remembered. "It was done so long ago." His eyebrows rose. "Honestly, I'd forgotten."

She flipped a few pages, folded them over. "Mitchell asked me to sign a power of attorney form last weekend, giving me the ability to make decisions on your behalf." Abby watched that sink in. "Along with my two percent in the company, I have the controlling interest. And I'm ready to use it."

Abby jerked when her father threw back his head and laughed. Outside the room, she could hear her mother's heels clicking down the hallway at a fast pace. She appeared at the door, one hand pressed to her chest as she ogled Abby's father. "Was that you . . . laughing?"

"Damn right." He wiped away tears of mirth. "God help anyone who ever underestimates my daughter. I certainly won't ever make that mistake."

Her mother moved into the room, arms crossed. "Meaning?"

Abby turned to the final document page and slid it across the desk toward her father. "Here is a list of New York hedge funds in the market to absorb funds of equal or lesser size. I've highlighted the candidates that appear most viable, based on the last four quarters and their client list." When her mother started to interrupt, Abby held up a finger. "If we sell for the amount I believe we're worth, this is what you'll walk away with and still be able to give a two-year severance to each employee."

"That's pretty generous," her father murmured, studying the document.

"Yeah, well." Abby smiled. "They all hate me, and this is my way of making them regret it."

Abby's mother leaned over the paperwork, one manicured finger smoothing over the number Abby had circled. A number that would ensure none of them ever had to work again and would keep them in the lifestyle to which they'd grown accustomed.

Her parents, anyway. She preferred her three-bedroom on Ninth Avenue.

Her father's relief was palpable across the table, tension ebbing from his shoulders with each passing second. "I . . . I think I've got it from here, Abby."

"Good. Because I think this is where I jump ship." Stress fell from her body in heavy clumps. "I love numbers, but I don't love adding and subtracting in my sleep."

"Fair enough," her father said, watching her closely as she backed toward the door. "Abby?"

"Yes?"

"Thank you. For everything."

"You're welcome." She rested her hand on the doorknob. "Um. You think maybe when you're feeling better . . . maybe both of you could come over to my place for dinner?"

Her stepmother looked startled—but cautiously pleased—and her father proud. "We'd love that."

Abby walked out of the building onto Park Avenue, sucked in a gulp of sunny, city air . . . and executed an awkward, but energetic pirouette.

Chapter 17

Russell leaned against the downtown subway entrance, across the street from the Longshoreman. The bright and breezy late Friday afternoon had allowed the bar to leave the doors and windows wide open, giving Russell a view inside. His friends were there at their usual table, minus Abby. It bothered him that she wasn't there. A lot. Was she sick? He'd been checking in on her via Ben, who got his information from Honey. At first, his so-called friend had refused to pass on a single detail, telling him to man up and go see Abby himself. Ben had finally taken pity on him after a drunk, desperate demand to know how Abby had worn her hair that day.

Yeah, he wouldn't be living that down anytime soon. Nor did he give a damn.

He'd been told Abby's workload would be easing soon, or so she'd told her roommates. His relief in hearing that was massive. The idea of Abby stuck inside, glued to a laptop with eight tons of pressure riding on her made him fucking crazy.

The blunt tips of his fingernails bit into his palm. He'd told himself he'd stop by after work wrapped for the day, just to get a glimpse of her. The letdown of not seeing her was the equivalent of being buried under an avalanche. Christ, how long had it been? Five days? It felt like five decades.

"Screw this," Russell growled, jaywalking across the avenue toward the Longshoreman. If he went back to Queens now, the dissatisfaction would be unbearable. Hell, he'd probably go back to the house, where he'd been working without cease, pick up the closest power tool, and destroy all his progress. It would only be a temporary distraction, though, and he'd be back to thinking about Abby. Replaying every word she'd ever spoken, every secret she'd ever confided, every smile she'd ever gifted him with.

When Russell walked into the Longshoreman, he wondered if he'd ever paid attention to the interior before. Nothing registered as familiar. Or maybe he'd just gotten so used to zeroing in on Abby when he walked inside, everything else usually fell away. Jesus, even his thoughts were goddamn pitiful. Stop thinking. That was the only option. Stop thinking and ask his friends about Abby. Just like ripping off a Band-Aid. He'd think later, when he could drink at the same time and mute the images that haunted him.

Four sets of eyebrows lifted when he sat down at the table. A reaction he'd expected since he'd left Southampton like it was on fire. Figuring he'd give them a minute to get used to his being there, Russell folded his arms and waited.

Roxy spoke up first, as if there'd been any doubt. "May we *help* you?"

"Where is she?"

Honey's chair scraped back, her intention to go for Russell's throat sparking in her eyes. Ben hooked an arm around her waist just in time, yanking her down onto his lap. "Easy, babe." He looked at Russell. "This better be good."

"Good?" He dropped his head into both hands. "I've got nothing good left. I just need to know how Abby is, please."

"What gives you the right to know?" Honey asked, still shooting daggers at him from across the table. "Whatever you did must have been pretty awful, Russell. She won't even talk to us about it."

He felt hollow. So goddamn hollow. "She didn't tell you why she was upset?" A huge part of him wished she had. When a man hurt her, she should tell someone. Oh God, that man had been *him*.

You bruise up a lot of girls, Hart?

Roxy traded a glance with her roommate. "She wasn't upset until she read your note and found out you'd split. Actually, she was singing the National Anthem in the shower. And I love the girl to death, but if she tried to carry a tune in a bucket, the bucket would sprout ears. Just so it could cover them."

Honey clucked her tongue at Roxy. "We thought you finally came clean about how you feel—"

"Wait. Abby wasn't upset before that?" Russell gave his head a hard shake. "The lawyer said she was . . . said she . . ."

Louis spoke up for the first time. "Mitchell? He left the night before."

"No, he didn't." A pit was yawning wide in Russell's stomach. "He was there on the road when I came up from the beach. He offered me money to leave . . . said it was best for Abby." An ache splintered his concentration. "He said the money was *from* Abby."

"Er. What now?" Roxy stared at him. "Have you not been wearing your hardhat in hazardous areas?"

"That sounds nothing like Abby, man," Ben said. "Are you sure?"

"The guy knew about Hart Brothers Construction. And the business-loan meeting with the bank. I only told Abby about the meeting." The protests sounded futile to Russell's ears, but he felt obligated to push on. If he didn't, it would mean he'd been wrong. Horrifically wrong. "I didn't blame her for it. I didn't even . . ." It had been the last thing on his mind, compared to hurting her. Anything she'd done to get away from him had seemed entirely justified, so he hadn't examined it too closely. Even if she *had* offered him money via the lawyer, he'd assumed she'd done it out of whatever remaining generosity she had left toward him. Never out of spite. Not his Abby. But . . . what if she'd never done it at all?

Louis cleared his throat. "I imagine it wouldn't be too difficult to get basic information about you. Not for someone who has connections in the financial world. And if he's the corporate counsel for a hedge fund that size . . ." Louis shrugged. "That's where he lives."

Russell's brain was struggling to play catch-up. Through the haze he'd been living in the last five days, holes started to form, letting in blinding light. Mitchell had known his last name. At the time, he'd barely been capable of registering it as odd, but now it told him how the lawyer's night had been spent. Protecting his asset, namely Abby, by getting rid of the man who could drag her down. Or drag her away from the world she lived in. The company that kept him driving the most current Mercedes. Yeah, that fucker had taken Russell's number by the pool, and again in the kitchen. *One of these things is not like the other. . .*

Had Mitchell taken it upon himself to separate them? If he *had* done so, was it justified? If Russell had really hurt Abby, then yes, it had been. But he didn't know because he'd left without even talking to her. Finding out how she felt.

"Why didn't you tell *us* about the bank meeting?" Ben asked, gaze narrowed on Russell. "Why keep it to yourself?"

"I've had *five* fucking bank meetings, Ben." The frustration burst out of Russell. Why were they asking him questions when his head was splitting in half? "You've known me for a while. Does listing my failures sound in character for me?" He pressed a hand to his right eye, hoping to prevent his skull from cracking. "I was trying for her. I've been trying for so long."

"For Abby," Louis said slowly, understanding clearing the confusion on his face. "While you were trying so hard, you pushed her away, man. She would have loved you all the more for it."

Honey leaned forward on Ben's lap. "What are you talking about?"

"I friend-zoned Abby," Russell said, tight-lipped.

Roxy gave a decisive headshake. "You can't friend-zone the friend zoner."

"I'm in love with you." Louis laid his head on Roxy's shoulder. "Have I told you that in the last hour?"

Ben and Russell traded a *Jesus Christ* glance.

"Roxy is right, but it doesn't explain what's wrong with Abby."

Honey pinned Russell with a look. "Unless there was illegal contact in the friend zone."

Russell banged his forehead against the table—and with that damning reaction—chaos erupted around him. "Did you know about this?" Roxy asked Louis, jerking her shoulder away, while Honey turned an accusing look on Ben at the exact same time.

Ben removed his glasses. "Fix it, Russell. Fix it now."

"She didn't even tell us." Honey traded a worried look with Roxy. "You two are always stuck together. There was nothing weird about that . . . but we should have tried harder to get it out of her."

Russell lifted his head to find Roxy glaring at him. "Do you know why she didn't tell us, Russell? Her best friends?"

"Why?" he croaked.

"She was probably ashamed." Roxy's words were a hot poker impaling his middle. They were enough on their own to drop him, but she wasn't finished. And he wanted to sit there and take it. Deserved every painful word. "And she wasn't ashamed because of whatever complex you have about . . . money or your company. Work *that* shit out, by the way. I certainly did." Roxy stabbed at the table with her finger. "She was ashamed because you cheapened something that could have been really beautiful. You made her a friend with benefits. *Abby.*"

Russell forced himself to swallow the anguish trying to capsize him because that final bullet would have done it. If he let himself perish from a wound now, he had no chance of seeing her again. And his sanity relied on that.

"Abby could care less about money, Russell," Honey pointed out.

"That's easy to say when you have it." Russell ignored Ben's and Louis's frantic slashing motions in front of their necks. "And it's different for a man—"

Roxy and Honey threw up their hands, tossing curses on the ceiling. "He didn't," Honey groaned. "He didn't just say that."

"Your grave is so fucking deep, man, you can see China," Louis muttered, shaking his head. "Stop digging. You're dragging us in with you."

Russell sat up straight and laid his hands flat on the table. "I need to see her. I—might be able to fix this now." He swallowed with difficulty. "At the very least, I need to make sure she doesn't feel . . ." He couldn't say the rest.

"Ashamed," Honey supplied. "Used. Cast aside."

"*Please.*" He felt gutted. "I only ever wanted her to be happy."

Roxy and Honey deflated a little. "She's her happiest with you, Russell. That's always been the case. Even we can't compete," Roxy said, unhooking the apartment key from her key ring and sliding it across the table. "Don't make me regret this."

Russell's chair was still wobbling when he vanished through the exit.

ABBY PULLED THE white sundress over her head as steam filled the bathroom. For once, the silence in the apartment was welcome. It matched the peace and quiet finally permeating her head after weeks of whizzing numbers and fear of failure. The corkscrew twisting into her temples from either side was gone . . . and she'd been the one to untwist it. She felt . . . proud of herself. Like right at that moment, she could fight a war and emerge victorious.

If her new, extra headspace allowed her other troubles to loom larger, that would change. Wouldn't it? Russell's abandonment and five-day silence had been sharing brain capacity with finding a way free of the company, all while maintaining the status quo at the office so as not to alert anyone of upcoming changes. Now the stark reminders of his absence rushed in to claim all the free real estate in her consciousness.

Determined to ride the high of what she'd accomplished that morning, Abby lifted her chin and went to work unclasping her bra, letting it fall at her feet. The heat from the shower steam attempting to ease the soreness in her neck and back, wrought from weeks over the computer. She tipped her head back and closed her eyes, breathing deeply—

Abby's spine snapped straight when she heard a creak outside the bathroom door. The steam went from comforting to a sight deterrent in a split second, her heart hammering as she whipped her attention toward the partially open door. Had she locked the front door? *Dammit.* She couldn't remember. And her roommates weren't due home until much later. Not to mention, they would call out to inform her of their presence, to save her the heart attack.

She started to reach for a towel. "Hello?"

Had the door moved?

"Abby. Can we talk?"

Her breath hitched, several emotions flooding her at once. Surprise. Awareness. Russell was right outside the bathroom, where she stood naked. She *hated* that a handful of gruff words from his mouth made her nipples tighten. What was he *doing* here? Frustration surged . . . and it surged *hard*. The anger at Russell she'd only just begun to process joined forces with the sexual energy his presence created. Whatever the reason, he was here? She didn't *want* to know. Just like she'd done this morning, she wanted to control this. To win the war. He couldn't come here and set her back like this. She wouldn't let him.

I'm sorry.

Abby saw the note he'd left in her mind's eye. She didn't want his pity. She wanted him to know how being left behind hurt. So she'd show him.

A frisson of alarm uncoiled in her belly when she caught sight of herself in the mirror. There was determination, sadness, lust. She could push open the door and walk into Russell's arms, as her instincts dictated. Might have followed through, too, if he hadn't hurt her so badly. But no. She *refused* to open herself up that way again.

With a deep breath, Abby pulled open the door, feeling the steam curl around her as Russell came into view. He fell back a step, the key in his hand dropping to the floor. "Oh God, angel." His gaze moved down her body, growing hungrier with every inch of flesh he covered. "Please. Go back in the bathroom. I-I'll wait until you're done."

His reaction made her a seductress for the first time in her life . . . and that power was an immediate addiction. It blew out the twin flames of dread and doubt, replacing them with a roaring blaze of want. Want she could assuage on her own terms. "Come with me," she murmured, the invitation twining with the steam. "Otherwise, you'll be waiting a while." Thrilled by her own boldness, Abby trailed a hand down her belly. "I'm going to be very thorough."

Russell's entire body visibly trembled. "You have every right to punish me, but I'm too weak right now to handle this." His tone reminded her of torn-up concrete. "Five days is a long fucking time without you. I needed to see how you are . . . if you're still tired. Still working too much. I came here to hear your voice."

God, she loved this man. Odd that her heart would pick this moment of asserting her independence to remind her. Odd and unacceptable. There it was, though. This bone-deep knowledge that if she could be this *furious* with him while still aching to hold him close and soothe his sadness . . . it was real, bone-deep love. The kind that would never go away unless she did something about it. Her heart told her to step back and examine the situation from all angles before trying to exorcise Russell's hold on her, but the newfound stubbornness that had served her so well of late smothered the inclination.

Abby tossed her hair and sailed toward Russell, who backed away with an expression that said he knew resistance was futile. When she slid a hand into the front waistband of his jeans and walked them backward, toward the bathroom, he came as if in a trance. "We need to *talk*, Abby."

They entered the bathroom, both of them immediately enveloped in steam. She used her free hand to close the door, then pushed Russell's big frame up against it. "Let's get the fun part out of the way first." She slipped her hands beneath his T-shirt and scratched his abs with her fingernails before dragging them lower, lower, and unfastening his belt. His erection was prominent beneath her hands, and she reveled in knowing the attraction ran deep, even if it was where their relationship ended. "Five days *is* a long time." She inwardly cursed at the quaver in her voice. "How are you going to make up for it?"

"Any way you want. As soon as you let me explain everything."

"No."

"*Yes.*"

She went up on her toes and got in his face. "*No—*"

Russell seized her wrists and pulled them behind her back, wrenching a gasp free from her mouth. The fight went out of her instantly. She sagged against him, as if her bones had liquefied, her body held up between his grip and muscular body. It shocked even *her* how swiftly every nuance of her being responded to the show of authority. Blood whizzed through her veins, rejoicing, anticipating an outlet for pent-up energy and tension she hadn't been aware of holding hostage.

Russell's breath was labored, gaze unfocused. "I'm trying to control this thing, angel. You have to help me." Tortured eyes fell to her parted mouth. "Show me where I hurt you, so I'll stop."

Her fingers twitched behind her back with the need to indicate the center of her chest. "What do you mean?"

"The bruises." He released Abby's hands, stacking his own atop his head, falling back against the door. "Show me how bad I am for you, as if I didn't already know. As if I don't think about it every hour of the day."

"Bruises," she whispered, a dull pain forming in her side. "How . . . who told you—" Her mouth snapped shut at the memory of Mitchell's shrewd, seemingly innocuous glance at her wrists the morning after they'd spent the night at the beach.

"The lawyer said you were upset. He asked me if I bruise up girls. I've been sick for days, Abby. So fucking sick."

Her knees almost buckled under the weight of relief. It all made sense now. Why he'd left without saying good-bye. Why he'd stayed away. Her big protector thought he'd hurt her. He'd been put through five days of torture for no reason. They both had.

"Russell." She smoothed her hands up the sides of his face. "You didn't hurt me. Or, when you did, it changed into something that felt good." Steam drifted between them, obscuring his face, so she moved closer. "I was coming back down to the beach so we could do it all again."

His long exhale of breath shifted the steam. "Is that true? You weren't upset?" He dropped his hands to his sides, and she could feel the effort he put into not reaching for her. "I was so rough for your first time . . . there are nail marks all over my back. I don't even remember your leaving them."

It turned her on hearing that. Made her feel possessive in a new, momentous way. "We left marks on each other, then." She swiped her rapidly dampening hair back from her face. "Is it wrong that I like that?"

"I don't *know*," he grated. "But I'm making a promise to you, Abby. If you give me a chance, we'll find out together. Find out everything about these things I feel and make sure they aren't bad for you."

"For us. Bad for *us*." She licked the condensation from her lips. "And I feel them, too, in a different way. In . . . reverse." Her voice sounded fainter in the drumming of her pulse. It was coming. They were going to be together again, and she could barely breathe around the eagerness. Praying he wouldn't protest or insist they talk more, Abby went up on her toes and lifted Russell's shirt over his head, dropping it to the floor. Oh boy. Had he gotten bigger, more cut? The heat inside the bathroom had caused him to perspire, making his rising and falling chest glow with masculine sweat. "Will you take a shower with me?"

His Adam's apple rose and dropped. "There's more to talk about."

No. She wasn't having that. Anticipation pumped too brightly, consuming her from the middle and radiating out. Keeping her gaze locked with Russell's fevered one, she unzipped his jeans and shoved them down, leaving him in a pair of white boxer briefs. She couldn't help perusing the body she'd revealed. The sweat dripping down his stomach, absorbing into the hem of his underwear, made her tongue jealous. "I have this fantasy where you . . ."

"What?" he prompted in a harsh voice.

"You wash me in the shower."

Chapter 18

Until now, he'd been attempting to keep his attention glued above Abby's neck, but with the uttering of those words, Russell broke. He groaned and swayed toward her, preying on her breasts with eyes starved for the sight of her flesh. She'd known—*known*—he'd have the corresponding desire. It was there in her knowing expression, the way she lowered her chin and regarded him through long eyelashes. Yeah, she'd known the act of caring for her would be the ultimate temptation. Caring for his Abby. *Doing* for her.

His cock stretched longer inside the damp boxer briefs, feeling strangled. He bent down and ripped a condom from his pants pocket, impatience spurring him toward Abby and *fuck*, somehow the way she backed away with that . . . *obedient* expression made him feel like a king. Her king. And her king was feeling thick below the waist and ready to blow.

"The way you're looking at me is a fucking hazard, Abby."

"Should I stop?"

Christ, with every word, every movement, she handed him

more and more control. After a week of solitary confinement, he was sprinting past the prison walls. *Not going back. I can't go back.* "I'll tell you if I want you to stop."

Her back hit the glass shower door, shaking it. "Okay."

She turned and started to climb into the running shower, but a vision of her slipping had Russell lunging forward to help. After that, touching her dewy, bare skin, he was totally fucked. With Abby's back to his front, he walked them under the spray, groaning louder with each step. Couldn't help it with the way her ass cheeks lifted and fell against his dick. "Getting ready to touch yourself, were you?" He tugged her head to the side and nipped hard at her ear. "Were you going to stroke where my fingers stroked? Push your fingers into that tight little space where my cock goes?" Her nod was jerky. "Turn around and see what you're getting instead."

He didn't wait for her to move but spun her himself. Droplets of water had the privilege of spotting her face, her neck, her tits, reminding him of where he'd come their first time together. How she'd looked wearing him in the filtered moonlight.

"I'm coming between your thighs this time, understand?" Russell nudged her belly with his pulsing dick. "Ah fuck, what I've got stored up for you . . ." He scraped the foil edge of the condom wrapper down Abby's spine and felt her shake, heard the whimper he'd missed like hell. *Craved.* "We'll catch it with this for now, but someday, there won't be a goddamn thing between us."

She nodded, her gaze dropping to his boxer briefs and the flesh they barely contained. Watching her closely, Russell jerked the waistband halfway down his length, letting the elastic hold it up against his stomach. Her tongue skated out, her body dipping, as if she meant to service him from her knees.

With a harsh noise, Russell gripped her arm and pulled her upright. "No, Abby." He steadied himself with a fortifying breath. "When I said I've got it stored up for you, I meant it. I haven't touched myself since we were together. I wouldn't last a second in that mouth."

She traced a finger down his chest, ending at his belly button, circling it once. Twice. "Later?"

His throat dried up. "Are you asking me if you can suck my cock later, Abby?"

"Yes," she breathed, hazel peeking out from beneath her eyelashes. "I'm asking you."

The way she made him feel in charge was again releasing the powerful urges he'd allowed to run free that night on the beach. He reminded himself that she hadn't been upset or hurt. That she'd wanted more. More. Russell reached behind Abby and gathered a handful of shower spray, bringing the water between their bodies and letting it wash over his erection. "Look down at me." He nudged the waistband down a little more, revealing another inch of himself. "Does it make you want to touch your pussy?"

"No. It makes me want *you* to touch it."

His moan echoed off the wet tiles. "You have that soap that makes you smell like white-grape sunlight? I'm going to rub it over every inch of you."

As if magnetized, their mouths hovered closer as Abby reached blindly for the plastic bottle. "Can I wash you, too?"

"Later." He brushed their steam-coated lips together. "A lot of things will have to wait until later, angel. Right now, I'm just trying not to jerk off to the sight of you." When her eyes went glassy, Russell laughed through the pain. "That turns you on, doesn't it? My girl isn't so innocent anymore."

She was staring at his lips, giving him no choice but to kiss her . . . *and kiss her and kiss her* until her thighs turned restless against his, her stomach pressing and lifting where it met his cock. Tight nipples dragged through his chest hair, making him feel too big for his skin all over. He rolled the condom on and dropped the wrapper, freeing his hand to palm her wet backside, massage the taut cheeks in time with his tongue dipping past her lips. The ends of her hair tickled his wrists and forearms, a product of her head falling back to receive the rapidly intensifying kiss. If he didn't break away from her mouth, he'd lift her onto his erection and take her too hard. But no. He wanted to take his time. It had been over too fast on the beach. He'd come here to fix everything, to reassure her. Had he accomplished that? No, not yet.

With a low groan, Russell tore away. "Everything is going to be okay now, Abby. No more games, okay? Everything is fixed now, okay?"

She slipped the bottle of body wash into his hand. "Talk after." Russell wanted to clasp both sides of her face and talk, talk, talk until everything poured out . . . but his body agreed with *after*. After he got over the worst of his lust and could focus. She needed it, too. As if to prove his thoughts true, she shoved his briefs down, making his dick drop heavily between his shower-dampened thighs. *Fuuuuuck.* "Stop thinking, okay? The way you look . . . it's making me so hot."

"*Stop.*" Russell slicked a hand down her belly, nudged her pussy with his knuckles. "I can't concentrate when you say things like that."

"*Good.*"

Stepping back to get an eyeful of her wet curves, Russell poured some body wash into his hands and set the bottle aside. "Is that where your fantasy ends? Being washed by me?"

Abby shook her head, making her sexy, palm-sized tits jiggle. "No."

"Good," he said, echoing her sentiment. His hands gravitated to those pretty mounds first, squeezing and lifting, rubbing her nipples with his palms. The harder he rubbed, the more she moaned, so he followed his instincts and pinched them between his index and middle fingers. He felt her knees shoot together, the rough touch affecting her where it counted. "I'm going to learn every little thing that gets you off. I want to know a hundred different ways." He grabbed the bottle and poured more body wash into his hand. She must have known what was coming because she held her breath as he reached down and cupped her pussy. "This is where your fantasy ends, isn't it?" He knelt in front of her, working her sensitive flesh, feasting on her with his eyes. "I'll never fuck you until you've been licked here, angel. It's a personal rule. Need to worship it before I take it."

"I can live with that," she gasped. He gathered a handful of shower spray to wash away the soap, his cock jerking at the sight of water rushing over her smoothness. Compelled, he licked out and took his first taste, just a gentle lapping of her clit. And *oh shit*. That white-grape scent that drove him crazy was now a flavor, going all the way back to his throat. His hands moved on their own, digging into her ass cheeks and yanking her forward, grinding her pussy against his mouth. He delved with his tongue and sucked, her cries to keep going entirely unnecessary. Making him stop would be like dragging an alcoholic from their first morning drink. "Russell, I'm . . . going to—"

When she broke off in a scream, the wet, shaking perfection against his lips would have sent him crashing to his knees if he weren't already there. His hand dropped from her ass to stroke his length, fast and rough, mind spinning in circles with the taste of Abby. But when her foot slipped on the bathtub floor, and she wobbled, Russell shot forward with a shout, wrapping his arms around her middle. Somehow, the residual fear of Abby's getting hurt only made his urgency to get inside her soar. "Need to get you out of this tub . . . you could slip—"

"No. Please, I need—"

"Can't chance it." He was already out of the shower, dragging Abby into his arms and carrying her to the sink vanity. And Jesus, Abby dripping wet, looking well pleasured and slightly miffed, was just about the sexiest goddamn thing he'd ever seen in his life. Feeling a surge of love and protectiveness so strong he could barely breathe, Russell pressed their foreheads together. "Do I need to remind you I'd lose my mind if something happened to you? *Do I?*"

"No," she whispered, the irritation fading from her eyes, once again being replaced with heat. "Even if I don't understand it . . . it's you. My Russell."

"Say that again," he begged, squeezing her hips in his hands.

She surprised him by turning around, locking her gaze on his reflection in the fogged-up mirror. Then she pressed her ass into his lap and twisted her hips, ruining him for any other experience life had to offer. "*My* Russell."

His cock surged under her declaration of ownership—ownership he hadn't known he'd been craving—blowing his restraint out of the water. He gripped his throbbing inches and tucked the head between her smooth thighs. "This how you want it, angel? A little dirty? You want to watch me try to hold back and fail?" He pushed the top half of her body forward, looked down at her sweet, perked-up ass. "Ah, Christ. This is going to end with you screaming."

She reached back and urged his hips forward. "I *want* to scream."

Goddamn. Russell wedged his forearm between her stomach and the vanity, refusing to leave a single mark on her body this time. He gripped her chin in the opposite hand, tilting her face up. "I don't ever want to be inside anyone else, Abby. I want you to unzip my pants whenever you're wet and know I've been waiting—just fucking *waiting*—to get inside my girl's pussy. I want you to forget how it feels to sit down anywhere but my lap, right on top of my dick. Yours. It's yours. I'm yours."

Her eyes had darkened with each word, her breath joining the steam to fog up the mirror. "I want that, too. All of it."

"You have it." He pressed his mouth to her ear, gave a quick pump of his hips against her still-slippery ass. "You're tight enough without your thighs squeezed together. Spread them for me, Abby."

She'd only put a sliver of room between her legs when Russell thrust his entire length inside her. His hand dropped from her chin to catch her when she fell forward with a muffled cry. "Oh my God. So big . . . so big."

"*Jesus*." He spoke through clenched teeth. "Don't say *that*."

Her breaths came out sounding more like sobs. "Y-you don't like hearing that?"

"*Every* guy likes hearing that, Abby." He ran his teeth up the side of her neck, struggling like hell to maintain some sense of control. Over his body. Over his emotions. "Just save it for next time, okay? When I don't have five days' worth of needing to fuck you weighing down my balls." He reared back and thrust deep, felt her pussy stretch around him. "You feel it?"

"*Yes*. I feel it, I feel it."

Knowing he only had a few minutes before he lost the battle with his lust, Russell dropped his forehead onto Abby's shoulder and set a slow rhythm. "It's got to be inside you this time. I'm not pulling out of all this tightness."

"I don't want you to," she breathed. "Please, don't."

Ah God, the little muscles in her pussy were gripping him, making each stroke mind-blowing. So fucking hot that his pace kicked up a notch, as he'd known it would. The heavy flesh hanging between his thighs slapped her with each pleasure-seeking drive, echoing off the slick bathroom tile. He was grunting like a goddamn animal, and he didn't give a fuck, it felt so good.

Abby pushed her legs apart a few more inches, and white light flashed in his vision. No way he'd just sunk even deeper. *No way.* He lifted his head to see her eyes closed tight, mouth open, tits bouncing as he broke her off.

And felt his control begin to slip. "Hips tilted back. The way you do when I'm giving you my mouth. I want your ass up on my stomach. *Do it.*" His hand found her backside, palm tingling with the need to slap it. But he tamped down on the impulse and drove into her harder, instead. Harder, *harder.* "Ask me for it, Abby. Ask me to give you what I've been storing up."

Her voice vibrated as she bounced. "Please, can I have it?"

"This?" He reached around and found her clit, teased the bud with his middle finger. "You want this?"

"Yes," she whimpered, imploring his reflection. "But I want . . . I want you to use your hand on me. I can tell . . . can tell you want it."

Russell cursed at the realization that his left hand held her ass in a punishing grip, to prevent himself from spanking that supple flesh. Fuck, the sight, her request, made him thrust all the harder. "No. Not until I know how not to hurt you."

She fell forward onto the sink, bracing herself on two elbows. "*Please.*"

Slap. Slapslapslap. The pinpricks of disappointment in his lack of restraint were eclipsed by Abby's response. She moaned, body writhing as the flesh that held him captive tightened on his cock, shaking the climax right out of him. Demanding he follow her into the oblivion she created. Russell buried his forehead into her upper back and growled as achy pressure drained from below his waist. His arms banded around Abby, dragging her upright. *Absorb her. Crawl inside her. Mine. Mine. Can't get close enough. Love her. Love her so much.*

ABBY CAME BACK to reality by degrees. Since that night at the beach, she'd been blocking the memory of what her body felt like postsex. Well used. Replete. Satiated. It was almost as good as the act itself because relief blanketed her mind, the pleasure of satisfying herself, satisfying a man making her limbs heavy. A smile curved her mouth. And there was the knowledge that another buildup would start right away, leading to more. More of Russell inside her.

One emotion she hadn't blocked successfully throughout the last five days? *Love.* That love for Russell had manifested itself in anger. Drive to break free of the debilitating work cycle. But it had been there, pushing at the backs of her eyelids, swimming in her stomach. Love so tangible that it eddied around her ankles, rising and rising like a warm current until she started to spin with it in slow circles. She wanted to throw her hands up to the sky and demand rain. It made no sense, and it also made her want to laugh.

But there was something. A tenacious . . . something, pacing in the background. Russell's words echoed as they'd done in the shower, pinging off the insides of her skull before finally sticking. *Everything is going to be okay now, Abby. No more games, okay? Everything is fixed now, okay?* Before today, she'd known Russell was holding back something from her. She'd *known*. It was a familiar feeling.

And she'd grown sick of it. Resentful, even. This morning had been her first step toward never feeling in the dark again. Taking control of her future. Owning her actions instead of other people's owning them for her. Hearing that Russell had "fixed" everything and it would all be okay . . . God, she was afraid to hear the rest. They had no choice but to talk about it, though. Impending dread made the bathroom seem darker, the steam thicker. Abby wanted to stay wrapped in his arms forever, but the longer she did, her chances of staying strong began to wane.

She laid a kiss on his bicep and eased away, wrapping a towel around her body on the way to shutting off the shower water. Feeling Russell's eyes on her, she pushed open the fogged-glass window to let the steam out and turned to face him. "I'm ready to talk now."

"Okay." He stood very still, obviously not caring about his nudity. Really, his confidence was entirely justified. It took a considerable effort on Abby's part not to stare at his sculpted thighs, his ridged abdomen. He was incredible, but his expression was anything but cocky. No, he looked wary. "You going to stand across the room while we talk, Abby? Because I have to tell you, it makes me nervous. Makes me wonder if you're going to listen."

"I'm listening." She pushed her wet hair back, an attempt to distract herself from the foreboding feeling using her heart as a trampoline. "But if you hold me while we talk, it could turn out different."

"That's what I'm afraid of." He stooped down and grabbed his boxer briefs, cursed to find them still damp, and dragged his jeans on without underwear. His forehead was marred as he completed the jerky actions, as if mentally preparing. When the task was complete, he faced her, bare-chested. "I got the business loan. I took your suggestion and reworked my ten-year plan into five—and I got it."

"Oh my God." Giant bird wings flapped in her chest. Happiness for her friend, and the man she loved. "That's amazing. Why didn't you say—" She pressed both hands to her cheeks. "You must be so excited. All the ways you can improve and expand. I—"

"*Abby.*" He looked almost pained by her enthusiasm. "I did it for us. Maybe it makes me an underachiever, but the business is a distant second to you. Everything is."

"I don't understand," she murmured, even though the picture was beginning to clear, just like the fog in the bathroom. "For us?"

His chest rose and fell with a heavy intake of breath. A bracing breath. "I know what kind of life you're used to, angel. Comfortable. Happy. I can give it to you now, okay? I *couldn't* before, so I kept away. Kept *you* away. Just until I was sure. I needed to be *sure.*" He took a step closer. "But I fixed everything. I'm going to work hard and give you everything you could ever ask for. If you'll just trust me and give me the chance."

It was almost too much to process at once, but some part of her had been prepared. With each realization that rushed in, she berated herself for not seeing. Not knowing. "Russell . . . I don't need the kind of life my parents have. I don't want it—"

"You say that now," he interrupted, taking a step toward her.

"And I know you believe it, too. But I've seen what happens when someone settles. When someone gets stuck. I didn't want that to be you. I couldn't fucking bear it."

"So this whole time, you wanted to be with me . . . but the money stopped you?" He nodded, the intensity in his eyes robbing her of oxygen. One masculine hand reached out for her, but she stepped back. "Was it your lack of money . . . or the fact that I have too much?"

His hesitation told her the answer. "Both." He tried to shrug, but his shoulders seemed so tense, it came off awkward. "That morning on the beach . . . I thought I could get past it. I could get past anything if you'd sleep beside me, right?" His hand flexed at his side. "Then the lawyer offered me the money, and I knew it would be in my face, every second of the day. Your parents, people you work with, would never stop reminding you how much better you could do. Better than me."

"What money—"

"So I went out, Abby. And I got better." His deep voice vibrated through the small space. "I'll never be good enough for you, but I'll try harder than *anyone*."

"What money are you talking about?"

It visibly took him a second to focus. "Mitchell flashed a bunch of hundred-dollar bills, told me you wanted me gone. That you wanted to help finance Hart Brothers. A parting gift."

She lowered herself onto the edge of the bathtub, her knees going weak. "And you believed him?"

"After I thought I hurt you, I wanted to keep feeling shitty,

Abby. I didn't deserve to feel any other way. So I believed anything that would keep me feeling shitty." His eyes were haunted as they ran over her, head to toe. "I'm sorry I believed it for even a second."

Her laughter didn't hold a trace of humor. "You're so worried about hurting me. Do you know how *awful* I've felt these last couple weeks? Do you? Not knowing why you couldn't just want me permanently? Why you kept disappearing?"

A rough noise burst from his mouth. "God, I didn't mean for you to feel that way. I'll never disappear on you again. I never want to be *away* from you." He dragged a hand over his shaved head. "I needed to know I could make you happy before I made you mine."

Abby shot to her feet. "I *was* yours! We've belonged to each other since we met." She gathered her towel closer. "Or did I imagine it?"

"No," Russell grated, his voice shaking. "You didn't imagine a damn thing. I've been *living* for you since you walked out onto the stoop."

"Only you didn't really want *me*, Russell. You wanted Abby minus the money and how the money made you feel." She felt tears threaten and forced them back. "The money is part of who I am, where I came from. It doesn't define me, though. But you let it define us." She slumped sideways onto the sink. Had she felt exultant only moments ago? How had everything crashed down around her so quickly? "And you didn't give me a say, Russell. That's the worst part. You maneuvered me from behind the scenes like everyone else in my life, putting me where you could be comfortable having me. An Abby your ego could handle."

"No." He was across the bathroom in a single, long stride, cupping her face like a cherished treasure. It made her want to throw herself on the floor and shatter into a million pieces, just to prove she *wasn't* something to be placed on a shelf, out of harm's reach. "I wouldn't change a single thing about you. How can you say that?"

"You *did* change me." She tugged away, staving him off with a hand when he followed. "Maybe the last month has changed me. I'm not sure yet, but I have to believe the change is for the better. I'm pissed as hell that you made decisions concerning us without me. *Porca troia*, Russell. I wanted *you* just as you are—"

"Don't. Don't say *wanted* like it happened in the past—"

"—but you want a different version of *me*. I'm capable of making calls concerning my life, and you took that away. I don't need you to give me a comfortable life. I can do that for myself. What I needed was someone to love. Someone to love me back. What would have mattered beyond that?"

She didn't see the Russell she knew anymore. He'd withdrawn into himself, staring back at her blankly. A painful rupturing took place inside her, self-hatred over hurting the man she loved warring with pride that she'd stood up for herself. But that pride was quickly being swallowed by the screaming need to take back everything and shake Russell until he returned from wherever he'd gone. If she took back her opinion, if she excused him for making her feel less-than for weeks, though, there was every chance it could happen again. Not to mention, she would lose a healthy amount of respect for herself.

"What are you saying?"

She reached deep and found the remaining dram of courage. "I'm saying, you should leave. I don't think there's anything more to say right now."

"Right now," he repeated dully.

"I don't want to lose you as a friend." Oh God, the pressure behind her eyelids was growing so tremendous, all her concentration went into making sure the tears didn't fall. Russell would feel compelled to comfort her, and she'd never survive that. "It might just take awhile."

"Friends." He backed away slowly, his gaze weighing her down like a boulder. Just before he reached the door, he leaned down to pick up his T-shirt and collect his shoes with methodical movements. She thought he meant to leave without another word, but he stopped. Without looking at her, he said. "I don't want to be your friend, Abby. I want to be your husband."

Moisture streamed down her cheeks, but Russell didn't see it because he walked from the apartment barefoot, without looking back a single time. As soon as the door closed behind him, Abby sank down onto the bathroom floor with a heart-wrenching sob, positive her lungs were caving in. She didn't get up again until darkness fell, and it was only to crawl into bed.

Chapter 19

Russell walked back to Queens. He moved uptown on autopilot, crossing the Queensboro Bridge as darkness fell. Apart from the odd bicyclist whizzing past toward Manhattan, the bridge was mostly empty of pedestrians, but a marching band could have passed him, and he wouldn't have flinched.

He'd lost Abby. Lost her completely. Before he'd gone and fucked their relationship all to hell, he'd at least had the privilege of being her friend. The guy she sat beside in restaurants or car rides as if it were a foregone conclusion. The first one she smiled at when walking into a room. At the time, he'd thought being that close without ending up in bed was pure torture. Right now, it sounded like the highest level of heaven one could achieve. And he would never, in his pathetic life, reach it again.

He wasn't even in a place yet where he could wrap his mind around the catastrophe of what had happened back at Abby's apartment. All he knew was the coldness wouldn't leave him alone. Ice lined his veins, made his muscles feel stiff and difficult to move. His heart . . . he wished it would just give in and stop working. Why wouldn't it just *stop working*? Tick . . . tick . . . tick. Every beat was pointless. Every fucking thing was pointless without her.

That saying, hindsight is twenty-twenty, was taunting him, ringing in his head like a fight bell. His experience had been somewhat different, though. The second—the goddamn second—Abby moved across the bathroom and away from him, he'd seen everything go up in smoke. She'd seen it, too. No. He was done lying to himself. He'd seen the flames even before walking into the bathroom, but he'd been so starved for her, nothing could have stopped him. Except the knowledge that he would lose her, and the notion terrified him so much, he'd pretended it didn't exist.

Every single thing she'd said had been right. He'd stood there absorbing every blow like a boxer with his hands bound behind his back. Some sick part of him had even welcomed the rejection because he deserved it for keeping her in the dark so long. *I was yours!* Those words might as well be a tattoo on his consciousness because they would never go away, popping up to remind him of his worst failure until he died. Which would be before he even arrived home if the torn-up feeling in his chest was any indication.

Russell became aware of his surroundings slowly. How long had he been standing outside his house? Taking the phone from his pocket to check the time felt like far too much effort, so he just stared at the two-story home, a sickening laugh working its way toward his throat. Had he actually envisioned carrying Abby over the threshold of this place? The place that held the very childhood memories that led him to fuck everything up? Yeah, he had.

His subconscious hadn't believed his bullshit about Abby's being a package delivered to the wrong doorstep. He might have fed himself the truth about not being worthy, but he'd been preparing for her since they'd met. The whole damn time.

"Hey, asshole."

He didn't even need to turn his head to know his brother had spoken. Not many people called a person of his size *asshole*. "Go away, Alec."

"What?" Alec stopped in front of him, holding a twelve-pack of Budweiser on his right shoulder. "Darcy is watching *The Bachelor*, so I'm home free for an hour or two. I don't want to know who gets a rose, so we're going to celebrate this bank loan, motherfucker."

His brother's words were little arrows spearing into his ears. "Fine," Russell heard himself say. "But I'm not going in there."

Alec split a curious look between Russell and the house. "You've spent every waking hour in there for the last week. Your gigantic outline has faded from my couch."

God. Russell buried his fingers into his temples. He'd been sleeping on a couch, and Abby had known it. She'd ridden in his rickety truck. *I was yours. I was yours.* The angel had wanted him exactly as he was, and he'd been so hung up on being the big bad provider, he'd missed the weight behind her every word. Every gesture. She'd accepted him, but he hadn't given her the same gift. He'd projected a need for a certain lifestyle onto her when she'd only proven at every turn that people were what mattered to her. Honey. Roxy. Him. He'd been important to her. But in the end, he'd only let her down.

With the coldness eating his insides, that reliable hindsight was more powerful now than ever. Abby was one in a million. He'd always known that, but his fear of her meeting the same fate as his mother had prevented him from acting like it. If *Abby* wasn't happy, she wouldn't blame other people. Her surroundings. She would just find a way to improve it. That was who she was. Nobody else. And the crazy truth was? Until the world fell down, before he'd tried to push her away, he'd *been* one of the things making her happy. He had the ability to do that. But he'd squandered it.

Gone. It was all gone now. All over money. Jesus, who cared about who paid for things, or if her relatives found him unsuitable? They would have worked it out together. Nothing had been bad enough that they couldn't overcome it with good. But the good was gone. He'd obliterated it.

Russell turned and dropped onto the lawn, barely noticing when Alec followed suit, until a cold can of beer was pressed into his hand. "Russell, will you accept this Budweiser?"

"I know you watch *The Bachelor* when Darcy isn't home." Russell nabbed the can and popped its top, surprised to find his hands working. "I caught you setting the TiVo once."

"Shut up and drink."

"It's a plan," Russell muttered, tipping back the can. His throat rejected the liquid, but he forced it down. God knew he'd have to find a way to get rip-roaring drunk, no matter how badly his body wanted to exist in the hurt, roll around in it like a masochist. His pain didn't deserve to be numbed so easily. Abby. He'd lost Abby, in every respect. Holy shit. *Holy shit. No.*

Alec watched as Russell shotgunned the beer. "Another?"

"I'm selling the house," Russell managed. "I'm never going in there again. I thought I could erase the bad with . . . with Abby, but it's fucking poisonous. It got to me, and now I'm poisonous, too."

"Hey, man—"

"Please. I don't want to talk about it." He was horrified to hear the crack in his voice, so he breathed through his nose for a minute. "There's nothing to say. It's too late. Just don't fight me on selling."

Alec sighed, turning the beer can in his hand. "It's your call."

The two brothers sat in silence, polishing off the twelve-pack as the familiar sounds of their childhood neighborhood decorated the air around them. It was unclear at what point Russell fell back on the grass and let unconsciousness replace his regret, at least until tomorrow.

Abby's image was the final thing he saw.

ABBY SAT ON the stoop of her building Sunday afternoon, passing a covert plastic bottle of mimosa between herself, Roxy, and Honey. Honey had just cooked brunch upstairs, but Abby had only forced down two bites of French toast before dragging the fork around her plate aimlessly. After an unknown amount of time, she'd looked up to find her roommates staring at her from the kitchen. She hadn't even put up a fight when they each took an arm and led her downstairs to get some fresh air for the first time in over a week.

The talk with her roommates was long overdue, and she knew it, so in the new, somewhat destructive spirit of not avoiding unpleasant conversations, she got the ball rolling. "I'm sorry I didn't tell you guys about Russell." Ouch. His name left her mouth feeling like the end of a lawn rake. "I didn't even know . . . what it was. What we were." She took a swallow of mimosa. "It doesn't matter now, anyway. Now, it's nothing."

It agonized her to say the words. They didn't feel like they could possibly be true. She'd spent the last ten days moderating a fight between her head and heart. One stubbornly clung to the belief she'd done the right thing, that if she'd given in to Russell, she would have lost the newfound respect she'd gained for herself. But the shuddering organ in her chest staunchly disagreed. It wanted back its counterpart.

"Abby . . ." Roxy blew out a long breath. "I'm not trying to call your bluff here . . . but I'm not sure you can call what's between you and Russell nothing. He's loved you since jump street. We've all known it."

Abby stared out at Ninth Avenue, waiting for the ache in her stomach to pass, but it never did. *I don't want to be your friend, Abby. I want to be your husband.* Words that should have made her cry happy tears, not bitter ones. "Russell made it nothing. All he had to do was be honest with me." She turned her attention to Honey, then Roxy. "And while we're on the subject of being honest, why didn't you just tell me? You let me float around in the dark, just like him. Did you think it was funny?"

Honey looked horrified. "No. God, Abby. That's not it at all." She appeared to be searching for the right words. "We wanted you to have the experience of having Russell tell you. Every girl should have that. It wouldn't have felt the same coming from us."

Roxy snagged the plastic bottle. "If we'd known he'd make a

jackass of himself and hurt you in the process, we would have told you months ago."

They meant it. Abby knew her friends wouldn't intentionally hurt her feelings, and honestly, she didn't have the capacity to be mad at anyone else. "All's forgiven. Just tell me next time someone is in love with me and decides friend-zoning me is a better idea than coming clean."

Honey cracked a sad smile. "It's a deal." She plucked at her frayed jeans skirt. "So we all agree Russell acted like a jackass, but . . ."

"But is this really permanent?" Roxy asked, squinting into the sun. "I can't imagine you two apart. You're . . . Russell and Abby. Rabby."

"That nickname never would have happened."

"Says you."

Abby massaged the back of her neck, wondering when her entire body would stop feeling trampled on. "It's permanent," she pushed out. "He doesn't want to be my friend, and I can't be with someone who's threatened by what my family has. Or moves me around into different categories when he feels like it." She crossed her arms over her middle. "He made me feel really horrible, okay? I know he didn't mean to, but he did. And I'm not past it yet."

Roxy laid a hand on her shoulder. "I get it. No one knows what you're feeling but you. We'll support you no matter what."

She nodded once. "Thanks."

"Hey, uh . . . Abby?"

All three girls turned to find a man in jeans and an *American Ninja Warrior* T-shirt at the base of their stoop. Although they had never met, Abby knew who he was immediately. His resemblance to Russell wasn't super noticeable, but it was there in the set of his shoulders, the square shape of his jaw. Russell's brother, Alec. All at once, worry crashed down on her head. The look on Russell's face when he'd walked out of the apartment two Fridays ago was all she could see. Why was his brother here and not him? Had something happened to him?

When Roxy cleared her throat, Abby realized she hadn't spoken. *Wake up.* She mentally shook herself and sat up straight. "Yes. I'm Abby."

Alec scratched the back of his neck, appearing to have difficulty looking her in the eye. "Jesus. My brother aimed high."

"Ohhhh," Honey and Roxy said at the same time, obviously discerning the stranger's identity.

"Would you mind if we talked alone for a minute?" Alec asked.

Abby felt glued to the step. She didn't want to hear what Russell's brother had to say, but craved it at the same time. How was he? *Where* was he? "Yeah. Okay," she said, standing on shaky legs.

Honey and Roxy stood with her, both of them leaning close. "You want us to stay with you?" Honey offered. "Or ask him to leave?"

"No." She gave them a grateful look. "It's fine. I'll be upstairs in a few minutes."

"We'll save you some champagne," Roxy said over her shoulder, as they climbed the stairs and disappeared inside.

Abby stared after her friends a beat, steeling herself, before descending the stoop to join Alec. Her upbringing had her extending a hand without thinking, and her breath caught when Alec's hard handshake reminded her so much of Russell. "How did you know where to find me?"

"You sent Russell a birthday card a couple months back . . . he kept it, envelope and all. He'd be pissed if he knew I'd gone through his stuff, but I didn't have a choice."

"Oh." Great. They had barely exchanged pleasantries and she already wanted to run upstairs, bury her face in a pillow, and wail. Who saved an envelope? "It's nice to meet you, finally."

"Yeah." Alec shifted side to side. "My brother would have brought you over for dinner, only our place is small, and my Darcy can't cook for shit."

An unexpected sob escaped Abby's lips, rendering them both horrified. "I'm sorry, I don't know why . . . you remind me of your brother, and—"

"If you don't mind me saying so, I'm pretty freakin' relieved you're upset." He made a frustrated noise. "That came out wrong. It's just that if I'd come here and seen you laughing it up, I would have had to bust Russell's chops for moping around over a girl who isn't even interested. And then I'd have to feel crappy about it, right? I feel crappy most of the time, as it is. But I digress."

A surge of irritation hit Abby that Russell had never introduced her to Alec. Five minutes in his company, and she already felt like they'd been friends for years. *I never introduced him to my parents, either.* The realization plowed over her like a bulldozer, but she struggled to respond. "What, um . . . brought you here? Is Russell okay?"

"No, I'd say he's pretty far from okay." Alec turned serious.

"Look, I don't know the details of what happened between you two, but I haven't always been there for my brother like I should have. This is me trying to correct that."

"Okay," Abby whispered, somehow already knowing she was toast.

Alec was silent a moment. "Our mother, she was depressed. Severely. My father didn't understand, didn't get her the help she needed. He worked all day. I cut school and dicked around, so I wouldn't have to go home." He sucked in a breath. "It was Russell with her most of the time. Listening to her cry. Making sure she ate enough food before she started drinking . . . he was the one who found her after the accident. And it affected him. We didn't get him the help *he* needed, either." He looked away. "He was the bravest one of us three, but that doesn't mean he's not scared. Scared of it happening again."

The summer sun held no warmth as Abby processed Alec's words. Her hands rose on their own, hugging the opposite elbows to keep herself from shattering. He'd told her only half the story that night in the water. Why? She would have understood everything if he'd just been honest. His insecurities made sense now. It had never been entirely about her *money*, even if he'd given that reason to himself. It had mostly been about her *happiness*. And she'd thrown him out before he could fully explain.

Oh God, she needed to see him. Abby realized she'd said the words out loud, when Alec nodded. "If you don't mind my being bossy, going *now* might be the best course of action."

Her pulse skipped a beat. "Why?"

"He's selling the house. That jerk moves fast." He checked his watch, as if he hadn't just ripped Abby's chest wide open and pulled out her beating heart. "There's an open house in forty-five minutes."

Through the urgency, Abby felt a sense of clarity as she ran beside Alec toward the truck he indicated. She knew exactly what she had to do. As soon as Alec pulled onto Ninth Avenue, she took out her phone and started dialing.

Chapter 20

Russell sat on the front porch of his house, wishing it were raining. The fact that is was eighty degrees without a cloud in the sky was some kind of fucked-up business when he felt flattened. He'd unlocked the front door for the Realtor so she could set up flowers for the open house although why flowers would convince someone to buy a house was beyond him. It should have bothered him that the Realtor had only hummed absently when he mentioned the custom banister, the restored crown molding. It *should* have, but it didn't. He'd only done those things for one person, so if the Realtor thought a pack of daisies would sell the damn place instead of his hard work, he couldn't find the strength to care.

The last ten days had been spent painting, making some final tweaks to the interior, and signing paperwork to get the house on the market. Those things should have distracted him from thoughts of Abby, but she'd been there, perched on his shoulder through each task. Sometimes she took mercy on him and talked in his ear the way she used to, asking him why he chose certain shades of paint or making adorable observations about his technique. Other times, he could only see her as she'd been in the bathroom, disappointed in him. He'd known that look a lot in his life, but coming from her, it had felt like a shotgun shell entering his sternum.

Jesus, he missed her. Not a day in his life would pass where he wouldn't. Even if by some miracle, they were able to hang out again as friends, the missing would only intensify. Because he'd see her and know what could have been if he'd given Abby enough credit to make her own choices. If he hadn't been so focused on *not* losing her rather than *keeping* her. Holding her close where she was supposed to be.

He registered the familiar sound of Alec's truck screeching to a stop at the curb but didn't look up. Alec had done a lot of hovering since last Friday night and frankly, Russell was growing weary of it. They weren't exactly adept at expressing their feelings, so there'd mainly been a lot of beer drinking and uncomfortable speculating about the Yankees' new left-handed pitcher. Abby had been there through all of it, reminding him of the times she'd taken the first sip of his beer. Or the time he'd pitched to her at Honey's baseball field, and she'd run the wrong direction around the bases. Everything reminded him of her. Everything.

"Russell?"

There she was again, talking into his ear. She sounded annoyed this time around, but he'd take whatever she dished out.

"Russell."

His chin jerked up and . . . there was Abby. Standing at the end of his stone walkway. *Oh God*, had he graduated to hallucinations? Maybe beer for breakfast hadn't been a good idea after all. It had sped up his descent into total madness. Still, he took in every detail of the mirage with greedy eyes, starting at the white sandals that showed her toes and scaling her legs. She wore a red-and-white-checkered dress he'd never seen before, which was odd. Usually, he pictured her in all white or yellow.

"I can't believe you're selling this house. After all the hard work you put in." Abby the Apparition came toward Russell on the path, and he held his breath, worried that if he moved, she would vanish. Right before she reached him, her attention was snagged by the For Sale sign posted in the yard. Russell watched in amazement as she marched toward the sign . . . and kicked the white pole holding it upright. She kicked it and kicked it until it fell over. *Holy shit, she's real. She's here.* Russell came to his feet slowly and watched real Abby—his sweet Abby—beat the hell out of the sign, cursing in Italian as she went. "I won't let you lose this house, Russell. You're staying. So just deal with it."

When Russell finally found his voice, it sounded rusty. "I don't want the house."

"Yes, you do. I saw how proud you were of it. I *saw*." She finally succeeded in knocking the sign over. Then she blew out a breath, smoothed her skirt, and tucked a stray hair behind her ear. "And you should be proud of it. All that work . . . the office, the custom banister—"

"You noticed the banister?"

"I'm not as oblivious as everyone thinks I am. Even if I was when it came to you." She turned and traded a nod with Alec, who turned and went back to his car with a shit-eating grin that Russell was too distracted to analyze. *Abby*. She was *right there*. And she sure as hell wasn't there for a friendly chat. "Why are you selling it? Why?"

Honesty exploded out of him. He never thought he'd get the chance to be truthful with her again and wouldn't pass up the opportunity. Anything to keep her standing in front of him a little longer. "Without you, Abby, this house is just some fucking wood I nailed together. It's meaningless." He swallowed hard. "Do you know when I started renovating this place?"

Her arms had uncrossed and dropped to her sides. "When?" she whispered.

"The day after we met, angel. The next damn day." He took a step in her direction, breathing a sigh of relief when she stayed put. "After my father left, it was just sitting here, waiting for us to sell it. But suddenly, I couldn't. Maybe it was wishful thinking, but I could picture us in these rooms. I could see you coming down the stairs in that robe hanging in your bedroom. The one with the flowers on it."

"It's a kimono," she said, so softly he barely heard her.

"Okay." He wanted to reach out and grab her but managed to hold back. She needed to hear everything. Deserved everything he'd been holding inside. "I love you, Abby. I've *loved* you. I didn't realize saying that might be all you needed to hear because I only understood action. If I were a smarter man, I would have said the words a million times. I've loved you. *I've loved you.* I've loved you.

And this house is useless unless you're inside it to make memories with me." He laid a fist over his heart. "My memories were supposed to be with you."

She didn't move. Or speak. For a really long time. And that was a goddamn blessing for Russell because it meant he got to be with Abby. Got to look at her. If he tried really hard, he could even catch a hint of white-grape sunlight on the summer breeze. His hands shook with the desire to touch her, so he shoved them into his jeans pockets. He'd barely started cataloging every detail of her face when she ran past him, up the stairs, and into the house.

A beat passed where he could only stare at the place where Abby had been standing. He quickly turned and followed, however, craving the sight of her within the four lonely walls. Russell paused on the threshold, because dammit, he'd never wanted to set foot inside again. But *she* was inside. She was *there*. So when he saw her red dress flash at the top of the staircase, he went after her.

Russell strode past the confused Realtor and scaled the stairs, turning right toward the office when he reached the landing. As he got closer to the office, his mouth went dry, pulse thundering with the knowledge of what Abby would find. He moved into the doorway, and there she was . . .

. . . bathed in the shine produced by eight oversized skylights. The ones he'd spent the last week installing. Hell, there was barely any ceiling left, but what little was there, he'd painted blue to match the sky. The walls were rose gold and high-gloss, so they could capture the sunlight, spin it into a glow, and surround her with it. As if she needed any help looking magical as she turned in a slow circle at the center of the room. He watched as she noticed the red and yellow roses he's set up along the window and placed around the room.

Then those hazel eyes were on him, eclipsing the sunlight. "You did this for me?"

"You said . . ." He cleared the rust from his throat. "You said you wanted it to feel like you were working outside."

Twin tears rolled down her cheeks, and Russell took an involuntary step forward to dry them, but her voice halted him in his tracks. "It's the most beautiful room I've ever seen. Anywhere. In my entire life."

Russell had to look away because the emotion that rolled through him was so potent, he was afraid to direct it toward her. Not unless she wanted it.

"Russell. You can't sell this house."

"Abby—"

"Where would we live?"

A shock of electricity struck him right in the chest, so powerful he couldn't breathe. Or speak. It was so obvious his fate lay with Abby, he could see it suspended between them in the air.

"We can't have a man living in the apartment. If you moved in, Ben and Louis would insist on moving in, too, and the whole place would be overcrowded. And since I need to be with you, the only option is for me to move here. So you can't sell it. No one gets this office but me. No one gets this house but us." She swiped at her eyes when more tears fell. "Are we getting married or living in sin? Because as long as I get you, Russell, I'm in either way. *Any* way."

He went down on his knees and crawled the remaining distance to Abby. She clutched his shoulders and tried to pull him up, but he refused, wrapping his arms around her waist and inhaling the scent that clung to her clothes. "How did I fuck this up so badly when I love you this much? How is that possible?"

She knelt on the floor in front of him, seized his face in her hands. "I love you, too." Her lips drifted over his forehead, cheeks. "I love you. You love me. And nothing else is more important than that."

He crushed her against his body, feeling alive for the first time in days. The oxygen he sucked in was laced with Abby, the staggering relief that he wouldn't have to live without her. *Thank God. Thank God.*

"We're going to go tell the Realtor you're not selling, okay?" He nodded into the crook of her neck. "Right after she rejects the offer I made."

Russell's head came up. "You made an offer?"

"I was afraid I wouldn't get here in time, and you'd accept someone else's offer." She searched his face. "If I'd bought the house, what would you have said?"

His answer was important to her. Important to them. After the way he'd pushed her away until he felt stable enough to give her things that could only be bought with money, she needed to know his insecurity had been obliterated by the reality of losing her. Russell tipped up her face. "If you'd bought my house, I would have asked you when I could move in, angel. Either way, it would have been ours."

The smile that spread across her face was so damn beautiful, he breathed her name. "Did you mean what you said about getting married? I can have a priest here in half an hour."

Her laughter wrapped around Russell as she eased him backward into a sitting position on the floor, wrapping her legs around his waist. "I meant it. *Of course*, I meant it. There's no one else for me in the world."

"Christ, me either, angel—" She rolled her hips and Russell saw sparks behind his eyes, but somehow found the wherewithal to reach over and slam the office door. "You need me now? God knows I need you so damn bad."

"Yes." She tugged down the straps of her dress to reveal her lack of bra. The sight sent Russell's erection surging between her legs, making her gasp. "I can't wait."

They both reached for his zipper at the same time with shaking hands, lowering it carefully to take out the arousal she'd inspired. Russell groaned against her mouth as he hurried to remove a condom from his wallet, quickly rolling it on. Abby's panties were shoved aside seconds later, and, *fuuuuck*, he was inside her. Neither one of them moved, simply breathing into one another's mouths. "Tell me you . . . love me again while . . . I'm inside you."

"I love you, Russell," she husked, looking him in the eye. "I'll never stop. I couldn't."

"Marry me, Abby." His voice was urgent, breaking as she started to move, her body undulating on his lap. The perfect feel of her made it difficult to focus, but he battled to stay present. "Tell me you'll marry me."

The way she looked at him spoke of love, more than words ever could. "Make me."

So he did.

Epilogue

See, there are obstacle courses, like the one the Army uses for training." Alec paused to make eye contact with Ben, Louis, and Russell. "And then you have the *real* deal. Not many men have attempted the *American Ninja Warrior* obstacle course and survived to be the best man at his brother's wedding." He spread his hands wide, pulling the lapels of his tuxedo wide. "Take a good look. I'm a rare breed, gents."

"I don't think anyone can argue that," Russell said, his tone dry but good-natured. There wasn't a damn thing that could bring him down. He was marrying Abby today. Making her his wife. Hell, he wasn't sure a single thing—even his brother—would exasperate him for the rest of his life. What was there to complain about when he had Abby at home?

Home. Russell hadn't known what the term meant until they'd moved in together. The first week of waking up in the same bed, eating breakfast in their own kitchen . . . he'd thought eventually they would stop smiling like crazy people when their eyes met across the dining-room table. Or while folding laundry on the living-room floor. But it hadn't happened yet. It never would, either. They would make sure of it.

The four men stood waiting in tuxedos at the base of the Ninth Avenue stoop where he'd seen Abby for the first time and fallen hard and permanently for her. They had spent the last four months since Abby had given him another chance looking at churches throughout Queens and Manhattan, but none of them had felt right. One morning, they'd driven across the bridge for breakfast, and it had hit them both at the same time as they climbed the steps. The stoop was the spot. Twenty minutes later, Louis had come downstairs to break up their kissing jag and haul them up to the apartment for pancakes.

Ben, looking perfectly at home in his tuxedo, nodded in his direction. "How are things at the office? We haven't been out since the grand opening."

"Great. *Better* than great," Russell responded, not bothering to hide his cheeseball grin. As if having Abby at home wasn't unbelievable enough, she'd fallen into the role of office manager for Hart Brothers Construction. In a matter of months, she'd turned them into a major contender for city contracts and developments they never would have tried for without her staunch confidence in the company. In him. "I don't know what we would do without Abby. She keeps the place running."

"Yeah," Alec chimed in, elbowing Russell in the side. "She works us a little harder than I'm used to, but it keeps this asshole happy. As soon as the lunch bell rings, he's peeling out of the site to get an hour in with her."

"Damn right," Russell said. It was true. In the beginning, he worried that Abby's being exposed to his overwhelming need for her day and night might be too much. For *her,* not him. He'd never get enough of Abby. Thankfully, every time he walked into the office on his lunch break, she was on him like white on rice, begging for a trip to the stockroom. And there were no words for how *that* made him feel.

True to his word, he'd done some exploring of the urges Abby tempted to his surface, and they'd learned together how to indulge both of their needs safely. He'd been relieved to find out that his nature didn't make him a threat to Abby, but rather, the dominant counterpart to her softer spirit. She loved the way he controlled what happened in the bedroom . . . required it, some days, it seemed. Giving her what she needed was a privilege he would never take for granted. Not for a single moment.

As it turned out, their bedroom was the *only* place where Abby liked to be controlled. Over the last four months, he'd watched her transform into a woman who didn't take no for an answer. She was . . . *dynamic* at work. More than once, he'd been late to a job because he couldn't tear himself away from listening to Abby negotiate over the phone. Or haggle with a supplier. God, she was amazing. He couldn't believe she was about to become his wife, but no way would he question her decision to be with him ever again. They needed each other.

Louis narrowed his eyes at the apartment-building door, as if willing them to open. "They say weddings put women in the frame of mind for marriage." He lifted his chin in Russell's direction. "You think you can convince Abby to toss the bouquet to Roxy?"

"You're too late," Ben said, looking smug. "I asked Abby weeks ago. She's throwing it to Honey."

"You slick motherfucker." Louis laughed and punched Ben in the shoulder. "I guess I deserve that for not being on the ball. At least Roxy agreed to move in with me. I'll have to trick her into marrying me another way. Maybe hypnosis . . ."

"Honey and I are looking for our own place, too. Somewhere between Columbia and NYU, so we have an equal commute." Ben slid his hands into the tuxedo pockets. "I can't believe we won't have this place to come to anymore. The storage room on the ground floor is where Honey and I . . . you know . . . kissed for the first time."

Alec groaned toward the sky. "This is about to get sappy, isn't it?"

Russell cleared the tightness from his throat. "I've carried Abby up these steps more times than I can count. I'm going to miss that."

"I picked Roxy up for our first official date upstairs." Louis ran a hand through his hair. "Ah, listen. We'll just take turns crashing each other's places. Probably wherever Honey is, though. She's the best cook."

A smile spread across Ben's face. "She'll love that."

"It's been a crazy year," Russell said under his breath. "The *best* year."

The three friends nodded, just as the building's door swung open to reveal Abby in a simple, long-sleeved white dress, a crown of flowers on her head. Russell's legs turned to glue on the spot, the air vanishing from his lungs. His nickname for her had never been more apt at that moment, elevated above him as she was like an angel, smiling into the pure, fall sunlight.

Abby's father stood to her left, his daughter's hand tucked into the crook of his elbow. Behind her, wearing bright red dresses were Honey and Roxy, beaming from ear to ear. Abby's stepmother was reserved as always, but Russell caught a hint of tears shining in her eyes before he quickly turned his attention back to Abby. God, he loved her. He'd *loved* her. Seeing her in the very same spot he'd first witnessed her beauty, knowing she had agreed to become his wife, filled him with so much contentment and gratefulness, he was surprised he didn't tip over and capsize.

Without taking his gaze off Abby, Russell spoke to the priest who'd been standing off to the side. "Make her my wife as fast as humanly possible, please."

Abby laughed, a bright, beautiful sound that floated down and grabbed Russell, forcing him to meet her halfway as she descended the stairs, retrieving her from her father. He'd gotten to know him in the months preceding the wedding, and the fact was, Abby's father hadn't *always* been richer than sin. He'd started with next to nothing, giving them more in common than Russell had ever expected. The relief of having Abby's father's approval was vast even if he was still working on the mother. Every time they had dinner together, though, he wore her down a little more. He'd even coaxed a smile out of her the last time.

Russell looked down at Abby and got lost in her, their surroundings blurring into background noise. "Every day I wake up thinking I can't possibly love you any more." He kissed her fore-head. "And then you look at me . . . and I'm proven wrong."

Her eyes went even softer as she pressed her cheek to his. "You're not alone." He felt her breath warm his ear. "I'm so happy. *You* make me so happy."

The pleasure of hearing that made his eyes closed. "I'll never stop. Marry me so I never have to stop."

Russell and Abby were married at the base of the Ninth Avenue stoop, surrounded by friends and the hazy, autumn breeze, after which Abby tossed *two* bouquets. One was caught by Honey, the other by Roxy, to the excessive delight of their boyfriends. And they all lived, deliriously happy, forever and ever.

Don't miss the other books in the
Broke and Beautiful series . . .

Chase Me and Need Me

The full series is available now wherever books are sold.

And keep an eye out for the next book from
#1 *New York Times* bestselling author Tessa Bailey . . .

Wreck the Halls

Coming October 2023
Read on for a sneak peek at this fun,
spicy holiday rom-com!

Prologue

2009

The second Beat Dawkins entered the television studio, it stopped raining outside.

Sunshine tumbled in through the open door, wreathing him in a halo of glory, pedestrians retracting their umbrellas and tipping their hats in gratitude.

Across the room, Melody witnessed Beat's arrival the way an astronomer might observe a once-in-a-millennium asteroid streaking across the sky. Her hormones activated, testing the forgiveness of her powder-fresh-scented Lady Speed Stick. She'd only gotten braces two days earlier. Now those metal wires felt like train tracks in her mouth. Especially while watching Beat breeze with such effortless grace into the downtown studio where they would be shooting interviews for the documentary.

At age sixteen, Melody was in the middle of an awkward phase—to put it mildly. Sweat was an uncontrollable entity. She didn't know how to smile anymore without looking like a constipated gargoyle. Her milk chocolate mane had been carefully styled for this afternoon, but her hair couldn't be tricked into forgetting about the humidity currently plaguing New York, and now it was frizzing to really *accentuate* the rubber bands connecting her incisors.

Then there was Beat.

Utterly, effortlessly gorgeous.

His chestnut-colored hair was damp from the rain, his light blue eyes sparkling with mirth. Someone handed him a towel as soon as he crossed the threshold and he took it without looking, rubbing it over his locks and leaving them wild, standing on end, amusing everyone in the room. A woman in a headset ran a lint brush down the arm of his indigo suit and he gave her a grateful, winning smile, visibly flustering her.

How could she herself and this boy possibly be the same age?

Not only that, but they'd also been named by their mothers as perfect complements to each other. Beat and Melody. They were the offspring of America's most legendary female rock duo, Steel Birds. Since the band had already broken up by the time Beat and Melody were born, their names were bestowed quite by accident, without the members consulting each other. Decidedly *not* the happiest of coincidences. Not to mention, children of legends with significant names were supposed to be interesting. Remarkable.

Obviously, Beat was the only one who was meeting expectations.

Unless you counted the fact that she'd chosen teal rubber bands.

Which had seemed a lot more daring in the sterility of the orthodontist's office.

"Melody," someone called to her right. The simple act of having her name shouted across the busy room caused Mel to be *bathed in fire*, but okay. Now the backs of her knees were sweating—and oh God, *Beat was looking at her*.

Time froze.

They'd never actually met before.

Every article about their mothers and the highly publicized band breakup in 1993 mentioned Beat and Melody in the same breath, but they were locking eyes for the very first time IRL. She needed to think of something interesting to say.

I was going to go with clear rubber bands, but teal felt more punk rock.

Sure. Maybe she could cap that statement off with some finger guns and really drive home the fact that he'd gotten all the cool rock royalty genes. Oh God, her feet were sweating now. Her sandals were going to squeak when she walked.

"Melody!" called the voice again.

She tore her attention off the godlike vision that was Beat Dawkins to find the producer waving her into one of the cordoned-off interview suites. Just inside the door was a camera, a giant boom mic, a director's chair. The interview about her mother's career hadn't even started yet and she already knew the questions she would be answering. Maybe she could just pop in very quickly, recite her usual responses, and save everyone some time?

No, I can't sing like my mother.

We don't talk about the band breakup.

Yes, my mother is currently a nudist and yes, I've seen her naked a startling number of times.

Of course, it would be amazing for fans if Steel Birds reunited.

No, it will never happen. Not in a million, trillion years. Sorry.

"We're ready for you," sang the producer, tapping her wrist.

Melody nodded, flushing hotter at the suggestion she was holding things up. "Coming."

She snuck one final glance at Beat and walked in the direction of her interview room. That was it, she guessed. She'd probably never see him in person again—

"Wait!"

One word from Beat and the humming studio quieted, ground to a halt.

The prince had spoken.

Melody stopped with one foot poised in the air, turning her head slowly. *Please let him be talking to me*, otherwise the fact that she'd stopped at his command would be a pitiful mistake. Also, *please let him be talking to someone else.* The train tracks in her mouth were approximately four hundred pounds per inch, the teal dress she'd worn—oh God—to match her rubber bands, didn't fit right in the boob region. Other girls her age managed to look normal. *Good*, even.

What was it *TMZ* had said about her?

Melody Gallard: always a before picture, never an after.

Beat *was* talking to her, however.

Not only that, but he was also jogging over in this athletic, effortless way, the way a celebrity might approach the mound at a baseball game to throw out the ceremonial first pitch, the crowd cheering him on. His hair had arranged itself back to a perfect coif, no evidence of the rain she could see, his mouth in a bemused half smile.

Beat slowed to a stop in front of her, rubbing at the back of his neck and glancing around at their rapt audience, as if he'd acted without thinking and was now bashful about it. And the fact that he could be shy or self-conscious with charisma pouring out of his eyeballs was astounding. Who *was* this creature? How could they possibly share a connection?

"Hey," he breathed, coming in closer than Melody expected, that one move making them coconspirators. He wasn't overly tall, maybe five eleven, but her eyes were level with his chin. His sculpted, clean-shaven chin. Wow, he smelled so good. Like a freshly laundered blanket with some fireplace smoke clinging to it. Maybe she should switch from powder fresh Speed Stick to something a little more mature. Like ocean surf. "Hey, Mel. Can I call you that?"

No one had ever shortened her name before. Not her mother, classmates, or any of the nannies she'd had over the years. A nickname was something that should be attained over time, after a long acquaintance with someone, but Beat calling her Mel somehow seemed totally normal. Their names were counterparts, after all. They'd been named as a pair, whether it had been intentional or not.

"Sure," she whispered, trying not to stare at his throat. Or inhale him. "You can call me Mel."

Was this her first crush? Was it supposed to happen this fast? She usually found members of a different sex sort of . . . .

uninspiring. They didn't make her pulse race, the way this one did. *Say something else before you bore him to death.*

"You stopped the rain," she blurted.

His eyebrows shot up. "What?"

I'm dissolving. I'm being absorbed by the floor. "When you walked in, the rain just . . . stopped." She snapped her fingers. "Like you'd turned it off with a switch."

When Melody was positive that he would cringe and make an excuse to walk away, Beat smiled instead. That lopsided one that made her feel funny *everywhere.* "I should have thought of switching it off before walking two blocks in a downpour." He laughed and exhaled at the same time, studying her face. "It's . . . crazy, right? Finally meeting?"

"Yeah." The word burst out of Melody and quite unexpectedly, her chest started to swell. "It's definitely crazy."

He nodded slowly, never taking his eyes off her face.

She'd heard of people like him.

People who could make you feel like you were the only one in the room. The world. She'd believed in the existence of such unicorns, she just never in her wildest dreams expected to be given the undivided attention of one. It was like bathing in the brightest of sunlight.

"If things had been different with our mothers, we probably would have grown up together," he said, blue eyes twinkling. "We might even be best friends."

"Oh," she said with a knowing look. "I don't think so."

His amusement only spread. "No?"

"I don't mean that to be offensive," Melody rushed to say. "I just . . . I tend to keep to myself, and you seem more . . ."

"Extroverted." He shrugged a single shoulder. "Yeah. I am." He waved a hand to indicate the room, the crew who were still captivated by the first—maybe only—meeting of Beat Dawkins and Melody Gallard. "You might think I'd be into this. Talking, being on camera." He lowered his voice to a whisper. "But it's always the same questions. Can you sing, too? Does your mother ever talk about the breakup?"

"Will there ever be a reunion?" Melody chimed in.

"Nope," they said at the same exact time—and laughed.

Beat eventually turned serious. "Look, I hope this isn't out of line, but I notice the way the tabloids treat you. Online and off. It's . . . different from how they treat me." Fire scaled the sides of her neck and gripped her ears. Of course he'd seen the cringe-inducing critiques of Melody. They were usually included in articles that profiled him, as well. The most recent one had whittled her entire existence down to the line, *In the case of Trina Gallard's daughter, the apple didn't just fall far from the tree, it's more of a lemon.* "I always wonder if it bothers you. Or if you're able to blow that bullshit off."

"Oh, I mean . . ." She laughed, too loudly, waved a hand on a floppy fist. "It's fine. People expect those gossip sites to be snarky. They're just doing their job."

He said nothing. Just watched her with a little wrinkle between his brows.

"I'm lying," she whisper-blurted. "It bothers me."

His perfect head tilted ever so slightly to one side. "Okay." He nodded, as if he'd made an important decision about something. "Okay."

"Okay what?"

"Nothing." His gaze ran a lap around her face. "You're not a lemon, by the way. Not even close." He squinted, but not enough to fully hide the twinkle. "More of a peach."

She swallowed the dreamy sigh that tried to escape. "Maybe so. Peaches do have pretty thin skin."

"Yeah, but they have a tough center."

Something grew and grew inside of Melody. Something she'd never felt before. A kinship, a bond, a connection. She couldn't come up with a word for it. Only knew that it seemed almost cosmic or preordained. And in that moment, for the first time in her life, she was angry with her mother for her part in breaking up the band. She could have known this boy sooner? Felt . . . *understood* sooner?

Someone in a headset approached Beat and tapped his shoulder. "We'd like to get the interview started, if you're ready?"

Unbelievably, he was still looking at Melody. "Yeah, sure."

Did he sound disappointed?

"I better go, too," Melody said, holding out her hand for a shake.

Beat studied her hand for several seconds, then gave her a narrow-eyed look—as if to say, *don't be silly*—and pulled her into the hug of a lifetime. The hug. Of a lifetime. In a millisecond, she was warm in the most pleasant, sweat-free way. All the way down to the soles of her feet. Light-headedness swept in. She'd not only been granted the honor of smelling this boy's perfect neck, he was encouraging her with a palm to the back of her head. He squeezed her close, before brushing his hand down the back of her hair. Just once. But it was the most beautiful sign of affection she'd ever been offered, and it wrote itself messily all over her heart.

"Hey." He pulled back with a serious expression, taking Melody by the shoulders. "Listen to me, Mel. You live here in New York, I live in LA. I don't know when I'll see you again, but . . . I guess it just feels important, like I need to tell you . . ." He frowned over his own discomposure, which she assumed was rarer than a solar eclipse. "What happened between our mothers has nothing to do with us. Okay? Nothing. If you ever need anything, or maybe you've been asked the same question forty million times and can't take it anymore, just remember that I understand." He shook his head. "We've got this big thing in common, you and me. We have a . . ."

"Bond?" she said breathlessly.

"*Yeah.*"

She could have wept all over him.

"We *do*," he continued, kissing her on the forehead hard and pulling Melody back into the second hug of a lifetime. "I'll find a way to get you my number, Peach. If you ever need anything, call me, okay?"

"Okay," she whispered, heart and hormones in a frenzy. He'd given her a *nickname*. She wrapped her arms around him and held tight, giving herself a full five seconds, before forcing herself to release Beat and step back. "Same for you." She struggled to keep her breathing at a normal pace. "Call me if you ever need someone who understands." The next part wouldn't stay tucked inside of her. "We can pretend we've been best friends all along."

To her relief, that lopsided smile was back. "It wouldn't be so hard, Mel."

A bell rang somewhere on the set, breaking the spell. Everyone flurried into motion around them. Beat was swept in one direction, Melody in the other. But her pulse didn't stop pounding for hours after their encounter.

True to his word, Beat found a way to provide her with his number, through an assistant at the end of her interview. She could never find the courage to use it, though. Not even on her most difficult days. And he never called her, either.

That was the beginning and the end of her fairy-tale association with Beat Dawkins.

Or so she thought.

Chapter 1

*B*eat stood shivering on the sidewalk outside of his thirtieth birthday party.

At least, he assumed a party was waiting for him inside the restaurant. His friends had been acting mysterious for weeks. If he could only move his legs, he would walk inside and act surprised. He'd hug each of them in turn, like they deserved. Make them explain every step of the planning process and praise them for being so crafty. He'd be the ultimate friend.

And the ultimate fraud.

When the phone started vibrating again in his hand, his stomach gave an unholy churn, so intense he had to concentrate hard on breathing through it. A couple passed him on the sidewalk, shooting him some curious side-eye. He smiled at them in reassurance, but it felt weak, and they only walked faster. He looked down at his phone, already knowing an unknown caller would be displayed on the screen. Same as last time. And the time before.

Over a year and a half had passed since the last time his blackmailer had contacted him. He'd given the man the largest sum of money yet to go away and assumed the harassment was over. Beat was just beginning to feel normal again. Until the message he'd received tonight on the way to his own birthday party.

I'm feeling talkative, Beat. Like I need to get some things off my chest.

It was the same pattern as last time. The blackmailer contacted him out of the blue, no warning, and then immediately became persistent. His demands came on like a blitz, a symphony beginning in the middle of its crescendo. They left no room for negotiation, either. Or reasoning. It was a matter of giving this man what he wanted or having a secret exposed that could rock the very foundation of his family's world.

No big deal.

He took a deep breath, paced a short distance in the opposite direction of the restaurant. Then he hit call and lifted the phone to his ear.

His blackmailer answered on the first ring.

"Hello again, Beat."

A red-hot iron dropped in Beat's stomach.

Did the man's voice sound more on edge than previous years? Almost agitated?

"We agreed this was over," Beat said, his grip tight around the phone. "I was never supposed to hear from you again."

A raspy sigh filled the line. "The thing about the truth is, it never really goes away."

With those ominous words echoing in his ear, a sort of surreal calmness settled over Beat. It was one of those moments where he looked around and wondered what in the hell had led him to this time and place. Was he even standing here at all? Or was he trapped in an endless dream? Suddenly the familiar sights of Greenwich Street, only a few blocks from his office, looked like a movie set. Christmas lights in the shapes of bells and Santa heads and holly leaves hung from streetlights, and an early December cold snap that turned his breath to frostbitten mist in front of his face.

He was in Tribeca, close enough to the Financial District to see coworkers sharing sneaky cigarettes on the sidewalk after too much to drink, still dressed in their office attire at eight P.M. A rogue elf traipsed down the street yelling into his phone. A cab drove by slowly, wheels traveling over wet sludge from the brief afternoon snowfall, "Have a Holly Jolly Christmas" drifting out through the window.

"Beat." The voice in his ear brought him back to reality. "I'm going to need double the amount as last time."

Nausea lifted all the way to his throat, making his head feel light. "I can't do that. I don't personally have that kind of liquid cash and I will not touch the foundation money. This needs to be *over.*"

"Like I said—"

"The truth never goes away. I heard you."

Silence was heavy on the line. "I'm not sure I appreciate the way you're speaking to me, Beat. I have a story to tell. If you're not going to pay me to keep it to myself, I'll get what I need from *20/20* or *People* magazine. They'd love every salacious word."

And his parents would be ruined.

The truth would devastate his father.

His mother's sterling reputation would be blown to smithereens.

The public perception of Octavia Dawkins would nose-dive, and thirty years of the charitable work she'd done would mean nothing. There would only be the story.

There would only be the damning truth.

"Don't do that." Beat massaged the throbbing sensation between his eyes. "My parents don't deserve it."

"Oh, yeah? Well, I didn't deserve to be thrown out of the band, either." The man snorted. "Don't talk about shit you don't know, kid. You weren't there. Are you going to help me out or should I start making calls? You know, I've had this reality show producer contact me twice. Maybe she would be a good place to start."

The night air turned sharper in his lungs. "What producer? What's her name?"

Was it the same woman who'd been emailing and calling Beat for the last six months? Offering him an obscene sum of money to participate in a reality show about reuniting Steel Birds? He hadn't bothered returning any of the correspondence because he'd gotten so many similar offers over the years. The public demand for a reunion hadn't waned one iota since the nineties and now, thanks to one of the band's hits going viral decades after its release, the demand was suddenly more relevant than ever.

"Danielle something," said his blackmailer. "It doesn't matter. She's only one of my options."

"Right."

How much had she offered Beat? He didn't remember the

exact amount. Only that she'd dangled a lot of money. Possibly seven figures.

"How do we make this stop once and for all?" Beat asked, feeling and sounding like a broken record. "How can I guarantee this is the last time?"

"You'll have to take my word for it."

Beat was already shaking his head. "I need something in writing."

"Not happening. It's my word or nothing. How long do you need to pull the money together?"

Goddammit. This was real. This was happening. *Again.*

The last year and a half had been nothing but a reprieve. Deep down, he'd known that, right? "I need some time. Until February, at least."

"You have until Christmas."

The jagged edge of panic slid into his chest. "That's less than a month away."

A humorless laugh crackled down the line. "If you can make your selfish cow of a mother look like a saint to the public, you can get me eight hundred thousand by the twenty-fifth."

"No, I can't," Beat said through his teeth. "It's impossible—"

"Do it or I talk."

The line went dead.

Beat stared down at the silent device for several seconds, trying to pull himself together. Text messages from his friends were piling up on the screen, asking him where he was. Why he was late for dinner. He should have been used to pretending everything was normal by now. He'd been doing it for five years, since the first time the blackmailer made contact. Smile. Listen intently. Be grateful. Be grateful at all times for what he had.

How much longer could he pull this off?

A couple of minutes later, he walked into a pitch-black party room.

The lights came on and a sea of smiling faces appeared, shouting, "*Surprise!*"

And even though his skin was as cold as ice beneath his suit, he staggered back with a dazed grin, laughing the way everyone would expect. Accepting hugs, backslaps, handshakes, and kisses on the cheeks.

Nothing is wrong.

I have it all under control.

Beat struggled through the inundation of stress and attempted to appreciate the good around him. The room full of people who had gathered in his honor. He owed them that after all the effort they'd clearly put in. One of the benefits of being born in December was Christmas-themed birthdays, and his friends had laid it on thick. White twinkling lights were wrapped around fresh garland and hanging from the rafters of the restaurant's banquet room. Poinsettias sprung from glowing vases. The scent of cinnamon and pine was heavy in the air and a fireplace roared in the far corner of the space. His friends, colleagues, and a smattering of cousins wore Santa hats.

As far as themes went, Christmas was the clear winner, and he couldn't complain. As far back as he could remember, it had been his favorite holiday. The time of year when he could sit still and wear pajamas all day and let his head clear. His family always kept it about the three of them, no outsiders, so he didn't have to be *on*. He could just be.

One of Beat's college buddies from NYU wrestled him into a playful headlock and he endured it, knowing the guy meant well. God, they all did. His friends weren't aware of the kind of strain he was under. If they did, they would probably try to help. But he couldn't allow that. Couldn't allow a single person to know the delicate reason why he was being blackmailed.

Or who was behind it.

Beat noticed everyone around him was laughing and he joined in, pretending he'd heard the joke, but his brain was working through furious rounds of math. Presenting and discarding solutions. Eight hundred thousand dollars. Double what he'd paid this man last time. Where would he come up with it? And what about next time? Would they venture into the millions?

"You didn't think we'd let your thirtieth pass without an obnoxious celebration, did you?" Vance said, elbowing him in the ribs. "You know us better than that."

"You're damn right I do." A glass of champagne appeared in Beat's hand. "What time is the clown arriving to make balloon animals?"

The group erupted into a disbelieving roar. "How the hell—"

"You ruined the surprise!"

"Like you said"—Beat saluted them, smiling until they all dropped the indignation and grinned back—"I know you."

They don't know you, *though. Do they?*

His smile faltered slightly, but he covered it up with a gulp of champagne, setting the empty glass down on the closest table, noting the peppermints strewn among the confetti. The paper pieces were in the shape of little B's. Pictures of Beat dotted the refreshment table in plastic holders. One of him jumping off a cliff in Costa Rica. Another one of him graduating in a cap and gown from business school. Yet another photo depicted him on-stage introducing his mother, world-famous Octavia Dawkins at a charity dinner he'd organized recently for her foundation. He was smiling in every single picture.

It was like looking at a stranger. He didn't even know that guy.

When he jumped off that cliff in Central America, he'd been in the middle of procuring funds to pay off the blackmailer the first time. Back when he could manage the sum. Fifty thousand here or there. Sure, it meant a little shuffling of his assets, but nothing he couldn't handle in the name of keeping his parents' names from being dragged through the mud.

He couldn't manage this much of a payoff alone. The foundation had more than enough money in its coffers, but it would be a cold day in hell before he stole from the charity he'd built with his mother. Not happening. That cash went to worthy causes. Well-deserved scholarships for performing arts students who couldn't afford the costs associated with training, education, and living expenses. That money did not go to blackmail.

So where would he get the funds?

Maybe a quick call to his accountant would calm his nerves. He'd invested in a few start-ups last year. Maybe he could pull those investments now? There had to be something.

There isn't, whispered a voice in the back of his head.

Feeling even more chilled than before, Beat forced a casual expression onto his face. "Excuse me for a few minutes, I just need to make a phone call."

"To whom?" Vance asked. "Everyone you know is in this room."

That was not true.

His parents weren't here.

But that was not who his mind immediately landed on—and it was ridiculous that he should still be thinking about Melody Gallard fourteen years after meeting her *one time*. He could still recall that afternoon so vividly, though. Her smile, the way she whisper-talked, as if she wasn't all that used to talking at all. The way she couldn't seem to look him in the eye, then all of a sudden she couldn't seem to look anywhere else. Neither had he.

And he'd hugged thousands of people in his life, but she was the only one he could still feel in his arms. They were meant to be friends. Unfortunately, he'd never called. She'd never used his number, either. Now it was too late. Still, when Vance said, *Everyone you know is in this room,* Beat thought of her right away.

It *felt* like he knew Melody—and she wasn't here.

She might know him the best out of everyone if he'd kept in touch.

"Maybe he needs to call a woman," someone sang from the other side of the group. "We know how Beat likes to keep his relationships private."

"When I find a woman who can survive my friends, I'll bring her around."

"Oh, come on."

"We'd be on our best behavior."

Beat raised a skeptical brow. "You don't have a best behavior."

Someone picked up a handful of B confetti and threw it at him. He flicked a piece off his shoulder without missing a beat, satisfied that he'd once again diverted their interest in his love life. He kept that private for good reason. "One phone call and I'll be back. Don't start the balloon animals without me. I'm going to see if the artist can create me a sense of privacy." He gave them all a grin to let them know he was joking. "It means a lot that you organized this party for me. Thank you. It's . . . everything a guy could hope for."

That sappy moment earned him a chorus of boos and several more tosses of confetti until he had to duck and cover his way out of the room. But as soon as he was outside, his smile slid away. Back on the sidewalk like before, he stood for a full minute looking down at the phone in his hand. He could call his accountant. It would be a waste, though. After five years of having the blackmailer on his back like a parasite, he'd wrung himself dry. There simply wasn't eight hundred thousand dollars to spare.

You know, I've had this reality show producer contact me twice. Maybe she would be a good place to start.

His blackmailer's words came back to him. Danielle something. She'd contacted Beat, too. Had a popular network behind her, if Beat recalled correctly. His assistant usually dealt with inquiries pertaining to Steel Birds, but he'd forwarded this particular request to Beat because of the size of the offer and the producer's clout.

Instead of calling his accountant, he searched his inbox for the name Danielle—and he found the email after a little scrolling.

Dear Mr. Dawkins,

Allow me to introduce myself. I'm your ticket to becoming a household name.

Since Steel Birds broke up in ninety-three, the public has been desperate for a reunion of the women who not only cowrote some of the world's most beloved ballads, but inspired a movement. Empowered little girls to get out there, find a microphone, and express their discontent, no matter who it pissed off. I was one of those little girls.

You're a busy man, so let me be brief. I want to give the public the reunion we've been dreaming about since ninety-three. There are no better catalysts than the children of these legendary women to make this happen. It is my profound wish for you, Mr. Dawkins, and Melody Gallard to join forces to bring your parents back together.

The Applause Network is prepared to offer each of you a million dollars.

Sincerely,
Danielle Doolin

Beat dropped the phone to his thigh. Had he seriously only skimmed an email that passionate? He hadn't even made it to the middle the first time he'd seen the correspondence. That much was obvious, because he would have remembered the part about Melody. Every time someone mentioned her, he got a firm sock to the gut.

He was getting one now.

Beat had zero desire to be a household name. Never had, never would. He liked working behind the scenes at his mother's foundation. Giving the occasional speech or social media interview was necessary. Ever since "Rattle the Cage" had gone viral, the requests had been coming in by the mother lode, but remaining out of the limelight was preferable to him.

However.

A million dollars would solve his problem.

He needed to solve it. *Fast.*

And if—and it was a *huge* if—Beat agreed to the reality show, he'd need to talk to Melody first. They might have grown up in the same weird celebrity offspring limelight, but they'd gotten vastly different treatment from the press. He'd been praised as some kind of golden boy, while every single one of Melody's physical attributes had been dissected through paparazzi lenses—all when she was still a *minor.* He'd watched it from afar, horrified.

So much so that the first and only time they'd met, he'd been rocked by protectiveness so deep, he still felt it to this very day.

Was there any way to avoid bringing her back into the spotlight if he attempted to reunite Steel Birds? Or would she be dragged into the story, simply because of her connection to the band?

God, he didn't know. But there was no way in hell Beat would agree to anything unless Melody was okay with him stirring up this hornet's nest. He'd have to meet with her. In person. See her face and be positive she didn't have reservations.

Beat's pulse kicked into a gallop.

Fourteen years had passed and he'd thought of her . . . a weird amount. Wondering what she was doing, if she'd seen whatever latest television special was playing about their mothers, if she was happy. That last one plagued him the most. Was Melody happy? Was he?

Would everything be different if he'd just called her?

Beat pulled up the contact number for his accountant, but never hit call. Instead, he reopened the email from Danielle Doolin and tapped the cell number in her email signature, with no idea the kind of magic he was setting into motion.

Chapter 2

Melody stood at the top of the bocce ball court, the red wooden ball in hand.

This throw would determine whether her team won or lost.

How? How had the onus of demise or victory landed on her birdlike shoulders? Who'd overseen the lineup tonight? She was their weakest player. They usually buried her somewhere in the middle. Her heartbeat boomed so loudly, she could barely hear the *Elf* soundtrack pumping through the bar speakers, Zooey Deschanel's usually angelic voice hitting her ears more like a witch's cackle.

Her team stood at the sides of the lane, hands clasped together like it was the final point at Wimbledon or something, instead of the bocce bar league. This was low stakes, right? Her boss and best friend, Savelina, had *assured* her this was low stakes. Otherwise, Melody wouldn't have joined the team and put their success at high risk. She'd be at home watching some holiday baking championship on the Food Network in an adult onesie where she belonged.

"You can do it, Mel," Savelina shouted, followed by several cheers and whistles from her coworkers at the bookstore. She hadn't known them well in the beginning of the season, considering she worked in the basement restoring young adult books and almost never looked up from her task. But thanks to this semitorturous bocce league, she'd gotten to know them a lot better. She *liked* them.

Oh, please God, grant me enough skill not to let them down.

Ha. If she didn't screw this up, it would be a miracle.

"Do you need a time-out?" asked her boss.

"What made you think that?" Melody shouted. "The fact that I'm frozen in fear?"

The sprinkle of laughter boosted her confidence a little, but not by much. And then she made the mistake of glancing backward over her shoulder and finding the entire Park Slope bar watching the final throw with bated breath. It was the equivalent of looking down at the ground while walking on a tightrope. Not that she'd ever experienced such a thing. The craziest risk she'd taken lately was hoop earrings. *Hoops!*

Now she was breathing so hard, her glasses were fogging up.

Was everyone looking at her butt?

They had to be. She looked at everyone's butts, even when she tried not to. What would make this crowd any different? Did they think her floor-length pleated skirt was a weird choice for bocce? Because it totally was.

"Mel!" Savelina gestured to the bocce lane with her pint of

beer. "We're going to run out of time. Just get the ball as close to the jack as possible. Slice of cake."

Easy for Savelina to say. She owned a bookstore and dressed like a stoned bohemian artist. She could pull off gladiator sandals and had a favorite brand of oolong tea. Of course she thought bocce was simple.

The crowd started cheering behind Melody in encouragement, which was honestly very nice. Brooklynites got a bad rap, but they were actually quite friendly as long as they were being offered drink specials and strangers regularly complimented their dogs.

"Okay! Okay, I'm going to do it."

Melody took a deep breath and rolled the red wooden ball across the hard-packed sand. It came to a stop at the farthest position possible from the jack. It wasn't even remotely close.

Their opponents cheered and clinked pint glasses, the home team bar heaving a collective sigh of disappointment. They probably thought an underdog-to-hero story was unfolding right in front of their eyes, but no. Not with Melody in the starring role.

Savelina approached with a sympathetic expression on her face, squeezing Mel's shoulder with an elegant hand. "We'll win the next one."

"We haven't won a game all season."

"Victory isn't always the point," her boss suggested. "It's trying in the first place."

"Thanks, Mom."

Savelina's tight, brown curls shook with laughter. "Two weeks from now, we have the final game of the season and I have a good feeling about it. We're going to head into Christmas fresh from a win and you're going to be a part of it."

Mel didn't hide her skepticism.

"Let me clarify," Savelina said. "You *must* be a part of it. We only have enough players if you show up. You're not taking off early to visit family or anything, are you?"

As a rare book restoration expert, Mel's work schedule was loose. She could take a project home with her, if needed, and her presence in the store largely depended on whether or not there was even a book that currently required tender loving care. "Uh, no." Mel forced a smile onto her face, even though a little dent formed in her heart. "No, I don't have any plans. My mother is . . . you know. She's doing her thing. I'm doing mine. But I'll see her in February on my birthday," she rushed to add.

"That's right. She always comes to New York for your birthday."

"Right."

Mel did the tight smile/nodding thing she always did when the conversation turned to her mother. Even the most well-intentioned people couldn't help but be openly curious about Trina Gallard. She was an international icon, after all. Savelina was more conscientious than most when it came to giving Mel privacy, but the thirst for knowledge about the rock star inevitably bled through. Mel understood. She did.

She just didn't know enough about her mother to give anyone what they wanted.

That was the sad truth. Trina love-bombed her daughter once a year and once a year only. Like a one-night sold-out show at the

Garden that left her with a hangover and really expensive merch she never wore again.

Melody could see Savelina was losing the battle with the need to ask deeper questions about Trina, probably because it was the end of the night and she'd had six beers. So Mel grabbed her kelly green peacoat from where it hung on the closest stool, tugged it on around her shoulders, and looked for a way to excuse herself. "I'm going to settle my tab at the bar." She leaned in and planted a quick kiss on Savelina's expertly highlighted brown cheek. "I'll see you during the week?"

"Yeah!" Savelina said too quickly, hiding her obvious disappointment. "See you soon."

Briefly, Mel battled the urge to give her friend something, anything. Even Trina's favorite brand of cereal—Lucky Charms—but the information faltered on her tongue. It always did. Speaking with any kind of authority on her mother felt false when most days, it felt as though she barely knew the woman.

"Okay." Mel nodded, turned, and wove through some Friday night revelers toward the bar, apologizing to a few customers who'd witnessed her anticlimactic underdog story. Before she could reach the bar, she made sure Savelina wasn't watching, then veered toward the exit instead—because she didn't really have a bar tab to settle. Customers who recognized her as Trina Gallard's daughter had been sending her drinks all night. She'd had so many Shirley Temples she was going to be peeing grenadine for a week.

Cold winter air chilled her cheeks as soon as she stepped out onto the sidewalk.

The cheerful holiday music and energetic conversations grew muffled behind her as soon as the door snicked shut. Why did it always feel so good to leave somewhere?

Guilt poked holes in her gut. Didn't she *want* to have friends? Who didn't?

And why did she feel alone whether she was with people or not?

She turned around and looked back through the frosty glass, surveying the bargoers, the merry revelers, the quiet ones huddled in darkened nooks. So many kinds of people and they all seemed to have one thing in common. They enjoyed company. None of them appeared to be holding their breath until they could leave. They didn't seem to be pretending to be comfortable when in reality, they were stressing about every word out of their mouth and how they looked, whether or not people *liked* them. And if they did, was it because they were a celebrity's daughter, rather than because of their actual personality? Because of who Melody was?

Melody turned from the lively scene with a lump in her throat and started to walk up the incline of Union Street toward her apartment. Before she made it two steps, however, a woman shifted into the light several feet ahead of her. Melody stopped in her tracks. The stranger was so striking, her smile so confident, it was impossible to move forward without acknowledging her. She had dark blond hair that fell in perfect waves onto the shoulders of a very expensive looking overcoat. One that had tiny gold chains in weird places that served no function, just for the sake of fashion. Simply put, she was radiant and she didn't belong outside of a casual neighborhood bar.

"Miss Gallard?"

The woman knew her name? Had she been lying in wait for her? Not totally surprising, but it had been a long while since she'd encountered this kind of brazenness from a reporter.

"Excuse me," Melody said, hustling past her. "I'm not answering any questions about my mother—"

"I'm Danielle Doolin. You might recall some emails I sent you earlier this year? I'm a producer with the Applause Network."

Melody kept walking. "I get a lot of emails."

"Yes, I'm sure you do," said Danielle, falling into step beside her. Keeping pace, even though she was wearing three-inch heels, her footwear a stark contrast to Melody's flat ankle boots. "The public has a vested interest in you and your family."

"You realize I was never really given a choice about that."

"I do. During my brief phone call with Beat Dawkins, he expressed the same."

Melody's feet basically stopped working. The air inside of her lungs evaporated and she had no choice but to slow to a stop in the middle of the sidewalk. Beat Dawkins. She heard that name in her sleep, which was utterly ridiculous. The fact that she should still be fascinated by the man when they hadn't been in the same room in fourteen years made her cringe . . . but that was the *only* thing about Beat that made her cringe. The rest of her reactions to him could best be described as breathless, dreamlike, whimsical, and . . . sexual.

In her entire thirty-year existence, she'd never experienced attraction like she had to Beat Dawkins at age sixteen when she spent a mere five minutes in his presence. Since then her hormones could only be defined as lazy. Floating on a pool raft with a mai tai, rather than competing in a triathlon. She had the yoga pants of hormones. They were fine, they definitely *counted* as hormones, but they weren't worthy of a runway strut. Her lack of romantic aspirations was yet another reason she felt unmotivated to go out and make human connections. To be in big, social crowds where someone might show interest in her.

It was going to take something special to make her set down the mai tai and get off this raft—and so far, no one had been especially . . . rousing. A fourteen-year-old memory, though? Oh mama. It had the power to make her temperature peak. At one time it had, anyway. The recollection of her one and only encounter with Beat was growing grainy around the edges. Fading, much to her distress.

"Well." Danielle regarded Melody with open interest. "His name certainly got your attention, didn't it?"

Melody tried not to stumble over her words and failed, thanks to her tongue turning as useless as her feet. "I'm sorry, y-you'll have to refresh my memory. The emails you sent me were about . . . ?"

"Reuniting Steel Birds."

A laugh tumbled out of Melody, stirring the air with white vapor. "Wait. Beat took a phone call about *this*?" Baffled, she shook her head. "As far as I know, both of us have always maintained that a reunion is impossible. Like, on par with an Elvis comeback tour."

Danielle lifted an elegant shoulder and let it drop. "Stranger things have happened. Even Pink Floyd set aside their differences for Live 8 in 2005 and no one believed it was doable. A lot of time has passed since Steel Birds broke up. Hearts soften. Age gives a different perspective. Maybe Beat believes a reunion wouldn't be such an impossible feat after all."

It was humiliating how hard her heart was pounding in her chest. "Did . . . did he say that?"

Danielle blew air into one cheek. "He didn't *not* say it. But the fact that he contacted me about the reunion speaks for itself, right?"

Odd that Melody should feel a tad betrayed that he'd changed his position without consulting her. Why would he do that? He didn't owe her anything. Not a phone call. Nothing. "Wow." Melody cleared her throat. "You've caught me off guard."

"I apologize for that. You're very difficult to get in contact with. I had to dig quite a bit to find out where you worked. Then I saw a picture of your bocce team on the bookstore's Instagram. Thank goodness for location tags." Danielle gestured with a brisk, gloved hand to the general area. "I assure you, I wouldn't have ventured into Brooklyn in twenty-degree weather unless I had a potentially viable project on the table. One that, if done correctly, could be a cultural phenomenon. And it *would* be done correctly, because I would be overseeing production personally."

What was it like to be so confident? "I'm afraid to ask what this project entails."

"That's why I'm not going to tell you until we're in my nice, warm office with espresso and a selection of beignets in front of us."

Melody's stomach growled reluctantly. "Beignets, huh?"

"They piqued Beat's interest, as well."

"They did?" Melody's breathless tone hit her ears, cluing her in to what was happening. The tactic that was being employed. "You keep bringing him up on purpose."

Danielle studied her face closely. "He seems to be my biggest selling point. Even more than the money the network is willing to pay, I'm guessing," she murmured. "If I hadn't mentioned his name, you never would have stopped walking. Surprising, since the two of you haven't maintained any sort of contact. According to him."

"No, I know," Melody rushed to blurt, heat clinging to her face and the sides of her neck. "We don't even know each other."

And that was the God's honest truth.

Fourteen years had passed.

However. Beat was a good person. He'd proven that to her— and he couldn't have changed so drastically. The kind of character it took to do what he'd done . . .

About a month after they'd met in that humid television studio, she'd passed through the gates of her Manhattan private school, expecting to walk to class alone, as usual. But she'd been surrounded by buzzing girls that morning. Had she seen Beat Dawkins on *TMZ*?

Considering she avoided that program like the plague, she'd shaken her head. They'd cagily informed her that Beat had mentioned her during a paparazzi ambush and she might want to watch the footage. Getting through first period without exploding was nearly impossible, but she'd made it. Then she'd rushed to the bathroom and pulled up the clip on her phone. There was Beat, holding a grocery bag, a Dodgers ball cap pulled down low on his forehead, being pursued by a cameraman.

Normally, he was the type to stop and suffer through their silly questions with a golden grin. But this time, he didn't. He halted abruptly on the sidewalk and, to this day, she could still remember what came out of his mouth, word for word.

I'm done talking. You won't get another word out of me. Not until you—and all the similar outlets—stop exploiting girls for clicks. Especially my friend Melody Gallard. You praise me for nothing and disparage her no matter how hard she tries. You can fuck right off. Like I said, I'm done talking.

That day, Melody hadn't come out of the bathroom until third period, she'd been so frozen in shock and gratitude. Just to be seen. Just to have someone speak up on her behalf. That clip had been shared all over social media. For weeks. It had started a conversation about how teenage girls were being portrayed by celebrity news outlets.

Of course, their treatment of her didn't change overnight. But it slowly shifted. It lightened in degrees. Bad headlines started getting called out. Shamed.

And shockingly, her experience with the press got better.

Melody was so lost in the memory, it took her a moment to notice the smile flirting with the corners of Danielle's glossy mouth. "He's coming to my office on Monday morning for a meeting. I've come all the way here to invite you, as well." She paused, seemed to consider her next words carefully. "Beat won't agree to the reunion project unless *you* are comfortable with it moving forward. He made your approval a condition."

Melody hated the way her soul left her body at Danielle's words. It was pathetic in so many ways.

Beat Dawkins was eons and galaxies out of her league. Not only was he blindingly gorgeous, but he had *presence*. He commanded rooms full of people to give speeches for his mother's foundation. She'd seen the pictures, the occasional Instagram reel. His grid was brimming with nonstop adventures. Equally glamorous friends were pouring out of his ears. He was loved and lusted after and . . . perfect.

Beat Dawkins was perfectly perfect.

And he'd taken her into consideration.

He'd thought of her.

This whole Steel Birds reunion idea would never fly—the feelings of betrayal between their mothers ran deeper than the Atlantic Ocean—but the fact that Beat had said her name out loud to this woman basically ensured another fourteen years of infatuation. *Sad, sad girl.*

"You mentioned money," Melody said offhandedly, mostly so it wouldn't seem her entire interest was Beat-related. "How much? Just out of curiosity."

"I'll tell you at the meeting." She smiled slyly. "It's a lot, Melody. Perhaps even by the standards of a famous rock star's daughter."

A lot of money. Even to her.

Despite her trepidation, Melody couldn't help but wonder . . . was it enough cash to make her financially independent? She'd been born into comfort. A nice town house, wonderful nannies, any material item she wanted, which had mainly turned out to be books and acne medication. Her mother's love and attention remained out of reach, however. Always had—and it was beginning to feel as though it always would.

Melody's brownstone apartment was paid in full. She had an annual allowance. Lately, though, accepting her mother's generosity didn't feel right. Or good. Not when they lacked the healthy mother-daughter relationship she would gladly take instead.

Could this be her chance to stand on her own two feet?

No. Facilitating a reunion? There had to be an easier way.

"At least take the meeting," Danielle said, smiling like the cat who'd caught the canary.

The woman had her and she knew it.

To be in the same room with Beat Dawkins again . . .

She wasn't strong enough to pass up the chance.

Melody shifted in her boots and tried not to sound too eager. "What time?"

About the Author

#1 *New York Times* bestselling author TESSA BAILEY can solve all problems except for her own, so she focuses those efforts on stubborn, fictional blue-collar men and loyal, lovable heroines. She lives on Long Island, avoiding the sun and social interactions, then wonders why no one has called. Dubbed the "Michelangelo of dirty talk" by *Entertainment Weekly*, Tessa writes with spice, spirit, swoon, and a guaranteed happily ever after. Catch her on TikTok @authortessabailey or check out tessabailey.com for a complete list of her books.